"*Deaver combines academic malfeasance, small-town police department politics, and family melodrama with all the requisite mystery and suspense for a double dose of pleasure.*"
—*Kirkus Reviews*

mistress of justice

"Excellent entertainment, with a resilient, astute paralegal as a likable heroine."
—*St. Louis Post-Dispatch*

"An intelligently written thriller . . . The characters are well-drawn [and] the plot is fast-paced."
—*Booklist*

"Fresh and funky; I loved it."
—*Alfred Hitchcock Mystery Magazine*

"A solid achievement . . . the ending packs a nice wallop."
—*Mystery News*

"Loaded with characters and action and a very devious plot . . . a top-notch legal thriller."
—*Mystery Lovers Bookshop News*

By the author of

THE BLUE NOWHERE

THE EMPTY CHAIR

SPEAKING IN TONGUES

THE DEVIL'S TEARDROP

THE COFFIN DANCER

THE BONE COLLECTOR

A MAIDEN'S GRAVE

PRAYING FOR SLEEP

THE LESSON OF HER DEATH*

MISTRESS OF JUSTICE*

DEATH OF A BLUE MOVIE STAR*

MANHATTAN IS MY BEAT*

BLOODY RIVER BLUES

SHALLOW GRAVES

HELL'S KITCHEN

*Available from Bantam Books

hard

JEFFERY DEAVER

news

BANTAM 🐓 BOOKS

NEW YORK TORONTO LONDON
SYDNEY AUCKLAND

hard news

A Bantam Book

PUBLISHING HISTORY
Doubleday original edition published December 1991
Bantam original edition published June 1992
Bantam revised edition / January 2001

ISBN 0-553-58329-8

Published simultaneously in the United States and Canada

Bantam Books are published by Bantam Books, a division of Random
House, Inc. Its trademark, consisting of the words "Bantam Books" and
the portrayal of a rooster, is Registered in U.S. Patent and Trademark
Office and in other countries. Marca Registrada. Bantam Books, 1540
Broadway, New York, New York 10036.

PRINTED IN THE UNITED STATES OF AMERICA

OPM   10 9 8 7 6 5 4 3 2 1

For Irene Miranker

Journalism without a moral position
is impossible. Every journalist is a moralist. . . .
She cannot do her work without
judging what she sees.

—MARGUERITE DURAS

hard news

chapter 1

THEY MOVED ON HIM JUST AFTER DINNER.

He didn't know for sure how many. But that didn't matter; all he thought was: Please, don't let them have a knife. He didn't want to get cut. Swing the baseball bat, swing the pipe, drop the cinder block on his hands . . . but not a knife please.

He was walking down the corridor from the prison dining hall to the library, the gray corridor that had a smell he'd never been able to place. Sour, rotten . . . And behind him: the footsteps growing closer.

The thin man, who'd eaten hardly any of the fried meat and bread and green beans ladled on his tray, walked more quickly.

He was sixty feet from a guard station and none of the Department of Corrections officers at the far end of the corridor were looking his way.

Footsteps. Whispering.

Oh, Lord, the man thought. I can take one out maybe. I'm strong and I can move fast. But if they have a knife there's no way. . . .

Randy Boggs glanced back.

Three men were close behind him.

Not a knife. Please. . . .

He started to run.

"Where you goin', boy?" the Latino voice called as they broke into a trot after him.

Ascipio. It was Ascipio. And that meant Boggs was going to die.

"Yo, Boggs, ain' no use. Ain' no use at all, you runnin'."

But keep running he did. Foot after foot, head down. Now only forty feet from the guard station.

I can make it. I'll be there just before they get me.

Please let them have a club or use their fists.

But no knife.

No sliced flesh.

Of course word'd get out immediately in general population how Boggs had run to the guards. And then everybody, even the guards themselves, would taunt him every chance they got. Because if your nerve breaks there's no hope for you Inside. It means you're going to die and it's just a question of how long it takes to strip away your body from your cowardly soul.

"Shit, man," another voice called, breathing hard from the effort of running. "Get him."

"You got the glass?" one of them called to another.

It was a whisper but Boggs heard it. Glass. Ascipio's friend would mean a glass knife, which was the most popular weapon in prison because you could wrap it in tape, hide it in you, pass through the metal detector and shit it out into your hand and none of the guards would ever know.

"Give it up, man. We gonna cut you one way or th'other. Give us you blood. . . ."

Boggs, thin but not in good shape, ran like a track star but he realized that he wasn't going to make it. The guards were in station seven—a room separating the communal facilities from the cells. The windows were an inch and a half thick and someone could stand directly in front of the window and pound with his bleeding bare hands on the glass and if the guard inside didn't happen to look up at the slashed prisoner he'd never know a thing and continue to enjoy his *New York Post* and pizza slice and coffee. He'd

never know a man was bleeding to death two feet behind him.

Boggs saw the guards inside the fortress. They were
concentrating on an important episode of St. Elsewhere
on a small TV.

Boggs sprinted as fast as he could, calling, "Help me,
help me!"

Go, go, go!

Okay, he'd turn, he'd face Ascipio and his buddies.
Butt his long head into the closest one. Break his nose, try
to grab the knife. Maybe the guards would notice by then.

A commercial on the TV. The guards were pointing at
it and laughing. A big basketball player was saying something. Boggs raced directly toward him.

Wondering: Why were Ascipio and his buddies doing
this? *Why?* Just because he was white? Because he wasn't
a bodybuilder? Because he hadn't picked up a whittled
broomstick along with the ten other inmates and stepped
up to kill Rano the snitch?

Ten feet to the guard station. . . .

A hand grabbed his collar from behind.

"No!" Randy Boggs cried.

And he felt himself start to tumble to the concrete
floor under the tackle.

He saw: the characters on the hospital show on TV
looking gravely at a body on the operating table.

He saw: the gray concrete rising up to slam him in
the head.

He saw: a sparkle of the glass in the hand of a young
Latino man. Ascipio whispered, "Do it."

The young man stepped forward with the glass knife.

But then Boggs saw another motion. A shadow coming out of a deeper shadow. A huge shadow.

A hand reached down and gripped the wrist of the
man holding the knife.

Snick.

The attacker screamed as his wrist turned sideways in the shadow's huge hand. The glass fell to the concrete floor and broke.

"Bless you," the shadow said in a slow, reverent voice. "You know not what you do." Then the voice snapped, "Now get the fuck outta here. Try this again and you be dead."

Ascipio and the third of the trio helped the wounded attacker to his feet. They hurried down the corridor.

The huge shadow, whose name was Severn Washington, fifteen to twenty-five for a murder committed before he had accepted Allah into his heart, helped Boggs to his feet. The thin man closed his eyes and breathed deeply. Then together they silently started to the library. Boggs, hands shaking desperately, glanced into the guard station, inside of which the guards nodded and smiled as the body on the operating table on the TV screen was miraculously revived and the previews for next week's show came on.

FOUR HOURS LATER RANDY BOGGS SAT ON HIS BUNK, LIS-tening to his cellmate, Wilker, James, eight years for receiving, second felony offense.

"Hear they moved on you, man, that Ascipio, man, he one mean fucker. What he want to do that for? I can't figure it, not like you have anything on him, man."

Wilker, James kept talking, like he always did, on and on and goddamn on but Randy Boggs wasn't listening. He sat hunched over a *People* magazine on his bunk. He wasn't reading the periodical, though. He was using it as a lap desk, on top of which was a piece of cheap, wide-lined writing paper.

"You gotta understand me, man," Wilker, James said. "I'm not saying anything about the Hispanic race. I mean, you know, the problem is they just don't see things the way normal people do. I mean, like, life isn't . . ."

Boggs ignored the man's crazy rambling and finally

touched pen to paper. In the upper left-hand corner of the paper he wrote, "Harrison Men's Correctional Facility." He wrote the date. Then he wrote:

> *Dear to who it may concern:*
> *You have to help me. Please.*

After this careful beginning Randy Boggs paused, thought for a long moment and started to write once more.

chapter 2

RUNE WATCHED THE TAPE ONCE AND THEN A SECOND
time. And then once more.

She sat in a deserted corner of the Network's newsroom, a huge open space, twenty feet high, three thousand square feet, divided up by movable partitions,
head-high and covered with gray cloth. The on-camera
sets were bright and immaculate; the rest of the walls and
floors were scuffed and chipped and streaked with old
dirt. To get from one side of the studio to the other, you
had to dance over a million wires and around monitors
and cameras and computers and desks. A huge control
booth, like the bridge of the Starship *Enterprise,* looked
out over the room. A dozen people stood in clusters
around desks or monitors. Others carried sheets of paper
and blue cardboard cups of coffee and videocassettes.
Some sat at computers, typing or editing news stories.

Everyone wore casual clothing but no one behaved
casually.

Rune was hunched over the Sony ¾-inch tape player
and small color TV that served as a monitor.

A tinny voice came out of the small speaker. *"I told
them back then just what I'm telling you now: I didn't do it."*

The man on the screen was a gaunt thirty-something,
with high cheekbones and sideburns. His hair was slicked
back and crowned with a Kewpie-doll curl above his forehead. His face was very pale. When Rune had first cued

up the tape and started it running, ten minutes before, she'd thought, This dude is a total nerd.

He wore a tight gray jumpsuit, which under other circumstances—say on West Broadway in SoHo—*might* have been chic. Except that the name of the designer on the label wasn't Giorgio Armani or Calvin Klein but the New York State Department of Correctional Services.

Rune paused the tape and looked at the letter once again, read the man's unsteady handwriting. Turned back to the TV screen and heard the interviewer ask him, *"You'll be up for parole, when?"*

"Parole? Maybe a few years. But hell . . ." The thin man looked at the camera quickly, then away. *"A man's innocent, he shouldn't be out on parole, he should just be out."*

Rune watched the rest of the tape, listened to him tell about how bad life in prison was, how nobody in the warden's office or the court would listen to him, how incompetent his lawyer had been. She was surprised, though, that he didn't sound bitter. He was more baffled—like somebody who can't understand the justice behind a plane crash or car wreck. She liked that about him; if anybody had a right to be obnoxious or sarcastic it was an innocent man who was in prison. But he just talked calmly and wistfully, occasionally lifting a finger to touch a glistening sideburn. He seemed scared of the camera. Or modest or embarrassed.

She paused the tape and turned to the letter that had ended up on her desk that morning. She had no clue how she'd happened to receive it—other than her being your typical low-level-person-of-indeterminate-job-description at a major television network. Which meant she often got bizarre letters dumped on her desk—anything from Publishers Clearing House award notices to fan mail for Captain Kangaroo and Edward R. Murrow, written by wackos.

It was this letter that had motivated her to go into the archives and dig up these old interview tapes.

She read it again.

Dear to who it may concern:
You have to help me. Please.

It sounded so desperate, pathetic. But the tone wasn't what affected her as much as the third paragraph of the letter. She read it again.

And what it was was that the Police which I have nothing against normally, didn't talk to all the Witnesses, or ask the ones they DID talk to the questions they should of asked. If they had done that, then I feel, in my opinion, they would have found that I was innocent of the Charges but they didn't do this.

Rune looked at the image freeze-framed on the screen. A tight close-up of Randy Boggs just after his trial several years ago.

Where was he born? she wondered. What was his history? In high school, had he been a—what did her mother call them?—a hood? A greaser? Did he have family? A wife somewhere? Maybe children? How would it be to have to visit your husband once a month? Was she faithful to him? Did she bake him cookies and send them to prison?

Rune started the tape again and watched the dull-colored grain on the screen.

"You want to hear what it's like to be in here?" Now, at last, bitterness was creeping into the thin man's voice. *"Let me tell you 'bout the start of my day. Do you want to hear about that?"*

"Tell me whatever you want," the invisible interviewer asked.

"You wake up at six and the first thing you think is Hell, I'm still here. . . ."

A voice from across the room: "Rune, where are you? Come on, let's go. We've got an overturned something on the Brooklyn-Queens Expressway."

The Model was standing up from his desk, pulling on a tan London Fog trench coat that would keep him ten degrees warmer than he needed to be on this April afternoon (but that would be okay because it was a *reporter's* coat). He was an up-and-comer—one of the hotshots covering metro news for the local O&O, the Network's owned-and-operated New York TV station, Rune's present employer as well. Twenty-seven, a round face, Midwest handsome (the word "sandy" seemed to apply to him in a vague way). He spent a lot of time in front of mirrors. Nobody shaved like the Model.

Rune worked as a cameraman for him occasionally and when she'd first been assigned to him he hadn't been quite sure what to make of this auburn-ponytailed young woman who looked a bit like Audrey Hepburn and was just a little over five feet, a couple ounces over a hundred pounds. The Model probably would have preferred a pickled, chain-smoking technician who'd worked the city desk from the days when they used sixteen-millimeter Bolex cameras. But she shot damn good footage and there was nobody better than Rune when it came to blustering her way through police barricades and past backstage security guards.

"What've you got there?" he asked, nodding at the monitor.

"I found this letter on my desk. From this guy in prison."

"You know him?" the Model asked absently. He carefully made sure the belt wasn't twisted then fitted it through the plastic buckle.

"Nope. It was addressed to the Network. Just showed up here."

"Maybe he wrote it a while ago." Nodding toward the screen, where Randy Boggs was freeze-framed. "Looks like you could carbon-date him nineteen sixty-five."

"Nope." She tapped the paper. "It's dated two days ago."

The Model read it quickly. "Sounds like the guy's having a shitty time of it. The prison in Harrison, huh? Better than Attica but it's still no country club. So, suit up. Let's go."

The first thing you think is, Hell, I'm still here. . . .

The Model took a call. He nodded. Looked at Rune. "This is great! It's an overturned ammonia tanker on the BQE. Boy, that is gonna screw up rush hour real nice. Ammonia. Are we lucky or are we lucky?"

Rune shut the monitor off and joined the Model at his cluttered desk. "I think I want to see her."

"Her? Who?"

"You know who I mean."

The Model's face broke into a wrinkleless smile. "Not Her, capital H?"

"Yeah."

The Model laughed. "Why?"

Rune had learned one thing about TV news. Keep your back covered and your ideas to yourself—unless the station pays you to come up with ideas, which in her case they didn't. So she said, "Career development."

The Model was at the door. "You miss this assignment, you won't have any career to develop. It's ammonia. You understand what I'm saying?"

"Ammonia," Rune repeated. She wound a paisley elastic silkie around her ponytail then pulled on a black leather jacket. The rest of her outfit was a black T-shirt, yellow stretch pants and cowboy boots. "Just give me ten minutes with capital H Her."

He took her by the arm, aimed her toward the door. "You think you're just going to walk into Piper Sutton's office?"

"I'd knock first."

"Uh-uh. Let's go, sweetheart. Double time. You can visit the lion's den after we get back and wrap the edits."

A figure stepped out of the corridor, a young man

in jeans and an expensive black shirt. He wore his hair long and floppy. Bradford Simpson was an intern, a Journalism School senior at Columbia, who'd started out in the mailroom his freshman year and was by now doing slightly more glamorous jobs around the station—like fetching coffee, handling deliveries of tapes and occasionally actually assisting a cameraman or sound crew. He was one of those madly ambitious sorts—Rune could identify with *that* part of him—but his ambition was to get his degree, don a Brooks Brothers suit and plunge into the ranks of corporate journalism. Sincere and well liked around the O&O and the Network, Bradford ("Don't really care for 'Brad'") was also cute as hell—in a preppy, Connecticut way. Rune had been shocked when he'd actually asked her out a few days ago.

But while she appreciated the offer, Rune had found she didn't do well dating people like Mr. Dockers Top-Sider here and, instead of his offer for dinner at the Yale Club, she'd opted to go film a fire in lower Manhattan for the *Live at Eleven* newscast. Still, she wondered if he'd ask her out again. No invitations were forthcoming at the moment, however, and he now merely looked at the screen, saw Randy Boggs's lean face on the monitor and asked, "Who's that?"

"He's in jail," Rune explained. "But I think he's innocent."

Bradford asked, "How come?"

"Just a feeling."

"Rune," said the Model. "We don't have time. Let's go."

She said to them both, "That'd be a pretty good story—getting an innocent man out of jail."

The young man nodded and said, "Journalists doing good deeds—that's what it's all about."

But the Model wasn't interested in good deeds; he was interested in ammonia. "Brooklyn-Queens Expressway, Rune," he said like an impatient professor. "Now."

"Oh, the tanker truck," Bradford said.

"See?" the Model said to Rune. "*Everybody* knows about it. Let's *move.*"

"It's a goddamn traffic accident," Rune protested. "I'm talking about an innocent man in jail for murder."

Bradford said, "There *is* something about him. . . ." Nodding at the screen. "He looks more like a victim than a killer, if you ask me."

But before she could agree, the Model led her firmly to the elevator. They descended to the ground floor of the four-story building that occupied a whole square block on the Upper West Side. The building had been an armory at one time then had been bought by the Network, gutted and rebuilt. Outside, it was scabby and dark and looked like it ought to be housing a thousand homeless people; inside was a half-billion dollars' worth of electronic equipment and TV celebrities. A lot of the space was leased to the local O&O station but most of it was for the Network, which recorded a couple of soap operas here, some talk shows, several sitcoms and, of course, Network News.

In the equipment room beside the parking garage Rune checked out an Ikegami video camera with an Ampex deck and a battery pack. Rune and the Model climbed into an Econoline van. She grabbed the lip of the doorway and swung up and in, the way she liked to do, feeling like a pilot about to take off on a mission. The driver, a scrawny young man with a long, thin braid of blond hair, gave a thumbs-up to Rune and started the van. Explosive strains of Black Sabbath filled the van.

"Shut that crap off!" the Model shouted. "Then let's move—we've got ammonia on the BQE! Go, go, go!"

Which the kid did, turning down the tape player and then squealing into the street hostilely, as if he were striking a blow for classic rock music.

As they drove through Manhattan, Rune looked absently out the window at the people on the street as they in turn watched the van, with its sci-fi transmission dish

on top and the call letters of the TV station on the side,
stenciled at an angle. People always paused and watched
these vans drive past, probably wondering if it was going
to stop nearby, if something newsworthy was happening,
if they themselves might even get to appear in the background of a news report. Sometimes Rune would wave at
them. But today she was distracted. She kept hearing
Randy Boggs's voice.

The first thing you think is, Hell, I'm still here. . . .
I'm still here. . . .
I'm still here.

"SO, WHY CAN'T I JUST WALK INTO HER OFFICE AND TALK
to her?"

The Model snapped, "Because she's the anchor."

As if nothing more need be said.

Rune trudged beside him through the scuffed corridor that led from the elevator back to the newsroom. The
worn carpet was sea-blue, the parent company's corporate
color. "So what *if* she's an anchorwoman. She's not going
to fire me for talking to her."

"Well, why don't you quit talking about it and make
an appointment." The Model was in a bad mood because,
yes, it had been an ammonia truck and, yes, it had tipped
over but no one had told the station that the truck was
empty. So, no spill. It had even had the courtesy to roll
over onto the shoulder so that rush-hour traffic wasn't dis-
rupted much at all.

They arrived in the studio and Rune replayed the
tape she'd shot of the truck. The Model looked at the
footage and seemed to be trying to think of something un-
pleasantly critical to say about her work.

She said enthusiastically, "Look, I got the sunset.
There on the side of the truck. That ridge of red, see—"

"I see it."

"Do you like it?"

"I like it."

"Do you mean it?"

"Rune."

As the tape was rewinding, Rune said, "But Piper's ultimately my boss, isn't she?"

"Well, in a way. She works for the Network; you work for the local owned-and-operated station. It's a strange relationship."

"I'm a single woman living in Manhattan. I'm used to strange relationships."

"Look," he said patiently. "The President of the United States is in charge of the Army and Navy, okay? But do you see him talking to every PFC's got a problem?"

"This isn't a problem. It's an opportunity."

"Uh-huh. Piper Sutton doesn't care diddly-squat for your opportunities, sweetheart. You have an idea, you should talk to Stan."

"He's head of local news. This is national."

"Nothing personal but you *are* just a camera girl."

"Girl?"

"Cameraperson. You're a *technician*."

Rune continued cheerfully. "What do you know about her?"

"Her with a capital H again?" The Model looked at Rune for a moment in silence.

Rune smiled coyly. "Come on, please?"

He said, "Piper Sutton started out where I am, right here—a reporter for the local O&O in New York. She went to the University of Missouri Journalism School. Anyway, she did beat reporting, then she moved up in the ranks and became head of radio news, then executive producer for radio. Then she got tapped as a reporter for the Network.

"She was overseas a lot, I know. She was in the Mideast and she got an award for covering the Sadat assassination. Then she came back here and anchored the weekend program then moved on to *Wake Up With the*

News. Finally they tried to move her into the parent. They offered her something pretty big, like executive VP in charge of O&Os. But she didn't want a desk job. She wanted to be on camera. She finagled her way into *Current Events.* And there she is. She makes a million dollars a year. Lives on Park Avenue. That lady is ground zero in the world of broadcast journalism and ain't gonna want to spend time having a confab with the likes of you."

"She hasn't met me yet," Rune said.

"And she devoutly wants to keep it that way. Believe me."

"How come everybody talks about her like she's some kind of dragon lady?"

The Model exhaled a sharp laugh through his nose. "I like you, Rune, which is why I'm not going to ruin your evening by telling you anything more about Piper Sutton."

chapter 3

"WHAT DO YOU WANT?" THE WOMAN'S RASPY ALTO VOICE barked. "Who *are* you?"

She was in her early forties, with a handsome, broad, stern face. Her skin was dry and she wore subtle, powdery makeup. Eyes: deep gray-blue. Her hair was mostly blonde though it was masterfully highlighted with silver streaks. The strands were frozen in place with spray.

Rune walked up to the desk and crossed her arms. "I—"

The phone rang and Piper Sutton turned away, snagged the receiver. She listened, frowning.

"No," she said emphatically. Listened a moment more. Uttered a more ominous "No."

Rune glanced at her cream-colored suit and burgundy silk blouse. Her shoes were black and glistened fiercely. Names like Bergdorf, Bendel and Ferragamo came to mind but Rune had no idea which name went with which article of clothing. The woman sat behind a large antique desk, under a wall filled with blotched and squiggly modern paintings and framed photos of Sutton shaking hands with or embracing a couple of presidents and some other distinguished, gray-haired men.

The phone conversation continued and Rune was completely ignored. She looked around.

Two of the walls in the office were floor-to-ceiling windows, looking west and south. It was on the forty-fifth floor of the Network's parent company building, a block away from the studio. Rune stared at a distant horizon that might have been Pennsylvania. Across from the desk was a bank of five 27-inch NEC monitors, each one tuned to a different network station. Though the volume was down, their busy screens fired an electronic hum into the air.

"Then do it," the woman snapped and dropped the phone into the cradle.

She looked back at Rune, cocked an eyebrow.

"Okay. What it is is this: I'm a cameraman for the local station and I—"

Sutton's voice rose with gritty irritation. "Why are you here? How did you get in?" Questions delivered so fast it was clear she had a lot more where they came from.

Rune could have told her she snuck in after Sutton's secretary went into the corridor to buy tea from the ten A.M. coffee service cart. But all she said was "There was nobody outside and I—"

Sutton waved a hand to silence her. She grabbed the telephone receiver and stabbed the intercom button. There was a faint buzz from the outer office. No one answered. She hung up the phone.

Rune said, "Anyway, I—"

Sutton said, "Anyway, nothing. Leave." She looked down at the sheet of paper she'd been reading, brows narrowing in concentration. After a moment she looked up again, genuinely surprised Rune was still there.

"Miss Sutton . . . Ms. Sutton," Rune began. "I've got this, like, idea—"

"A like idea? What is a like idea?"

Rune felt a blush crawl across her face.

"I have an idea for a story I'd like to do. For your show. I—"

"Wait." Sutton slapped her Mont Blanc pen onto the desk. "I don't understand what you're doing here. I don't know you."

Rune said, "Just give me a minute, please."

"I don't have time for this. I don't care if you work here or not. You want me to call security?" The phone rose once more.

Rune paused a moment. Took a figurative breath. Okay, she told herself, do it. She said quickly, "*Current Events* came in at number nine in nationwide viewership according to the CBS/TIME poll last week." She struggled to keep her voice from quavering. "Three months ago it was rated five in the same poll. That's quite a drop."

Sutton's unreadable eyes bore into Rune's. Oh, Christ, am I really saying these things? But there was nothing to do but keep going. "I can turn those ratings in the other direction."

Sutton looked at Rune's necklace ID badge. Oh, brother. I'm going to get fired. (Rune got fired with great regularity. Usually her reaction was to say, "Them's the breaks," and head off to Unemployment. Today she prayed this wouldn't happen.)

The telephone went back into the cradle. Sutton said, "You've got three minutes."

Thank you thank you thank you. . . .

"Okay, what it is, I want to do a story about—"

"What do you mean *you* want to do a story? You said you're a cameraman. Give the idea to a producer."

"I want to produce it myself."

Sutton's eyes swept over her again, this time not recording her name for referral to the Termination Division of the Human Resources Department but examining her closely, studying the young, makeupless face, her black T-shirt, black spandex miniskirt, blue tights and fringy red cowboy boots. Dangling from her lobes were earrings in the shape of sushi. On her left wrist were three wristwatches with battered leather straps, painted gold and silver. On her right were two bracelets—one silver in the shape of two hands gripped together, the other a string friendship bracelet. From one shoulder dangled a leopard-skin bag; out of one cracked corner it bled an ink-stained Kleenex.

"You don't look like a producer."

"I've already produced one film. A documentary. It was on PBS last year."

"So do a lot of film students. The lucky ones. Maybe you were lucky."

"Why don't you like me?"

"You're assuming I don't."

"Well, do you?" Rune asked.

Sutton considered. Whatever the conclusion was she kept it to herself. "You've got to understand. This . . ." She waved her hand vaguely toward Rune. ". . . is déjà vu. It happens all the time. Somebody blusters their way in— usually after hiding by the filing cabinet until Sandy goes to get coffee." Sutton lifted an eyebrow. "And says, Oh, I've got this *like* idea for a great new news program or game show or special or God knows. And of course the idea is very, very *boring*. Because young, enthusiastic people are very, very *boring*. And nine times out of ten—no, ninety-nine times out of a hundred, their great idea has been thought of and discarded by people who really work in the business. You think hundreds of people just like you haven't come in here and said exactly the same thing to me? Oh, note the proper use of the word 'like.' As a preposition. Not an adjective or adverb."

Both phones rang at once and Sutton spun around to take the calls. She juggled them for a while, jamming a short-nailed finger down on the hold button as she switched from one to the other. When she hung up she found Rune sitting in a chair across from her, swinging her legs back and forth.

Sutton gave a harsh sigh. "Didn't I make my point?"

Rune said, "I want to do a story on a murderer who was convicted only he didn't do it. I want my story to get him released."

Sutton's hand paused over the phone. "Here in New York?"

"Yep."

"That's metro, not national. Talk to the local news director. You should've known that in the first place."

"I want it to be on *Current Events*."

Sutton blinked. Then she laughed. "Honey, that's the Net's flagship news magazine. I've got veteran producers lined up for two years with programs they'd kill to air on *C.E.* Your *like* story ain't getting slotted on my show in this lifetime."

Rune leaned forward. "But this guy has served three years in Harrison state prison—three years for a crime he didn't commit."

Sutton looked at her for a moment. "Where'd you get the tip?"

"He sent a letter to the station. It's really sad. He said he's going to die if he doesn't get out. Other prisoners are going to kill him. Anyway, I went to the archives and looked through some of the old tapes about his trial and—"

"Who told you to?"

"No one. I did it myself."

"Your time or our time?"

"Huh?"

" 'Huh?' " Sutton repeated sarcastically. Then, as if explaining to a child: "Were you on *your* time or on *our* time when you were doing this homework?"

"Sort of on my lunch hour."

Sutton said, "*Sort of.* Uh-huh. Well, so this man is innocent. A lot of innocent people get convicted. That's not news. Unless he's famous. Is he famous? A politician, an actor?"

Rune blinked. She felt very young under the woman's probing eyes. Tongue-tied. "It's sort of, it's not so much *who* he is as it is the fact he was convicted of a crime he didn't commit and he's sort of going to just rot in jail. Or get killed or something."

"You think he's innocent? Then go to law school or set up a defense fund and get him out. We're a news department. We're not in the business of social services."

"No, it'll be a really good story. And it'll be sort of like . . ." Rune heard her clumsy words and froze. She must think I'm a total idiot. Sutton raised her eyebrows and Rune continued carefully, "If we get him released then all the other stations and newspapers'll cover *us*."

"Us?"

"Well, you and *Current Events*. For getting the guy out of jail."

Sutton waved her hand. "It's a small story. It's a local story." Sutton began writing on the sheet of paper in front of her. Her handwriting was elegant. "That's all."

"Well, if you could maybe just keep this." Rune opened her bag and handed Sutton a sheet of paper with a synopsis of the story. The anchorwoman slipped it underneath her china coffee cup on the far side of her desk and returned to the document she'd been reading.

Outside the woman's office the secretary looked up at Rune in horror. "Who are you?" Her voice was high in panic. "How did you get in here?"

"Sorry, got lost," Rune said gloomily and continued toward the dark-paneled elevator bank.

The elevator doors had just opened when Rune heard a voice like steel on stone. "You," Piper Sutton shouted, pointing at Rune. "Back in here. Now."

Rune hurried back to the office. Sutton, close to six feet, towered over her. She hadn't realized the anchorwoman was so tall. She hated tall women.

Sutton slammed the door shut behind them. "Sit."

Rune did.

When she too was seated Sutton said, "You didn't tell me it was Randy Boggs."

Rune said, "He's not famous. You said you weren't interested in somebody who wasn't—"

"You should've given me all the facts."

Rune looked contrite. "Sorry. I didn't think."

"All right. Boggs *could* be news. Tell me what you've found out."

"I read the letter. And I watched those tapes—of the trial and one of him in prison a year ago. He says he's innocent."

Sutton snapped. "And?"

"And, that's it."

"What do you mean, 'that's it'? That's why you think he's innocent? Because he *said* so?"

"He said the police didn't really investigate the crime. They didn't try to find many witnesses and they didn't really spend any time talking to the ones they did find."

"Didn't he tell that to his lawyer?"

"I don't know."

"And that's *all*?" Sutton asked.

"It's just that I . . . I don't know. I looked at his face on the tape and I believe him."

"You *believe* him?" Sutton laughed again. She opened her desk and took out a pack of cigarettes. She lit one with a silver lighter. Inhaled for a long moment.

Rune looked around the room, trying to think up an answer to defend herself. Being studied by Piper Sutton knocked most of the thoughts out of her head. All she said was "Read the letter." Rune nodded toward the file she'd given the woman. Sutton found it and read. She asked, "This is a copy. You have the original?"

"I thought the police might need it for evidence if he ever got a new trial. The original's locked in my desk."

Sutton closed the file. Said, "I guess I'm looking at quite a judge of human character. You're, what, some justice psychic? You get the vibes that this man's innocent and that's that? Listen, dear, at the risk of sounding like a journalism professor let me tell you something. There's only one thing that matters in news: the truth. That's all. You've got a goddamn feeling this man is innocent, well, good for you. But you go asking questions based on rumors, just because you get some kind of psychic fax that Boggs is innocent, well, that bullshit'll sink a news department real fast. Not to mention your career. Unsupported claims're cyanide in this business."

Rune said, "I was going to do the story right. I know how to research. I know how to interview. I wasn't going to go with anything that wasn't . . ." Oh, hell: *corroborated* or *collaborated*? Which was it? Rune wasn't good with sound-alike words. ". . . backed up."

Sutton calmed. "All right, what you're saying is you have a hunch and you want to check it out."

"I guess I am."

"You guess you are." Sutton nodded then pointed her cigarette at Rune. "Let me ask you a question."

"Shoot."

"I'm not suggesting that you not pursue this story."

Rune tried to sort out the *not*s.

Sutton continued, "I'd never suggest that a reporter shouldn't go after a story he feels strongly about."

Rune nodded, wrestling with *this* batch of negatives.

"But I just wonder if your efforts aren't a little misplaced. Boggs had his day in court and even if there were some minor irregularities at trial, well, so what?

"But I just have this feeling he's innocent. What can it hurt to look into it?"

Sutton's matte face scanned the room slowly then homed in on the young woman. She said in a low voice, "Are you sure you're not doing a story about *you*?"

Rune blinked. "Me?"

"Are you doing a story about Randy Boggs or about a young, ambitious journalist?" Sutton smiled again, a smile of fake innocence, and said, "What're you concerned with most—telling the truth about Boggs or making a name for yourself?"

Rune didn't speak for a minute. "I think he's in-nocent."

"I'm not going to debate the matter with you. I'm sim-ply asking the question. Only you can answer it. And I think you've got to do a lot of soul-searching to answer it honestly. . . . What happens if—I won't say it turns out he's innocent because I don't think he is—but if you find some new evidence that can convince a judge to grant him a new trial? And Boggs gets released pending that trial? And what if he robs a convenience store and kills the clerk or a customer in the process?"

Rune looked away, unable to sort out her thoughts. Too many tough questions. What the anchorwoman said made a lot of sense. She said, "I think he's innocent." But her voice was uncertain. She hated the sound. Then she said firmly, "It's a story that's got to be done."

Sutton gazed at her for a long moment, then asked, "You ever budgeted a segment on a news program? You ever assigned personnel? You ever worked with unions?"

"I'm union. I'm a camera—"

Sutton's voice rose. "Don't be stupid. I know *you're* union. I'm asking if you've ever *dealt* with the trades, as management?"

"No."

Sutton said abruptly, "Okay, whatever you do, it isn't going to be as sole producer. You're too inexperienced."

"Don't worry, I'm, like, real—"

Sutton's mouth twisted. "Enthusiastic? A fast learner? Hard working? Is that what you were going to say?"

"I'm good. That's what I was going to say."

"Miracles can happen," Sutton said, pointing a long ruddy finger at Rune. "You can be assistant producer. You can report and you can . . ." Sutton grinned. " 'like' write the story. Assuming you write more articulately than you speak. But I want somebody who's been around for a while to be in charge. You're way too—"

Rune stood up and put her hands on the desktop.

Sutton leaned back and blinked. Rune said, "I'm not a child! I came here to tell you about a story I think is going to be good for you and for the Network and all you do is insult me. I didn't *have* to come here. I could've gone to the competition. I could've just sat on the story and done it myself. But—"

Sutton laughed and held her hand up. "Come on, babes, spare me, please. I don't need to see your balls. Everybody in this business has 'em or they'd be out on their ear in five minutes. I'm not impressed." She picked up her pen, glancing down at the document in front of her. "You want to do the story, go see Lee Maisel. You'll work for him."

Rune stayed where she was for a moment, her heart pounding. She watched as Sutton read a contract as dense as the classified section in the Sunday *Times*.

"Anything else?" Sutton glanced up.

Rune said, "No. I just want to say I'll do a super job."

"Wonderful," Sutton said without enthusiasm. Then: "What was your name again?"

"Rune."

"*Is that a stage name?*"

"Sort of."

"Well, Rune, if you're really going to do this story and you don't give up halfway through because it's too much work or too tough or you don't have enough chutzpah—"

"I'm not going to give up. I'm going to get him released."

Sutton barked, "No, you're going to find the *truth*. Whatever it is, whether it gets him released or proves he kidnapped the Lindbergh baby too."

"Right," Rune said. "The truth."

"If you're really going to do it don't talk to anybody about it except Lee Maisel and me. I want status reports regularly. Verbally. None of this memo bullshit. Got it? No leaks to anyone. That's the most important thing you can do right now."

"The competition isn't going to find out."

Sutton was sighing and shaking her head the same way Rune's algebra teacher had when she'd flunked for the second time. "It's not the competition I'm worried about. I'm worried that you're wrong. That he really is guilty. If we lose a story to another network, well, that happens; it's part of the game. But if there're rumors flying around about a segment we're doing and it turns out to be wrong it's my ass on the line. *Comprende,* honey?"

Rune nodded and quickly lost the staring contest.

Sutton broke the tension with a question. She sounded amused as she asked, "I'm curious about one thing. "Do you know who Randy Boggs was convicted of killing?"

"I read his name but I don't exactly remember. But what I'll do—"

Sutton cut her off. "His name was Lance Hopper. Does that mean anything to you?"

"Not really."

"It ought to. He was head of Network News here. He was our boss. Now you see why you're playing with fire?"

chapter 4

LEE MAISEL WAS A LARGE, BALDING, BEARDED MAN IN HIS fifties. He wore brown slacks and a tweed jacket over a tie-less button-down dress shirt and a worn burgundy-and-beige argyle sweater. He smoked a meerschaum pipe, yellowed from smoke and age. The pipe was one of a dozen scattered over his desk. He didn't look like a man who made, as executive producer of one of the country's most popular TV newsmagazines, over one million dollars a year.

"I mean, how was I supposed to know who Lance Hopper was?" Rune asked.

"How indeed?"

Maisel and Rune sat in his large office in the Net-work's portion of the old armory building. Unlike Piper Sutton's office in the parent's high-rise, Maisel's was only thirty feet in the air and overlooked a bowling alley. Rune liked it that he was down here with his troops. Maisel even looked like a general. She could picture him in khaki shorts and a pith helmet, sending tanks after Nazis in North Africa.

Rune sat next to a large Mr. Coffee machine. She looked at it uncertainly—as if the pot contained the nu-clear sludge that the coffee resembled. He said, "Turk-ish." He poured a cup for himself and raised an eyebrow. She shook her head.

"Piper really rides on hyper, doesn't she?" Rune asked. Then it occurred to her that maybe she shouldn't be talking about Sutton this way, at least not to him.

Maisel didn't say anything, though. He asked, "You don't grasp the significance? About Hopper?"

"All I know is Piper said he was head of the Network. Our boss."

Maisel turned and dug through a stack of glossy magazines on his credenza. He found one and handed it to her. It wasn't a magazine, though, but an annual report of the Network's parent company. Maisel leaned forward and opened it to a page near the center, then rested a thick, yellow fingertip on one picture. "That's Lance Hopper."

Rune read, *Lawrence W. Hopper, executive vice president.* She was looking at a tall, jowly businessman in a dark suit and white shirt. He wore a red bow tie. He was in his fifties. Handsome in a businessman sort of way. Rock-hard eyes.

"You understand what you've done?" Maisel said.

"No, not exactly."

Maisel's tongue touched the corner of his mouth. He toyed with one of his pipes, replaced it. "Boggs was convicted of killing a man I knew and worked with. A man Piper knew and worked with. Lance could be a son of a bitch but he was one hell of a journalist and he turned the Network around. He was in the Walter Cronkite and David Brinkley and Mike Wallace pantheon of broadcast journalism gods. He was that good. Everybody respected Lance Hopper. When Boggs was convicted of killing him you should've heard the applause in the newsroom. Now here *you* come and say Boggs isn't guilty. That's going to cause problems around here. Loyalty problems. And it could get you and everybody involved in the project in a lot of trouble."

Maisel continued. "Look, I interviewed Boggs myself. He's a drifter. He's never had a decent job in his life. Everybody agrees with the jury that he did it. If you're right and he's innocent you're going to be pretty unpopular around here. And you aren't going to win any awards from the judge and prosecutor either. And if you're wrong you'll still be pretty unpopular but not around here because you won't be *working* here anymore. See the significance?"

"But what difference does popularity make? If he's innocent he's innocent."

"Are you as naive as you seem to be?"

"*Peter Pan's* my favorite play."

Maisel smiled. "Maybe it *is* better to have balls than brains." Rune smelled sweet-sour whisky on his breath. Yes, Maisel certainly fit the mold of an old-time journalist.

"Why don't you find a *nice* criminal who's been wrongly imprisoned and get him out of jail. Why do you have to crusade for an asshole?"

Rune said, "Innocent assholes shouldn't be in jail any more than innocent saints."

Which earned an outright laugh. Rune could tell he didn't want to smile but he did. He looked at her for a minute. "Piper called me and said there was a, well, an eager young thing from the local station who—"

Rune asked, "Is that how she described me? Eager?"

Maisel dug into his pipe with a silver tool that looked like a large flattened nail. "Not exactly. But let's let it go at that. And when she told me that, I thought, Oh, boy, another one. Eager, obnoxious, ambitious. But she won't have grit."

"I have grit."

Maisel said, "I think you may. And I have to tell you—even though I think he's guilty the Boggs case went a little too smoothly. Too fast."

"Did the media hang him out to dry before the trial?" Rune asked.

Maisel leaned back. "The media hangs *all* defendants out to dry before the trial. That's a constant. No, I'm just speaking of the cops and the court system. . . . I think this may be—*may* be—a story worth telling. If you do it right."

"I can do it. I really can."

"Piper said you're a cameraman. You have any other experience?"

"I did a documentary. It was on PBS."

"Public Broadcasting?" he asked derisively. "Well, *Current Events* is a hell of a lot different from PBS. It costs over a half-million dollars a week to produce. We don't get grants; we survive because of advertising revenue geared to our Nielsen and Arbitron. We *earn* our way. Last week we had ten-point-seven rating points. You know what a point represents?"

"Not exactly."

"Each point means that nine hundred and twenty-one thousand homes are watching us."

"Awesome," Rune said, losing the math, but thinking that a lot of people were going to see her program.

"We're fighting against some of the biggest-drawing shows in the history of television. This season we're up against *Next Door Neighbors* and *Border Patrol.*"

Rune nodded, looking impressed, even though she'd only seen one episode of *Neighbors*—the season's big hit sitcom—and thought it was the stupidest thing on TV, full of wisecracking and mugging for the camera and idiotic one-liners. *Border Patrol* had great visuals and a super sound track, though all that ever happened was that the cute young agent and the older, wiser agent argued about departmental procedures, then saved each other's ass on alternate weeks while administering large doses of political correctness to the audience.

Current Events, on the other hand, she watched all the time.

Maisel continued. "We've got four twelve-minute segments each week, surrounded by millions of dollars of commercials. You don't have time to be leisurely. You don't have time to develop subjects and give the audience mood shots. You'll shoot ten thousand feet of tape and use five hundred. We're classy. We've got computer graphics coming out of our ears. We paid ninety thousand dollars for synthesized theme music by this hotshot New Age musician. This is the big time. Our stories aren't about sex-change operations, dolphins saving fishermen's lives, three-year-old crack dealers. We report *news*. It's a magazine, the way the old *Life* and *Look* were magazines. Remember that."

Rune nodded.

"Magazine," Maisel continued, "as in pictures. I'll want lots of visuals—tape of the original crime scene, old footage, new interviews."

Rune sat forward. "Oh, yeah, and how about claustrophobic prison scenes? You know, small green rooms and bars? Maybe the rooms where they hose down prisoners? Before-and-after pictures of Boggs—to see how thin and pale he's gotten."

"Good. I like that." Maisel looked at a slip of paper. "Piper said you're with the local station. I'll have you assigned to me."

"You mean I'll be on staff? Of *Current Events*?" Her pulse picked up exponentially.

"Temporarily."

"That's fantastic."

"Maybe. And maybe not," Maisel said. "Let's see how you feel about it after you've interviewed a hundred people and been up all night—"

"I stay up late all the time."

"Editing tape?"

Rune conceded, "Dancing usually."

Maisel said, "Dancing." He seemed amused. He said, "Okay, here's the situation. Normally we assign a staff producer but, for some reason, Piper wants you to work directly with me. Nobody else. I don't have anybody to spare for camera work so you're on your own there. But you know how the hardware works—"

"I'm saving up to buy my own Betacam."

"Wonderful," he said with a bored sigh, then selected a pipe and took a leather pouch of tobacco from his desk.

A secretary's spun-haired head appeared. She said that Maisel's eleven o'clock appointment had arrived. His phone started ringing. His attention was elsewhere now. "One thing," he said to Rune.

"What?"

"I'll support you a hundred percent if you stick to the rules, wherever the story takes you. But you fuck with the facts, you try to *create* a story when there isn't one there, you speculate, you lie to me, Piper or the audience, and I'll cut you loose in a second and you'll never work in journalism in this city again. Got that?"

"Yessir."

"So. Get to work."

Rune blinked. "That's it? I thought you were going to, like, tell me what to do or something."

As he turned to the phone Maisel said abruptly, "Okay, I'll tell you what to do: You think there's a story out there? Well, go get it."

"THIS AIN' YOU."

"Sure it is. Only what I did with my hair was I used henna and this kind of purple stuff then I'd use mousse to get it spiky. . . ."

The security guard at the New York State Department of Correctional Services' Manhattan office looked at Rune's laminated press pass from the Network, dangling a chrome chain tail. It showed a picture of her with a wood-peckery, glossy hairdo and wearing round, tinted John Lennon glasses.

"This ain' you."

"No, really." She dug the glasses out of her purse and put them on then grabbed her hair and pulled it straight up. "See?"

The guard looked back and forth for a moment from the ID to the person, then nodded and handed the pass back to her. "You want my opinion, keep that stuff outta yo hair. That ain' healthy for nobody."

Rune put the chain necklace over her head. She walked into the main office, looking at the bulletin boards, the government-issue desks, the battered water fountains. It seemed like a place where people in charge of prisons should work: claustrophobic, colorless, quiet.

She thought about poor Randy Boggs, serving three years in his tiny cell.

The first thing you think is Hell, I'm still here. . . .

A tall man in a rumpled cream-colored suit walked past her, glancing down at her pass. He paused. "You're press?"

Rune didn't understand him at first. "Oh, press. Yeah. I'm a reporter. *Current Events*. You know, the news—"

He laughed. "Everybody knows *Current Events*." He stuck his hand out. "I'm Bill Swenson. Head of press relations here."

She shook his hand and introduced herself. Then she said, "I guess I'm looking for you. I have to talk to somebody about interviewing a prisoner."

"Is this for a story?"

Rune said, "Uh-huh."

"Not a problem. But you don't have to go through us. You can contact the warden's office directly for permission and then the prisoner himself to arrange a time to meet if the warden agrees."

"That's all?"

"Yes," Swenson said. "What facility?"

"Harrison."

"Doing hard time, huh?"

"Yeah, I guess it would be."

"Who's the prisoner?"

She was hesitating. "Well . . ."

Swenson said, "We've got to know. Don't worry— I won't leak it. I didn't get where I am by screwing journalists."

She said, "Okay, it's Randy Boggs. He was convicted of killing Lance Hopper."

Swenson nodded. "Oh, sure, I remember that case. Three years ago. Hopper worked for your company, right? Wait, he was *head* of the Network."

"That's right. Only the thing is, I think Boggs is innocent."

"Innocent, really?"

Rune nodded. "And I'm going to try to get the case reopened and get him released. Or a new trial."

"That's going to make one hell of a story." Swenson glanced up and down the halls. "Off the record?"

"Sure." Rune felt a chill of excitement. Here was her first confidential source.

"Every year there're dozens of people wrongly convicted in New York. Sometimes they get out, sometimes they don't. It's a scary thing to think it could happen."

"I think it'll make a good story."

Swenson started down the hall back toward the exit. Rune followed him. He said, "They'll give you the phone number of the warden in Harrison at the main desk." He escorted her through the security gate and to the door. She said, "I'm glad I ran into you."

"Good luck," he said. "I'll look forward to that show."

chapter 5

WHEN RUNE CLIMBED UP THE GANGWAY ONTO HER HOUSE-
boat, which was rocking gently in the Hudson River off the
west side of Greenwich Village, she heard crying inside. A
child's crying.

Her hand hesitated at the deadbolt then she un-
locked the door and walked inside.

"Claire," Rune said uncertainly. Then, because she
couldn't think of anything else to say, she added, "You're
still here."

In the middle of the living room the young woman
was on her knees, comforting three-year-old Courtney.
Claire nodded at Rune and gave her a sullen smile, then
turned back to the little girl.

"It's okay, honey."

"What happened?"

"She just fell. She's okay."

Claire was a few years older than Rune. They looked
a lot alike, except that Claire was into a beatnik phase,
while Rune shunned the antique look for New Wave.
Claire dyed her hair black and pulled it straight back in a
severe ponytail. She often wore pedal pushers and black-
and-white-striped pullovers. Her face was deathly white
and on her lips was the loudest crimson lipstick Max Fac-
tor dared sell. The only advantage in her rooming here—
since she'd stopped paying rent—was that her fashion
statement added to the houseboat's decor, which was
1950s suburban.

After Claire had lost her job at Celestial Crystals on Broadway and been evicted from her fifth-floor East Village walk-up she'd begged Rune to take her and her daughter in. Claire had said, "Come on. Just a day or two. It'll be fun. Like a pajama party."

That had been six weeks ago—and what had followed had been like no pajama party Rune had ever been to.

That morning, before Rune went to work, Claire had told her that she'd gotten a new job and promised that she and Courtney would be gone by dinnertime.

Now, Claire stood up and shook her head in disgust. "What it is, that guy, he backed out. Some effing people!"

Rune didn't exactly remember who "that guy" was or what he was backing out of. But Rune was now even madder at him than Claire was. She's gotta go. . . . Talk now or later? Now, she decided. But her courage broke. Shit. She dropped her leopard-skin bag on the purple shag kidney-shaped scrap of carpet that she'd found on the street then bent down and kissed the three-year-old's forehead.

Courtney stopped crying. "Rune," she said. "Story. Read me a story?" She was dressed in blue jeans and a dirty yellow pullover.

"Later, honey, it's time for dinner," Rune said, crouching down and smoothing the girl's curly dark hair. "This hair is like totally audacious." She stood up and walked into the galley of the houseboat. As she poured Grape-Nuts into a large bowl and added chocolate chips and cashews she shouted to Claire, "Her hair, I was saying. What it is is all that garbage we use. We dye it and we mousse it and we perm it. I'll bet if you never touch your hair it'd be as nice as that forever."

Claire said sourly, "Well, sure, but that would like be *so* boring."

Rune came back into the living room, eating the cereal and drinking a Molson Golden. "You eaten?"

"We ate Chinese."

"Courtney too? Is that good for her?"

Claire said, "Are you kidding? There are a billion people in China and whatta you think they grew up on?"

"I don't know—"

"*You're* eating that crap?" Claire glanced at the cereal.

"I'm not a three-year-old. Don't you watch commercials? She's supposed to be eating that gross stuff that comes in jars. You know, like pureed carrots and spinach."

"Rune," Claire said, "she's not an infant. She's got teeth."

"I like spinch," Courtney said.

Rune said, "I was you, I'd get that book. Spock."

"The guy on the old *Star Trek*?" Claire asked.

"Different Spock."

Claire said, "The Vulcan nerve pinch. That's what I'd like to learn. Put 'em right to sleep."

"What's a Vulcan?" Courtney asked. Then she disappeared into the bedroom without waiting for an answer. She returned a few minutes later, pulling a stuffed dragon by the tail.

Rune made the dragon dance, then hugged Courtney. She asked the little girl, "What's her name? Do you remember?"

"Persephy."

"Very good. Persephone. And who was Persephone?"

Courtney held up the dragon.

"No, I mean in real life?"

Claire said, "Real life?"

"She was a goddess," Courtney answered. "She was Zeus's little girl."

Claire said, "I don't think it's a good idea you're teaching her that stuff like it's true."

"What isn't true about it?"

"About the gods and goddesses and fairies and all that shit."

"Shit," said Courtney.

Rune said to Claire, "You're saying it's not true?"

"You believe in Roman goddesses?"

"Persephone was Greek. I'm not saying I believe and I'm not saying I don't."

"I want her to grow up to be a highly grounded person," Claire said.

"Oh, get real," Rune said. "Your goal in life is to get to every club in downtown Manhattan and never pay for a drink yourself. *That's* reality?"

"I want her to be an adult."

Rune whispered, "She's three years old. She'll grow up fast enough."

Claire cocked an eyebrow at Rune. "Some people I know have resisted adulthood totally successfully." She smiled sweetly. "Favor, please?"

"I'm broke."

"Naw, what it is is I gotta go out tonight. Babysit, will you?"

"Claire—"

"I met this guy and he was talking about a job. He might hire me."

"Which *club're* you going to meet him at?" Rune asked wryly.

"S.O.B.'s," Claire admitted. "But he really thinks he can get me work. Come on, please. . . ." Nodding at her daughter. "You two get along so good."

Rune looked at Courtney. "We *do* get along, don't we, dude? Gimme five high." She held up her hand and Courtney crawled forward. They slapped upraised palms.

"Dude," the little girl said then crawled back to Persephone. Rune looked at her face and didn't see much of Claire in it. She wondered who the father was. Claire, she knew, occasionally wondered the same.

After a moment Rune said, "You know, I'm not, like, too good with saying things like this. . . ." Rune paused, hoping Claire would pick up on the hint. But she was concentrating on putting a fake diamond earring into one of the holes on the side of her nose. Rune continued, "What I'm saying is you really've *got* to find a place to live."

"I didn't plan on staying this long. It's not that easy to find a place to live in Manhattan."

"I know," Rune said. "Look, I don't want to kick you out."

Claire got solemn for a moment. "The truth is I'm thinking about going back to Boston. Just to get my act together for a while. What do you think?"

Hallelujah!

Rune said, "I think that's a very mature thing to do."

"Really?"

"I do. Absolutely."

"I'll stay with my mother. She's got a nice house. I can have the upstairs to myself. The only thing that bothers me is I don't know what I could do there exactly."

Rune wasn't sure what Claire could do here in Manhattan either, except hang out and go to clubs, which she could probably do in Boston just as easily and for a lot less money. But she said, "Boston's supposed to be a wonderful place. History, lots of history."

"Yeah, history. But, excuse me, what do you do with history?"

"You don't have to *do* anything with it. It's just neat." Rune hefted Courtney to the windowsill, propped her on her hip. "Just look out there, honey, and picture it three hundred years ago. You know who lived there? Indians! The Canarsie Indians. And there were bears and deer and everything."

"Like the zoo," the girl said. "Can we go to the zoo?"

"Sure we can. Maybe tomorrow. And see over there, all those roads? They used to be tobacco fields. They called the place Sapokanikan. It means the tobacco plantation. Then the settlers came up here from New York City—which was all down by the Battery then. They came up here because they had all these terrible plagues or epidemics—and they saw all these fields and farmland and the place got called Green Village—"

Claire interrupted, "And now it's Greenwich Village and it's got bagels and coffeehouses and ATM machines and the Antique Clothes Boutique."

Rune shook her head. "Oh, you're just so sitcom, it's disgusting."

Claire said, "So—Boston . . . You mind if I spend some time there?"

Mind? Rune felt as if she'd just gotten a package in a turquoise Tiffany's box. "I'd say: Do it."

"Then I will," Claire said lethargically. She yawned and pulled a vial out of her purse. "You want some coke?"

"Coke," said Courtney.

Rune took Claire by the arm roughly, whispering viciously: "Are you crazy? Look what you're teaching her." She snatched the vial and spoon away from Claire and tossed them back into the purse.

Claire pulled away angrily. "Coke is real. Dragons and goddesses aren't."

"You keep your reality." Rune stood up and took Courtney by the hand and led her up onto the outer deck. "Come on, honey, I'll read you a story."

AN HOUR LATER COURTNEY ASKED, "ONE MORE, PLEASE."

Rune debated, flipping through the book of fairy stories. She glanced down into the galley and saw Claire doing a small line of coke off her compact mirror.

"Okay," Rune said. "One more, then off to bed."

She looked at the story the book had fallen open to and laughed. "The Snow Princess." Which seemed like a good choice since Claire had a nose blizzard going at the moment.

" 'Once upon a time—' "

"In a land far away," Courtney yawned and lay down with her head in Rune's lap.

"That's right. '. . . in a land far away, there lived an old couple who never had any children.' "

"I'm a children."

" 'The man and woman loved each other dearly but dreamed about how happy they would be if only they had a daughter to share their life with. Then one winter, as the husband was walking home through the forest, he saw a snowman that some children had built and he had an idea. He went home and together, with his wife, they built a little princess out of snow.' "

"What's snow?"

"Last winter, that white stuff."

"I don't remember," the girl said, frowning.

"It comes out of the sky and it's white."

"Feathers."

"No, it's like wet."

"Milk."

"Never mind. Anyway, the couple went to bed and all night long they wished and wished real hard and what do you think happened?"

"They got a little girl?"

Rune nodded. " 'In the morning when they woke up there was the most beautiful little princess, who looked just like the girl the couple had made out of snow the night before. They hugged her and kissed her, and they spent all their time playing with her and taking the little girl for walks in the forest. The couple was so happy. . . .

" 'Then one day a handsome prince came riding along through the snow, and saw the snow princess playing in a snow-filled field beside the couple's house. They looked at each other and fell in love.' "

"What's—?" Courtney began.

"Never mind that. The thing is he wanted the snow princess to come live with him in his castle at the foot of the mountain. The snow princess's parents were very sad and begged her not to go but she married the prince and went off to live with him in the castle.

" 'They were very happy throughout the winter, then one day in early spring the sun came out, strong and hot, as the snow princess was walking with her husband. . . .' "

Rune paused and read ahead in the story—to the part where the sun gets hotter and hotter and the princess melts, the water running through her husband's fingers into the ground until there's nothing left of her. She looked up at the girl's expectant face and thought: We've got a problem here.

"Go on," Courtney said.

Pretending to read, Rune said, "Well, the sun was so hot that the snow princess remembered how much she missed her parents and she kissed her husband good-bye and climbed back up to the mountain village, where she moved back in with her parents, and got a job and met a neat guy, who was also made out of snow, and they lived happily ever after."

"I like that story," Courtney said in her tone of an official pronouncement.

Claire came out on deck. "Time for bed."

Courtney didn't complain much. Rune kissed her good night then helped Claire put her pajamas on her and get her into bed.

"You know, if you're interested," Claire said, "it's much easier to meet men in Boston."

"You want me to go to Boston with you? Just to meet men?"

"Sure, why not?"

"Because most men are damaged to start with. Why should I go somewhere where it's *easier* to meet men? I'd think you'd want to go where it's harder."

"What's wrong with men?"

"Haven't you noticed something?" Rune asked. "How many men do you know whose IQ matches their age?"

"You gonna marry Sam?"

"He's a great guy," Rune said defensively, uneasy with the *M* word. "We have a good time. . . ."

Claire sighed. "He's twenty years older than you, he's going bald, he's married."

"He's separated," Rune said. "Anyway, what twenty-five-year-olds with hair have you met that're such good catches?" Admitting to herself, though, that the married part was definitely an ongoing problem.

"You move to Boston, you'll be married in six months. I guarantee it." Claire pirouetted. "How do I look?"

Like a hooker, circa 1955.

Rune said, "Stunning."

Claire grabbed her bag and slung it over her shoulder. "I owe you one."

"I know you do," Rune said and watched her clatter unsteadily down the gangplank on high-heeled saddle shoes.

chapter 6

THE NOTE ON HER DESK THE NEXT MORNING, FROM MAI-
sel, was to the point.

Sutton's office. The minute you come in!
                                        —*Lee*

Rune had received a lot of notes like this and they were
usually the preface to flunking a course, getting fired or
getting yelled at.

Heart pounding, she left her Morning Thunder tea
on her desk and walked out of the studio. In ten minutes
she was standing in front of Piper Sutton's secretary. Yesterday's look of terror at Rune's unauthorized entry had
been replaced by a subtle gloat.

Rune said, "I'm supposed to see—"

"They're waiting for you."

"Is it okay to—?"

"They're waiting for you," the woman repeated cheerfully.

Inside, Sutton and Maisel turned their heads and
stared as she approached. Rune stopped halfway into the
big office.

"Close the door," Sutton ordered.

Rune obeyed then walked into the room. She smiled
at Maisel, who avoided her eyes.

Oh, boy, she thought. Oh, boy.

Sutton's eyes were flint. She said, "Sit down," just as

Rune was dropping into the chair across from the desk.
Rune felt a shiver down her back and the hairs on her
neck stirred. Sutton tossed a copy of one of the city's
tabloids on her desk. Rune picked it up and read a story
circled in thick, red ink that bled into the fibers of the
newsprint.

NETWORK WANTS TO FREE KILLER OF ITS EXEC

By Bill Stevens

The story was short, just a few paragraphs. It recounted
how a reporter from *Current Events* was investigating
Randy Boggs's conviction for Lance Hopper's murder.
Boggs's defense lawyer, Fred Megler, had no comment
other than to say that his client has always maintained his
innocence.

"Oh, shit," she muttered.

"How?" Sutton tapped her glossy fingernails on the
desktop. They were as red and hard as the finish on a
Porsche. "How did this happen?"

"It's not my fault. He lied to me."

"Bill Stevens?"

"That wasn't the name he gave me. I was at the Department of Corrections and this guy came up and said he
worked for the press department and could he help me
and he was real nice and he even told me things off the
record so I assumed it was okay to—"

"Assumed it was okay?" Sutton's voice rose. She lifted
her eyes to the ceiling. "I don't believe it."

Maisel sighed. "This's the oldest trick in the book.
Jesus, Rune, you fucked this one up. Stevens is a beat reporter for the paper. He covers the government agencies.
When he sees a reporter who's new and doesn't recognize
him he finds out what their assignment is then scoops
them."

"You walked right into his arms." Sutton lit a cigarette

and slapped the lighter down on the desktop. "A fucking babe in the woods."

"He seemed like a nice guy."

"What the hell does 'nice' have to do with anything?" Maisel asked, exasperated. "This is journalism."

All ruined. My one big chance and I blew it, right out of the gate.

Sutton asked Maisel, "Damage assessment?"

"None of the other nets are that interested." He touched the tabloid. "Even Stevens didn't follow up on Boggs. The focus of the story was that *we're* trying to get him released. So we look like idiots if it doesn't pan out." He toyed with an unlit pipe and stared at the ceiling. "The story's hit some syndicated news services but so far all we've had are a couple of junior reporters call Publicity for statements. Nobody on Wallace's or Rather's level. Nobody from *Media in Review*. It's a pain in the ass but I don't think it's critical."

Sutton kept her eyes on Rune as she said, "I've already gotten a call from Semple."

Maisel closed his eyes. "Ouch. I thought he was in Paris."

"He is. The *Herald Tribune* picked up the story in their third edition."

Dan Semple was the current head of Network News. He'd taken over when Lance Hopper was killed. He was, give or take a few miracles, God. One of the reasons that Hopper was so sorely missed was that he was an angel compared with Semple, who was known for his vicious temper and cut-throat business practices. He'd even punched a junior producer who'd carelessly lost an exclusive to CNN.

Maisel asked, "What was his reaction?"

"Not fit for human consumption," Sutton said. "He'll be back in a few days and he wants to talk about it." She sighed. "Corporate politics . . . just what we need now.

And with the budgets coming up in a month . . ." Sutton looked at the newspaper, gestured at it then glanced at Rune. "But the big danger of this is what?"

Maisel was nodding. But Rune didn't get it.

"I . . ."

"Think," Sutton snapped.

"I don't know. I'm sorry."

Maisel supplied the answer. "That another magazine or feature program'll pick up the lead and bring out the story at the same time we do. It's a news policy—we don't spend time and money on a story if there's a chance we'll be preempted."

Rune rocked forward in the chair. "It won't happen again. I promise. I'll be so skeptical you won't believe it."

"Rune," Sutton began.

"Look, what I'll do is ask people when I interview them if anybody from any other station has been asking them questions. If they have been I'll tell you. I promise. That way you can decide if you want to go ahead with the story or not."

Maisel said, "The only weapon journalists have is their minds. You've got to start using yours."

"I will. Just like the Scarecrow."

Sutton asked, "The what?"

"You know, *The Wizard of Oz*. He wanted a brain and—"

"Enough." Sutton waved her hand, managing to make her face both blank and hostile at the same time. Finally she said, "All right. Keep on it. But if anybody beats us to the punch—I'm talking *anybody*: a rap station, MTV, Columbia's student station—we drop the project. Lee?"

"Okay with me," Maisel said.

Lighting another cigarette, Sutton nodded and said, "All right. But this was your last strike, babes."

"I thought you got three," Rune said, standing up, retreating to the door.

Sutton tossed the lighter onto her desk; it skidded into a crystal ashtray. "We play by *my* rules around here. Not the American League's."

THE CHAMELEON SAT ON THE WALL, AT AN ANGLE, FROzen in space, hardly breathing.

Jack Nestor lay in bed and watched it.

He liked chameleons. Not the way they changed color, which wasn't so spectacular when it came right down to it. It was more the way they were fragile and soft. He sometimes could get up real close to them—the ones around the Miami Beach Starlite Motor Lodge were used to people. He'd pick one up and let it walk along his massive, tanned forearm. He liked feeling the baby-skin of the lizard and the pleasant tickle of its feet.

Sometimes he'd plop one down on his dark blurred tattoo, hoping it would turn to that deep blue color, but it never did. They didn't change to flesh color either. What they did was they jumped the hell off his arm and scurried away like long roaches.

Nestor was forty-eight years old but looked younger. He still had a thick wavy mass of hair, which he kept in place with Vitalis and spray. It was dark blond though contained some timid streaks of gray. Nestor had a squarish head and a hint of a double chin but the only thing about his body that bothered him was his belly. Nestor was fat. His legs were strong and thin and he had good shoulders but his large chest sat above a round belly that jutted out and curled over his waistband, hiding his Marine Corps belt buckle. Nestor didn't understand why he had this problem. He couldn't remember the last time he'd sat down to a proper meal, roast beef and potatoes and bread and vegetables and pie for dessert (he thought it was probably Christmas Day six years ago, when the prison cooks had laid out a really good spread). What he ate now was just Kentucky Fried and Whoppers and Big

Macs. He missed Arthur Treacher's Fish 'N Chips and wondered if they were still in business anywhere. Anyway, he thought it wasn't fair that all he was eating was these fucking tiny meals and he was still gaining weight.

Nestor noticed two red-and-white-striped boxes in bed. The Colonel grinned at him. Nestor kicked the boxes onto the floor. They tumbled open and bones and coleslaw shreds scattered on the floor.

The chameleon took off.

"Ooops," Nestor said.

He pulled on his T-shirt and smoothed his hair back. He yawned and groped on the bedside table for a cigarette. The pack was empty but he found a used one, still an inch long, lit it and stacked the cheap pillows against the headboard. He sat back, yawned again, and coughed.

Flashes of sun shot off speeding cars and burst against the wall. The room's window, as advertised, did overlook the beach; that much was true. However, the view had to get across six lanes of highway, two access roads and the hotel parking lot before it eased through the streaked window of room 258. Nestor listened to the sticky rush of the traffic for a few minutes, then reached over and squeezed the butt of the young woman lying next to him.

The third time, when he got a little rougher, she stirred.

"No," she mumbled with a thick Cuban accent.

"Rise and shine," Nestor said.

She was in her mid-thirties, with a body that looked ten years younger and a face that went ten years the other way. Her eye shadow and mascara were smeared. The lipstick, too, was a mess and it looked as if her lips had slid to the side of her face. She opened her eyes briefly, rolled over on her back and pulled a thin sheet up to her navel.

"No, not again."

"What?"

"Not again. It hurt last night."

"You didn't say nothing about it hurting."

"So? You wouldn't have stopped."

That was true but he would at least have asked if she felt better before they went to sleep.

"You all right now?"

"I just don't wanna."

Nestor didn't want to either. What he wanted was breakfast—two Egg McMuffins and a large coffee. He crushed out the cigarette and bent down and kissed her breast.

Mumbling, eyes closed, she said, "No, Jacky, I don't wanta. I have to go to the bathroom."

"Well, I gotta have either you or breakfast. So, what's it gonna be?"

After a moment: "What you want for breakfast?"

He told her and five minutes later she was in her orange spandex miniskirt struggling along the glisteningly hot sidewalk to the McDonald's up the street.

Nestor took a shower, spending most of the time rubbing his stomach with this green-handled pad with bumps on it. Somebody'd told him that if you did that, it broke up the fat cells and flushed them away. He thought he noticed a difference already even though on the scale he hadn't lost any weight yet. He kneaded the large glossy star-shaped scar six inches to the left of his navel, a memento of the time a hollow-point 7.62mm slug had made a journey through his abdomen. Nestor had never gotten used to the leathery feel of the flesh. He had a habit of squeezing and running his fingers over it.

He rinsed off, stepped out of the shower and spent a lot of time shaving then getting his hair into shape. He dressed in a dark-green, short-sleeved knit shirt and the gray pants he always wore. Dungarees. He wondered why anybody would call pants anything that started in *"dung."* *Shitarees, Craparees*. He pulled on thin black nylon socks, sheer like women's stockings, then strapped on black sandals.

He stepped out of the bathroom, which was filled

with steam and hair spray mist, and smelled the food, resting on the TV. The woman was sitting at the chipped desk putting on her makeup. For a minute, looking at her buoyant breasts in the tight yellow sweater, Nestor's hunger for food wavered, but then the McMuffins won and he sat on the bed to eat.

He ate the first one quickly and then, with the edge off his appetite, lay back on the bed to read the paper and sip his coffee while he worked on the second one. He noticed she'd bought some insurance; a third McMuffin was also in the bag—to keep his appetites and his hands occupied. He laughed but she pretended she didn't know he'd caught on.

He'd gotten halfway through the front section of the *Miami Herald,* reading the national news, when he sat upright in bed. "Oh, shit."

She was curling her eyelashes. "Huh?"

But Nestor was standing up, walking to his dresser, wiping his mouth with the back of his hand. He pulled out a jumble of underwear and socks and knit shirts.

"Hey, iron these for me?" He handed her the shirts.

"Jacky, what is it?"

"Just get the iron out, okay?"

She did and spread a thin towel on the desk for an ironing board. She ironed each shirt, then folded it precisely.

"Whatsa matter?"

"I've got to go away for a little while."

"Yeah, where you going? Can I come too?"

"New York."

"Oh, Jacky, I've never been—"

"Forget about it. This's business."

She handed him the shirts then snorted. "What business? You got no business."

"I got a business. I just never told you about it."

"Yeah, so what do you do?"

Nestor began to pack a suitcase. "I'll be back in a

week or two." He hesitated then took out his wallet and handed her two hundred and ten dollars. "I'm not back then pay Seppie for the room for next couple weeks, okay?"

"Sure, I'll do that."

He looked at the dresser again then said to her, "Hey, check in the bathroom, see if I left my razor?"

She did this and when she wasn't looking Nestor reached way back into the bottom drawer of the dresser and took out a dark-blue Steyr GB 9mm pistol and two full clips of bullets. He slipped these into his bag. Then he said, "Hey, never mind, I found it. I packed it already."

She came up to him. "You gonna miss me?"

He picked up the paper and tore out the story. He read it again. She came up and read over his shoulder. "What that about? Somebody getting some guy outta jail in New York?"

He looked at her with irritation and put the scrap in his wallet.

She said, "Who is that guy, Randy Boggs?"

Nestor smiled in an unamused way and kissed her on the mouth. Then he said, "I'll call you." He picked up the bag and walked outside into the blast of humid heat, glancing at a tiny chameleon sitting motionless in a band of shade on the peeling banister.

chapter 7

"IF HE DIDN'T DO THIS CRIME HE DID *SOMETHING*."

The man's voice went high at the end of the sentence and threatened to break apart. He was in his late forties, so skinny that his worn cowhide belt made pleats in slacks that were supposed to be straight-cut.

"And if he did *something* the jury says, 'What the hell, let's convict him of *this*.'"

Rune nodded at the taut words.

Randy Boggs's lawyer sat at his desk, which was piled high—yellow sheets, court briefs, Redweld folders, letters, photographs of crime scenes, an empty yogurt carton crusty on the rim, a dozen cans of Diet Pepsi, a shoe box (she wondered if it contained a Mafia client's fee). The office was near Broadway on Maiden Lane in lower Manhattan, where the streets were grimy, dark, crowded. Inside, the building was a network of dirty, green corridors.

The office of Frederick T. Megler, J.D., P.C., was at the end of a particularly dirty and particularly green corridor.

He sat back in his old leather chair. His face was gray and mottled and would make occasional forays into exaggerated expressions (wonder, hatred, surprise) then snap back into its waiting state of innocent incredulity, punctuated with a breathy, nasal snort.

"That's what I have to deal with." The bony fingers of

his right hand made a circuit of the air as he explained the judicial system in New York to Rune. "The way it works . . ." He looked at Rune and his voice rose in volume for emphasis. "The way the system works is that the jury can *only* convict you for the crime for which you've been accused. They can't convict you because you're an asshole or because of the three guys you wasted last year or because of the old lady you're *going* to mug tomorrow for her social security check. Just for the particular crime."

"Got it," Rune said.

Megler's other set of bony fingers joined in. They pointed at her. "You get things like this true story. My client's arrested for killing some poor son of a bitch. An ADA—assistant district attorney—bless her young, virginal soul, brings him up on four counts. Murder two, manslaughter one and two, criminally negligent homicide. Those last three counts are what they call lesser-included offenses. They're easier to prove. If you can't get a conviction on murder—which is hard to prove to the jury— maybe you can get the manslaughter. If you can't get that maybe you'll get criminally negligent homicide. Okay? So. My client—who's got a rap sheet a mile long—had a grudge against the victim. When the cops arrested him based on an informer, he was in a bar in Times Square, where four witnesses swore he'd been drinking for the past five hours. The victim was killed two hours before. Shot five times in the head at close range. No murder weapon."

"So your client had a perfect alibi," Rune said. "And no gun."

"Exactly." The voice dipped from its screech and sounded earnest. "I grill the informant in court and by the time I'm through his story's as riddled as the vic's forehead, okay? But what happens? The jury *convicts* my guy. Not of murder, which is what they should've done if they believed the informant, but of criminally negligent homicide. Which is total bullshit. You don't *negligently* shoot

five bullets into somebody's head. Either you don't believe
the alibi and convict him of murder or you let him off
completely. The chickenshit jury didn't have the balls to
get him on murder but they couldn't let him walk because
he's a black kid from the Bronx who had a record and'd
said on a number of occasions he wanted to cut the vic's
spleen out of his body."

Rune sat forward in her chair. "See, that's just what
I'm doing my story on—an innocent man got convicted."

"Whoa, honey, who said my client was innocent?"

She blinked and mentally reviewed the facts for a
moment. "I thought *you* did. What about the gun, what
about the alibi?"

"Naw, he killed the vic, ditched the gun, then paid
four buddies a couple six-packs of crack to perjure themselves. . . ."

"But—"

"But the point is not is he guilty? The point is you
gotta play by the rules. And the jury didn't. You can only
convict on the evidence that was presented. The jury
didn't do that."

"What's so wrong with that? He was guilty and the
jury convicted him. That sounds okay to me."

"Let's change the facts a little. Let's pretend that
young black Fred Williams, National Merit Scholar with a
ticket to Harvard Medical School, who all he's ever done
bad is get a parking ticket, is walking down a Hundred
and Thirty-fifth Street when two of New York's finest
screech up behind him, get him in a choke hold then drag
him to the precinct and book him for rape. He gets picked
out of a lineup because they all look alike, et cetera, and
the case goes to trial. There the DA describes to a predominantly Caucasian middle-class jury how this kid
beat, raped and sodomized a mother of two. Then a predominantly Caucasian middle-class witness describes the
perp as a black kid with razor-notched hair and basketball
sneakers and the predominantly Caucasian middle-class

doctor gets up and describes the victim's injuries in horrifying detail. What the fuck do you think is going to happen to Fred? He's going to jail and he ain't gonna be just visiting."

Rune was quiet.

"So every time a shooter who Glocks some poor asshole five times in the head gets convicted by a cheating jury—i.e., a flawed legal system—that means there's a risk that Fred Williams is gonna go down for something he *didn't* do. And as long as that's a risk then the world's got to put up with people like me."

Rune gave him a coy look. "So's that your closing argument?"

Megler laughed. "A variation on one of them. I've got a great repertoire. Blows the jury away."

"I don't really believe what you're saying but it looks like you do."

"Oh, I do indeed. And as soon as I stop believing it then I'm out of the business. I'll go into handicapping or professional blackjack. The odds are better and you still get paid in cash. Now, I've got some truly innocent clients arriving in about a half hour. You said you wanted to ask me about the Boggs case? Anything about that article I read?"

"Yes."

"You're doing the story?"

"Right. Can I tape you?"

His thin face twisted. He looked like Ichabod Crane in her illustrated copy of *Sleepy Hollow*. "Why don't you just take notes."

"If you'd feel more comfortable . . ."

"I would."

She pulled out a notebook. She asked, "You represented Boggs by yourself?"

"Yep. He was a Section Eighteen case. Indigent. So the state paid my fee to represent him."

"I really think he's innocent."

"Uh-huh."

"No, I really, really think so."

"You say so."

"You don't?"

"My opinion of my clients' innocence or guilt is completely, totally irrelevant."

She asked, "Could you tell me what happened? About Hopper's death, I mean."

Megler sat back in a thoughtful pose. He studied the grimy ceiling. The window was open a crack and exhaust-scented April air riffled stacks of paper.

"The district attorney's case was that Boggs was in Manhattan, just driving through from, I don't know, upstate someplace. Some witness said Boggs was standing on the sidewalk talking with Hopper and then they got into a fight over something. Hopper'd just gotten home from work and had just pulled into the courtyard of his building on the Upper West Side. The prosecutor speculated it was a traffic dispute."

Rune's eyes made a sardonic circuit of the room. "Traffic? But he was on the sidewalk, you said."

"Maybe he parked after Hopper cut him off and got out of the car. I don't know."

"But—"

"Hey, you asked what the assistant district attorney said. I'm telling you. I'm trying to be helpful. Am I being helpful?"

"Helpful," Rune said. "What was Randy's story?"

"Part of the problem was that he *had* a story."

"Huh?"

"I tell all my clients, if you're arrested don't take the stand. Under any circumstances. The jury can't—the judge tells them this—the jury can't draw any conclusions from the defendant's not taking the stand. But Randy—against my advice, I wanta point out—did. If you do that the prosecutor can introduce evidence of prior convictions for the purpose of attacking your honesty. Only that—not to prove you have a criminal tendency. Just to show that you might lie. But what does the jury hear? Fuck credibility—all they hear is his string of arrests for petty crimes. Next thing you know, Boggs, who's really a pretty decent guy who's had some bad luck, is sounding like Hitler. He's got a petty larceny bust in Ohio, some juvie bullshit down in Florida, GTA in—"

"What's that?"

"Grand theft auto. So suddenly, the ADA's making him sound like he's head of the Gambino family. He—"

"Where was the gun?"

"Let me finish, willya? He said he was with this guy picked him up hitchhiking, a guy who was into some kind of credit card scam. This guy goes to buy some hot plastic and Boggs is waiting in the car. He hears a shot up the street. He gets out of the car. He sees Hopper lying there, dead. He turns and runs smack into a police car."

"He had the gun?"

"The gun was off a ways, in some bushes. No prints but they traced it to a theft in Miami about a year before the killing. Boggs had spent time in Miami."

"Who was this other guy?"

"Boggs didn't know. He was hitchhking along the Taconic and the man picked him up. They drove into the city together."

"Good," Rune said. "A witness. Excellent. Did you find him?"

Megler looked at her as if enthusiasm and the flu were pretty much the same thing. "Yeah, right. Even if he's real, which he isn't, a guy who's involved in a credit card boost's gonna come forward and testify? I don't think so, honey."

"Did Randy describe him?"

"Not very well. All he said was his name was Jimmy. Was a big guy. But it was late, it was dark, et cetera, et cetera."

"You don't believe him?"

"Believe, not believe—what difference does it make?"

"Any other witnesses?"

"Good question. You want to go to law school?"

If you're the end product I don't think you want to hear my answer, Megler. She motioned for him to continue.

The lawyer said, "That was the big problem. What fucked him—excuse me, what did him in was this witness. The cops found someone in the building who described Boggs and then later she IDed him in a lineup. She saw him pull out a gun and ice Hopper."

"Ouch."

"Yeah, ouch."

"What was the name?"

"How would I know?" Megler opened a file cabinet and retrieved a thick stack of paper. He tossed it on the desk. Pepsi cans shook and dust rose. "It's in there someplace. You can have it, you want."

"What is it?"

"The trial transcript. I ordered it as a matter of course but Boggs didn't want to appeal so I just filed it away."

"He didn't want to appeal?"

"He kept claiming he was innocent but he said he wanted to get the clock running. Get his sentence over with and get on with his life."

Rune said, "I saw in the story that the conviction was for manslaughter."

"The jury convicted on manslaughter one. He showed reckless disregard for human life. Got sentenced to fifteen years. He's served almost three. He'll be eligible for parole in two. And he'll probably get it. I hear he's a good boy."

"What do you think?"

"About what?"

"Is he one of your guilty clients?"

"Of course. The old I-was-just-hitchhiking story. You hear it all the time. There's always a mysterious driver or girl or hit man or somebody who pulled the trigger and then disappears. Bullshit is what it is. Yeah, Boggs is guilty. I can read them all."

"But if I found new evidence—"

"I've heard this before."

"No, really. He wrote me a letter. He said the police dropped the ball on the investigation. They found the witnesses they wanted and didn't look any further."

Megler snorted cynically. "Look, in New York it's almost impossible to get a conviction overturned because of new evidence." He squinted, recalling the law. "It's got to be the kind of evidence that would've changed the outcome of the case in the first place and, even then, you have to be able to show you made diligent efforts to find the evidence at the time of the trial."

"But if I do find something would you handle the case?"

"Me?" He laughed. "I'm available. But you're talking a lot of hours. I bill at two twenty per. And the state ain't picking up *this* tab."

"But I really think he's innocent."

"So you say. Come up with fifteen, twenty thousand for a retainer, I'll talk to you."

"I was hoping you'd do it for free."

Megler laughed again. Since he had no belly, it seemed to be his bones that were jiggling under the slick polyester skin of his shirt. "Free? I don't believe I'm familiar with that word."

FOR THE FIRST TIME IN HER LIFE RUNE HAD AN ASSISTANT.

Bradford Simpson volunteered to help her. She suspected he was motivated partly by his desire to go out with her—though she couldn't for the life of her guess why he'd want her and not some beautiful Connecticut debutante who was tall and blonde (two of her least-favorite adjectives when applied to other women). On the other hand, he hadn't exactly asked her out again after she'd turned him down and she supposed that his reappearance had more to do with journalistic crusading than romance.

"What can I do to help?" he'd asked.

And she'd gotten a little flustered, since she didn't have a clue—never having had anyone work for her.

"Hmm, let me think."

He'd offered, "How about if I dig through the archives for information about Hopper?"

"That sounds good," she'd said.

He was now at her cubicle with another armful of files. He laid them out on her desk as neatly as his Robert Redford hair was combed and his penny loafers were polished.

"Did you know Lance Hopper?" she asked him.

"Not real well. He was killed a month after I started my first summer internship here. But I worked for him once or twice."

"*You* worked for the head of Network News?"

"Well, I wasn't exactly an anchorman. But he gave assignments to all the interns. Scut work usually. But he also spent a lot of time with us, telling us about journalism, getting stories, editing. He's the one who started the intern program. I think he would've made a good professor." Bradford fell quiet for a moment. "He did a lot for me, for all of us interns."

Rune broke the somber spell by saying, "Don't worry. We'll pay him back."

Bradford turned his blue eyes toward her questioningly.

She said, "We're going to find who really killed him."

chapter 8

WHAT'S THAT?

Rune opened her eyes, stared up at the ceiling of her houseboat's bedroom, watching the ripples of the morning sun reflecting onto the off-white paint.

She turned her head, squinting.

What's wrong?

She felt the boat gently rocking in the Hudson, water lapping against the hull. Heard the baritone grind of a boat engine that seemed near but was probably two hundred yards away—she'd learned how noise carries on the water. The sound of rush-hour traffic too.

So what was it? What was missing? What wasn't here that ought to be?

The tie-dye sheet had tangled around her feet, a percale Gordian knot. Her white Joy of Movement T-shirt had ridden up to her neck and her hair was in her face. Rune was a restless sleeper. She untangled her feet and pulled the shirt down. She brushed a crescent of pizza crust out of the bed and sat upright.

Well, part of it was the silence—a special kind of silence, the sort that comes from the *absence* of a human being.

Rune realized that Claire was gone.

The young woman always had her Walkman plugged in by nine A.M. Even upstairs, in the houseboat's bedroom, Rune usually could hear the raspy chunk of decibels murdering Claire's eardrums.

But today, nothing.

Rune went into the white-enameled head, thinking: Maybe she got up early to go shopping. But no, none of her stores—clothing and cosmetics—opened before ten or eleven.

Which meant that maybe she'd left for Boston!

Which is exactly what happened. Rune, downstairs, stood in the middle of the living room and read the note Claire had left. As she scanned the words she grinned like a kid on Christmas Eve.

Excellent! she thought. Thank you, thank you, thank you. . . .

The note was all about how Claire appreciated (spelled wrong) everything Rune had done for her in the past couple of weeks (six and a half) even though she was a moody bitch a lot but that was good because if she could live with her she could live with anybody (Rune, trying to figure who the *she*s were and not liking the conclusion).

Claire explained that she was going home to her mother's in Boston, like she'd said, and how she was going to think about going back to school. She spent a long paragraph, the last one, talking about how happy she was that Rune and Courtney were such good friends and how they'd gotten along so well because—

The smile vanished.

—she knew Rune would take good care of the girl.

Oh, shit . . .

Rune ran into the small storeroom in the bow of the boat, the room that Claire and Courtney had shared.

Goddamm it!

The little girl was lying, asleep, on top of Claire's futon, clutching a mutant stuffed animal that might, at one time, have been a rabbit.

Son of a bitch. Claire, how could you?

Rune did a fast survey. The room was pretty much cleared out. Claire had taken her clothes and jewelry and whatever other objects had filled the dust-free squares and circles and trapezoids on the top of the dresser.

Everything, gone—except for Courtney's toys and clothes and a poster of the Jackson 5 that Claire had kept, waiting for it to become chic enough to put up again.

Son of a—

Rune ran outside to find the letter again.

—bitch!

The letter said only that she hoped to be back to pick up Courtney sometime and to give her the home she needed and deserved.

Sometime?

Rune was sweating. She actually felt her scalp prickle. Her fingers left stains on the paper.

No address. No phone number.

She didn't even remember Claire's real last name—the girl kept trying on stage names for the day when she became a professional model.

Rune went back to the room and searched carefully. The only clue she found was a bra under the bed with initials penned on the side—C.S. But Rune thought it looked a little small for Claire and remembered that one of her boyfriends had been a transvestite.

Hopeless, Rune sat down in the middle of the room and picked up a toy, a wooden penguin on a stick. His broad plastic feet were on wheels. She ran him back and forth, the webbed feet slapping on the wooden deck.

I don't want to be a mother.

Claire . . .

Slap, slap, slap.

The jogging penguin woke up Courtney.

Rune sat down on the futon, kissed the girl's cheek. "Honey, did you talk to your mommy this morning?"

"Uh-huh."

The little girl rubbed her eyes. Oh, they're so damn cute when they do that. Come on, kid, get ugly.

"Did she say where she was going?"

"Uh-huh. Can I have some juice?"

"Honey, did your mother say where she was going?"

"Bawden."

"Boston, I know. But where?"

"Uh-huh. Juice?"

"Sure. We'll get some Ocean Spray in a minute. Where in Boston?"

"Grandma's house."

"Where *is* your grandmother's house?"

"Bowden. I want some juice."

"Honey, what's your mother's name?"

"Mommy." The little girl started to squirm.

"No, I mean her last name?"

"Mommy. I want some juice!"

Rune said, "Did she say anything before she left?"

Courtney stood up in bed, pulled away from Rune. "Zoo."

"The zoo?"

"She said you'd take me to the zoo."

"That's what your mommy said?"

"Uh-huh. I want juice!"

"Did she say how long she'd be gone?"

Courtney frowned for a moment then extended her arms as wide as they'd go. She said, "Long, long time."

Rune picked up the stuffed rabbit. Oh, shit.

Courtney stuck her lower lip out threateningly and said, "Juice."

SAM HEALY WAS IN HIS LATE THIRTIES, OVER SIX FEET tall and lean. His thinning hair was combed straight back and his moustache drooped over the corners of his mouth. He resembled a cowboy, at least when he was wearing what he now wore—a plaid shirt, jeans and black boots. His profession: a detective with the NYPD Bomb Squad.

They sat in Rune's houseboat, where he spent an occasional night, and she leaned forward, listening to him as intensely as if he were telling a rookie how to dismantle a C-4 demolition charge. She asked, "How often should I feed her?"

Healy said, "You're too nervous about this, Rune. Three times a day'll work fine."

"How about medicine?" Rune's palms were glistening with sweat. "Should she be taking medicine?"

"Well, is she sick?"

"No."

"Then why would she need medicine?"

Rune said, "She's a baby. I thought you always gave medicine to babies."

"Not if she's not sick."

Rune gazed out over the river. "Oh, Sam, it was fun playing with her and reading to her but this—this is, like, really, really serious."

"They're very resilient."

"Oh, God. What if she falls?" she asked, panicked.

Healy sighed. "Pick her up. Comfort her. Dust her off."

"I'm not ready for this, Sam. I can't be a mother. I'm trying to do my story. I'm . . . Oh, God, does she wear diapers?"

"Ask her."

"I can't ask her. I'd be embarrassed."

"She's what? About three? She's probably toilet-trained. If not, you should start pretty soon."

"Me? No way. Forget about it."

"Rune, kids are wonderful. When you and Adam and I go out we have a great time."

"But he's *your* son. That's different. I don't want one of my own. I'm too young to be a mother. My life is over with already."

"It's only temporary, isn't it?"

"That's the part I'm not too sure about." Rune looked toward Courtney's room. Her voice was panicky when she said, "You think she drinks too much juice?"

"Rune."

"She drinks a lot of juice."

"You should worry a lot less."

"Sam, I can't have a kid with me when I interview people. What am I—?"

"I'm going to give you the name of the day-care center Cheryl and I used to take Adam to. It's a good place. And some of the women there work nights as baby-sitters."

"Yeah?"

"Look at the bright side: You didn't have to go through labor."

Rune sat close to him and laid her head on his chest. "Why do I get myself into things like this?"

"She's a sweet little girl."

Rune put her arms around him. "They're all sweet when they're asleep. The thing is they wake up after a while."

He began rubbing her shoulders.

"That's nice."

"Yeah," he said, "it is."

He rubbed for five minutes, his strong fingers working down her spine. She moaned. Then he untucked her T-shirt and began working his way up, under the cloth.

"That's nicer," she said and rolled over on her back.

He kissed her forehead. She kissed his mouth, feeling the tickle of the moustache. It was a sensation she'd gotten used to, one she liked a lot.

Healy kissed her back. His hand, still inside her T-shirt, worked its way up. He disarmed bombs; he had a very smooth touch.

"Rune!" Courtney shouted in a shrill voice.

They both jumped.

"Read me a story, Rune!"

Her hands covered her face. "Jesus, Sam, what'm I going to do?"

chapter 9

THE TRAIN UP TO HARRISON, NEW YORK, LEFT ON TIME and sailed out of the tunnel under Park Avenue, rising up on the elevated tracks like an old airplane slowly gaining altitude. Rune's head swiveled as she watched the red-brick projects and clusters of young men on the street. No one wore colorful clothing; it was all gray and brown. A woman pushed a grocery cart filled with rags. Two men stood over the open hood of a beige sedan, hands on their wide hips, and seemed to be confirming a terminal diagnosis.

The train sped north through Harlem and the scenes flipped past more quickly. Rune, leaning forward, climbing onto her knees, felt the lurch as the wheels danced sideways like a bullfighter's hips and they crossed the Harlem River Bridge. She waved to passengers on a Dayliner tour boat as they looked up at the bridge. No one noticed her.

Then they were in the Bronx—passing plumbing supply houses and lumberyards and, in the distance, abandoned apartments and warehouses. Daylight showed through the upper-story windows.

You wake up in the morning and you think . . .

Rune tried to doze. But she kept seeing the tape of Boggs's face, broken into scan lines and each scan line a thousand pixels of red, blue and green dots.

. . . Hell, I'm still here.

. . .

THE WAY THEIR EYES LOOKED AT HER WAS WEIRD.

She'd figured the prisoners would lay a lot of crap on her—catcalls or whoops of "Yo, honey," or long slimy stares.

But nope. They looked at her the way assembly line workers would glance at a plant visitor, someone walking timidly between tall machines, careful not to get grease on her good shoes. They looked, they ignored, they went back to mopping floors or talking to buddies and visitors or not doing much of anything.

The warden's office had checked her press credentials and guards had searched her bag and the camera case. She was then escorted into the visitors' area by a tall guard—a handsome black man with a moustache that looked like it was drawn above his lip in mascara. Visitors and inmates at the state prison in Harrison were separated by thick glass partitions and talked to each other on old, heavy black telephones.

Rune stood for a moment, watching them all. Picturing what it would be like to visit a husband in prison. So sad! Only talking to him, holding the thick receiver, reaching out and touching the glass, never feeling the weight or warmth of his skin. . . .

"In here, miss."

The guard led her into a small room. She guessed it was reserved for private meetings between lawyers and their prisoners. The guard disappeared. Rune sat at a gray table. She studied the battered bars on the window and decided that this particular metal seemed stronger than anything she'd ever seen.

She was looking out the greasy glass when Randy Boggs entered the room.

He was thinner than she'd expected. He looked best straight on; when he turned his head to glance at a guard his head became birdish—like a woodpecker's. His hair was longer than in the tape she'd studied and the Dairy Queen twist was gone. It still glistened from the oil or cream he used to keep it in place. His ears were long and narrow and he had tufts of blond, wiry hair growing out of them. She observed dark eyes, darkened further by an overhang of bone, and thick eyebrows that reached toward each other. His skin wasn't good; in his face were patches of wrinkles like cities in satellite photos. But this appeared to be a temporary unhealthiness—the kind that good food and sun and sleep can erase.

Boggs looked at the guard and said, "Could you leave us?"

The man answered, "No."

Rune said to the guard, "I don't mind."

"No."

"Sure," Boggs said, as cheerful as if he'd been picked for first baseman in a softball game. He sat down and said, "What for d'you want to see me, miss?"

As she told him about receiving his letter and about the story she grew agitated. It wasn't the surroundings; it was Boggs himself. The intensity of his calmness. Which didn't really make sense but she thought about it and decided that was what she sensed: He was so peaceful that she felt her own pulse rising, her breath coming quickly—as if her body were behaving this natural way because his couldn't.

Still, she ignored her own feelings and got to work. Rune had interviewed people before. She'd put the camera in front of them, washed them in the hot light from Redhead lamps and then asked them a hundred questions. She'd gotten tongue-tied some and maybe asked the wrong questions but her talent was in getting people to open up.

Boggs, though, took a lot of work. Even though he'd written the letter to the station he was uneasy around reporters. "Don't think I'm not grateful." He spoke in a soft voice; a slight southern accent licked at his words. "But I'm . . . Well, I don't mean this personal, directed at you, miss, but you're the people convicted me."

"How?"

"Well, miss, you know the expression 'media circus'? I'd never heard that before but when I read about my trial afterwards I found out what they mean. I wasn't the only person who felt that way. Somebody who got interviewed in *Time* said that's what my trial was. I wrote a letter to Mr. Megler and to the judge saying that I thought it was a media circus. Neither of them wrote back."

"What was a circus about it?"

He smiled and looked off, as if he was arranging his thoughts. "The way I see it, there was so many of you reporters all over the place, writing things about me, that the jury got it into their head that I was guilty."

"But don't they . . ." There was a word she was looking for. "You know, don't they keep the jury in hotel rooms, away from papers and TV?"

"Sequester," Boggs said. "You think that works? I was on *Live at Five* the day I was arrested and probably every other day up till the trial. You think there was one person in the area that didn't know about me? I doubt it very much."

Rune had told him she worked for *Current Events* but there was no visible reaction; either he didn't watch the program or he didn't know that it was on the Network, the employer of the man he'd supposedly killed. Or maybe he just wasn't impressed. He glanced at the Betacam sitting on the table beside Rune. "Had a film crew in the other day. Were shooting some kind of cop movie. Everybody was real excited about it. They used some of the boys as extras. I didn't get picked. They wanted people looked like convicts. I looked more like a clerk, I guess. Or . . . What would you say I look like?"

"A man who got wrongly convicted."

Boggs smiled an interstate cloverleaf into his face. "You got some good lines. I like that. Yeah, that's a role I've been acting for a long time. Nobody's bought it yet."

"I want to get you released."

"Well, miss, seems like we've got a lot in common." He was definitely warming up to her.

"I talked to Fred Megler—"

Boggs nodded and his face showed disappointment but not anger or contempt. "If I had money to hire me a real lawyer, like those inside traders and, you know, those coke kingfishers you see on TV, I think things might've been different. Fred isn't a bad man. I just don't believe his heart was in my case. I reckon I'd say he should've listened to some of my advice. I've had a little experience with the law. Which I'm not proud of but the fact remains I've seen the inside of a courtroom several occasions. He should've listened to me."

Rune said, "He told me your story. But I knew you were innocent when I saw you."

"When would that've been?"

"On film. An interview."

The smile was now wistful. He kept evading her eyes, which bothered her. She believed this was shyness, not guile, but she didn't want shifty eyes on tape.

Boggs was saying, "I appreciate your opinion, miss, but if that's all you have to go on I'm still feeling like a six-ounce bluegill on a twenty-pound line."

"Look at me and tell me. Did you do it or not?"

His eyes were no longer evasive; they locked onto hers and answered as clearly as his words, "I did not kill Lance Hopper."

"That's enough for me."

And Boggs wasn't smiling when he said, "Trouble is, it don't seem to be enough for the people of the state of New York."

• • •

TWO HOURS LATER RANDY BOGGS GOT TO: "THAT'S WHEN I decided to hitch to New York. And that was the biggest mistake of my life."

"You were tired of Maine?"

"The lobster business didn't work out like I'd hoped. My partner—see, I'm not much for figures—he kept the books and all this cash coming in didn't no way equal the cash going out. I suspicioned he kept the numbers pretty obscured and when he sold the business he told me he was letting it go to a couple creditors but I think he got paid good money. Anyways, I had me maybe two, three hundred bucks was all and two new pair of jeans, some shirts. I figured I'd be leaving that part of the country before another winter come. Snow belongs in movies and in paper cones with syrup on it. So I begun thumbing south. Rides were scarce's hens' teeth but finally I got me some rides and ended up in Purchase, New York. If that isn't a name I don't know what is." He grinned. "Purchase . . . It was raining and I had my thumb out so long it was looking like a bleached prune. Nobody stopped, except this one fellow. He pulled over in a—we call them—a Chinese tenement car. Big old Chevy twelve or so years old—you know, could ride a family of ten. He said, 'Hop in,' and I did. Biggest mistake of my life, miss. I'll tell you that."

"Jimmy."

"Right. But then I told him *my* name was Dave. I just had a feeling this wasn't a person I wanted to open up with a real lot."

"What happened after you got in?"

"We drove south toward the city, making small talk. 'Bout women mostly, the way men do. Telling how you get put down by women all the time and how you don't understand them but what you're really doing is bragging that you've had a ton of 'em. That sort of thing."

"Where was Jimmy going? Further south?"

"He said he was only going so far as New York City but I was thankful I was getting a ride at all. I figured I could buy a Greyhound ticket to get me on my way to Atlanta. In fact I was thinking just that very thing when he looks over at me in the car and says, 'Hey, son, how'd you like to earn yourself a hundred bucks.' And I said, 'I'd like that pretty well, particularly if it's legal but even if not I'd still like it pretty well.'

"He said it wasn't *real* illegal. Just picking up something and dropping it off. I told him right away, 'I've got a problem if that'd be drugs you were talking about.' He said it was credit cards and since I've done a little with them myself in the past I said that wasn't so bad but could he maybe consider two hundred. He said he'd more than consider it and said if I drove he'd make it two hundred fifty. And I agreed was what I did. We drive to this place somewhere. I didn't know New York but at the trial I found out it was on the Upper West Side. We stopped and he got out and I scooted over behind the wheel. Jimmy, or whatever his name was, walked into this courtyard."

Rune asked, "What did he look like?"

"Well, I wasn't too sure. I oughta be wearing glasses but I'd lost them overboard in Maine and couldn't afford to get new ones. He was a big fellow, though. He sat big, the way a bear would sit. A moustache, I remember. It was all in profile, the look I got."

"White?"

"Yes'm."

"Describe his clothing."

"He wore blue jeans with cuffs turned up, engineer boots—"

"What are those?"

"Short buckled boots, you know. Black. And a Navy watch coat."

"Weren't you a little nervous about this credit card thing?"

Boggs paused for a minute. "I'll tell you, miss. There've been times in my life—not a lot, but a few— when two hundred fifty dollars hasn't been a lot of money. But back then it was. Just like it would be now and when somebody is going to give you a lot of money you'd be surprised what stops becoming funny or suspicious. Anyway, I sat for about ten minutes in the car. I had me a cigarette or two. I was real hungry and was looking around for a Burger King. That's what I really wanted, one of those Whoppers. There I am, feeling hungry, and I hear this shot. I've fired me enough pistols in my life to know a gunshot. They don't boom like in the movies. There's this crack—"

"I know gunshots," Rune said.

"Yeah, you shoot?"

"Been shot at, matter of fact," she told him. This wasn't ego. It was to let him know more about her, make him trust her more.

Boggs glanced at her, decided she wasn't kidding, and nodded slowly. He continued. "I walk carefully into the courtyard. There's a man lying on the ground. I thought it was Jimmy. I run up to him and see it's *not* Jimmy and I lean down and say, 'Mister, you okay?' And of course he isn't. I see he's dead. I stand up fast and I just panic and run."

Boggs smiled with a shallow twist of his lips. "And what happens? The story of my life. I run into a police car cruising by outside. I mean, I really run right into it, bang. I fall over and they pick me up and collar me and that's it."

"What about Jimmy?"

"I glanced around and seen the car but Jimmy wasn't inside. He was gone."

"Did you see any gun?"

"No, ma'am. I heard they found it in the bushes. There wasn't any of my prints on it but I was wearing gloves. The DA made a big deal out of it that I was wearing gloves in April. But I got me small hands . . ." He held one up. "I don't have a lot of meat on me. It was real cold."

"You think Jimmy shot Mr. Hopper?"

"I pondered that a lot but I don't see why he would have. He didn't have any gun that I saw and if it was just a credit card scam Mr. Hopper wouldn't've been in on that, credit cards're small potatoes. I think Jimmy had the cards on him and just panicked when he heard the shot. Then he just took off."

"But you told the cops about Jimmy?"

"Well, not the credit card part. It didn't seem that was too smart. So I kept mum on that. But, sure, I told them about Jimmy. Not one of them—to a man—believed me."

Not even your own lawyer, Rune thought. "Assuming Jimmy didn't shoot Hopper, you think he might've *seen* the killer?"

"Could've."

"There isn't a lot to go on, what you've told me."

"I understand that." He sighed. "I was just biding my time, waiting for parole. But there're people here I got on the bad side of somehow. I'm really worried they're going to move on me again."

"Move on you?"

"Kill me, you know. They tried once. I don't know why. But that's life here in prison. Don't need to be a reason."

Rune asked, "How bad do you want to get out?"

Boggs glanced at the camera. Rune stood up and looked through the viewfinder to frame him better. What she saw troubled her because she wasn't looking at animal eyes, or criminal's eyes, which would have been scary but expected; she saw gentleness and pain and—even harder to bear—a portion of him that was still a lonely, frightened young boy. He said, "I'll answer that by telling you what it's like in here. It's like your heart is tied 'round and 'round with clothesline. It's like every day is waking up the morning after a funeral. It's like you welcome fear because when you're afraid you can't think about being free. It's a sadness so bad you want to howl when you see a plane flying by going to a place you can imagine but can't ever get to, no matter how close it might be."

Randy Boggs stopped and cleared his throat. "Do what you can for me, miss. Please."

chapter 10

RUNE GAVE MOTHERHOOD HER BEST SHOT.

She really did.

Courtney was probably three-fourths toilet-trained. The remaining quarter was tough to cope with but Rune managed as best she could.

She bought healthy food for the girl.

She bathed her twice a day.

She also leapt right in to improve the little girl's wardrobe.

Claire, who had super-crucial taste in her own fashion, had bought the poor kid mostly sweats, blouses with bears or Disney cartoon characters on them and corduroy jeans (corduroy! In New York!). Rune took her straight down to SoHo, to a kids' store where Rune knew one of the salesclerks. She dropped some bucks on real clothes: A black Naugahyde miniskirt and a couple of black T-shirts. Yellow and lime-green tights. A wad of lacy tooling for her hair. Jewelry was risky—you never knew what kids would swallow—but Rune found an outrageous studded belt and black cowboy boots (which were slightly too big but she figured there was only one way the girl's feet were going to grow and why not buy something that would last more than a month). The finishing touch was a plastic leopard-skin jacket.

Rune paid the two hundred twenty-seven dollars but decided the results were worth it. She said, "All right, dude, you're looking crazy good."

"Crazy," Courtney said.

But it wasn't long before problems developed.

They'd left the store, bought some ice cream and gone window-shopping. Then Rune wondered if you could take three-year-olds dancing. There was a super late-night club just opening up down on Hudson in the old building where the famous Area had been years before, a totally historical place. She hadn't seen too many children there. None, in fact. But she wondered if you could sneak one in early, say, just after work, about six or seven. It seemed a shame to have a kid who looked like a miniature Madonna and not expose her to some real New York life.

"You want to go dancing?"

"I want to go to the zoo!" the girl said fiercely.

"Well, the zoo's closed now, honey. We can go in a day or so."

"I wanta see the animals."

"In a day or two."

"No!" Courtney started to scream and ran into Comme de Garçon, where she threw the ice cream into a rack of eight-hundred-dollar suits.

The day-care center didn't work out either.

Rune did the math and figured out that if she dropped Courtney off at eight and picked her up at seven—the hours Piper Sutton insisted that her crew work, at a minimum—and then got a night sitter twice a week, she would have one hundred and eight dollars a month left out of her paycheck.

So the little girl spent half the week at day care, half at the Network.

And when Piper Sutton called Rune one night at what was, for the rest of the world, quitting time and demanded an update on the Boggs story ("Now, Rune. Now now now!), Rune had to park the little girl with Bradford Simpson, who took up the task sportingly even though she could tell by the furtive phone call he made that he was breaking a date to help her out. It was clear that she'd soon run out of friends if she tried to conscript last-minute baby-sitters very often.

But what finally did it was the honey.

Rune had spent all Thursday taking footage of the exteriors of the building where Lance Hopper had been killed and of the crime scene itself. She'd picked up Courtney just before the day-care center closed and had to spring for a cab to get fifty pounds of equipment and thirty pounds of child back to the houseboat.

Rune plopped her in front of the old Motorola console TV, queued up *The Wizard of Oz* and took a shower.

Courtney, who didn't like the black-and-white Kansas portion of the film, wandered off to find something to play with. What she located was a jar of clover honey, sitting on the galley table. She climbed up on a chair and pulled it down carefully then sat on the floor and opened it.

Courtney loved honey. Not so much because of the taste but because of the great way it poured so slowly down the stairs. Which was a lot of fun but what was even better was the way she could use it to paste together Rune's videotape cassettes. She made a wall out of them, and pretended it was the Wicked Witch's castle.

Then the water in the shower shut off and it occurred to Courtney that playing with the honey might be one of those things she shouldn't be doing. So she hid the rest of the evidence, pouring it into the Ikegami video camera case.

Courtney closed the door, then slipped the empty jar under the coffee table. At that point Dorothy arrived in full-color Oz and the little girl settled down to watch the film.

Rune surprised herself by actually screaming when she saw the camera. She was trying to shout that the camera had cost fifty thousand dollars but the words weren't even getting out of her mouth. Courtney looked down at the camera, bleeding honey, and started to cry.

Rune then dropped to her knees and surveyed the ruined tapes. She cradled the camera like a hurt pet. "Oh, God, oh, no . . ."

"Oh-oh," Courtney said.

"I can't take it," Rune gasped.

ONLY TWO PHONE CALLS.

She was surprised to find that when it came to children, you could cut through city bureaucracy pretty fast. The administrator she was speaking to told her that a protective diagnostic caseworker could be on her way in a half hour. Rune said not to bother, she'd come to *their* offices tomorrow. The woman gave Rune the address.

The next morning she packed up the girl's few possessions and they walked to the subway. After transferring three times they got off at the Bleecker Street stop and climbed to the sidewalk.

"Where're we going?" Courtney asked.

"To see some nice people."

"Oh. Where? At the zoo?"

"I'm sure they'll take you to the zoo."

"Good."

The building looked like one of those massive, grimy factories in ten shades of gray—a set from a 1930s movie about a tough, slick-haired industrialist who learns that life with floozy blondes and martinis can be pretty unsatisfying.

But when Rune considered it again she decided that the building on LaGuardia Place looked more like a prison. She almost turned around. But then she free-associated: prison, Randy Boggs. . . . And she realized that she had a responsibility to do her story and save him. And that having Courtney in her life was going to make that impossible. She shifted the girl's fingers, still slightly sticky from the honey, into her left hand and led her toward the squat, dark building.

Rune glanced at the granite slab above the front door

to the building, which would have been a good place to carve the words, *Abandon Hope, All Ye Who Enter.*

Instead of: *New York Child Welfare Administration.*

Rune and Courtney walked slowly toward the main office, through green corridors, over green linoleum. Through fluorescent light that started life white but turned green when it hit the skin. It reminded her of the shade of lawyer Megler's office. A guard pointed to a thin black woman in a red linen suit, sitting behind a desk covered with recycled files and empty cardboard coffee cups.

"May I help you?" the woman asked.

"You're Ms. Johnson?"

The woman smiled and they shook hands. "Sit down. You're . . . ?"

"Rune."

"Right. You called last night." Paper appeared and civil servant Johnson uncapped a Bic pen. "What's your address?"

"West Village."

Johnson paused. "Could you be more specific than that?"

"Not really. It's hard to explain."

"Phone number?"

Rune said, "No."

"Beg pardon?"

"I don't have a phone."

"Oh." So far she hadn't written anything. "Is this Courtney?"

"That's right."

"We're going to the zoo," the little girl said.

"What it is is this: I have a roommate, I mean *had* a roommate—her mother—and I don't know her last name and she left me with Courtney. She just took off—can you believe it? I mean, I woke up and she was gone."

Johnson was frowning painfully, more mom than civil servant for the moment.

"Anyway, she went to Boston and what she did, she . . ."

Rune's voice fell. ". . . ditched you know who. And I'm like, what am I going to do? See, I wouldn't mind if I wasn't working, which is usually what I'm doing—not working, I mean—only now I—"

Johnson had stopped writing. "Apparent abandonment. Happens more often than you'd think."

Courtney said, "Rune, I'm hungry."

Rune dug into her shoulder bag and pulled out a can of sardines. Johnson watched her. A can opener appeared and Rune began cranking. "I liked it better when they had that little key on them." Rune looked at a bewildered Ms. Johnson. "You know, the key. On the cans? Like in the cartoons you always see."

"Cartoons?" Johnson asked. Then: "You think those are good for her?"

"Water-packed. I wouldn't give her oil." She held up the can.

Rune tucked a napkin into Courtney's collar, then handed her a plastic fork. "Anyway, her mother's gone and I don't know how to find her."

"You don't have any idea? No last name?"

"Nope. Just know she's in Boston."

"Bawden."

Johnson said, "Usually what happens in cases like these is the police get involved. They'll contact the Boston Police and do a standard missing person search. First name, C-L-A-I-R-E?"

"Right. I just don't have any leads. Claire took everything with her. Except this too-disgusting old poster and some underwear. You could fingerprint it, maybe. But they probably wouldn't be *her* fingerprints on it."

"Who's Courtney's father?"

Rune frowned and shook her head.

Johnson asked, "Unknown?"

"Highly."

"Describe her mother to me."

"Claire's about my height. Her hair's dark now but

we're talking it started life pretty light. Kind of dirty brownish." Rune thought for a minute. "She's got a narrow face. She isn't pretty. I'd say more cute—"

"I'm really more interested in a general description that'll help the police locate her."

"Okay, sure. Five-three, jet-black hair. About a hundred and ten. Wears black mostly."

"Grandparents or other relations?"

"I can't even find her mother—how'm I going to know the aunts and uncles?"

Johnson said, "She's really adorable. Does she have any health problems? Is there any medicine she takes?"

"No, she's pretty healthy. All she takes is vitamins in the shape of animals. She likes the bears best but I think that's only because they're cherry-flavored. You like bears, don't you, honey?"

Courtney had finished the sardines. She nodded.

"Okay, well, let me tell you a little about the procedure from here on out. This's the Child Welfare Administration, which is part of the city's Human Resources Administration. We've got a network of emergency foster homes where she'll be placed for a week or so until we can get her into a permanent foster home. Hopefully, by then we'll have found the mother."

Rune's stomach thudded. "Foster home?"

"That's right."

"Uhm, you know what you hear on the news. . . ."

"About the foster homes?" Johnson asked. "It's the press that made up most of those stories." Her voice was crisp and Rune had a flash of a different Ms. Johnson. Beneath the ruby lipstick and pseudo Ann Taylor did not beat a timid heart. She probably had a tattoo of a gang's trademark on the slope of her left breast.

The woman continued. "We spend weeks investigating foster parents. If you think about it, who scrutinizes natural parents?"

Good point, Rune thought. "Can I visit her?"

The answer was no—Rune could see that—but Johnson said, "Probably."

"What happens now?"

"We have a diagnostic caseworker on call. She'll take Courtney to the emergency home tonight."

"I don't have to do anything else?"

"That will be the end of your involvement."

Rune hated civil-servant language. It was as if they took the words and quick-froze them.

She turned to Courtney and said, "Will you miss me?"

The girl said, "No."

No?

Johnson said to her, "Honey, would you like to go stay with a nice mommy and daddy? They have some children just like you and they'd love for you to visit."

"Yeah."

Rune said to her, "You'll be happy there."

Why isn't she sobbing?

Johnson said, "I'll take her now. You have her things?"

Rune handed over the bag containing the ratty stuffed animals and her new clothes. Johnson looked at Rune's face and said, "I know how you feel but, believe me, you did the right thing. There wasn't any choice."

Rune squatted down and hugged the girl. "I'll come visit you."

It was then that Courtney sized up what was happening. "Rune?" she asked uncertainly.

Johnson took her by the hand and led her down the corridor.

Courtney started to cry.

Rune started to cry.

Johnson remained dry-eyed. "Come on, honey."

Courtney looked back once and called, "Zoo!"

"We'll go to the zoo, I promise."

Rune left the ugly slab of a building, feeling an intense freedom.

And feeling too the weight of a guilt that matched her own 102 pounds ounce for ounce. But that was okay. She had a story to do.

SPRING IN PRISON IS LIKE SPRING IN THE CITY. WEAK, AL-most unnoticeable. You only sense it because of the air. You smell it, you taste it, you feel an extra portion of warmth. It flirts with you once or twice, then that's it. Back to work, or back to the prison yard. Crocuses can't break through concrete.

Randy Boggs was waiting for Severn Washington in the prison gym when the smell of spring hit him. And, damn, it made him feel bad. He'd never been to college. School for him meant high school and this battered prison gym reminded him a lot of the one at Washington Irving High where, twenty years earlier, he'd have been working out on the parallel bars or struggling to do an iron cross on the rings, and, bang, there would be that smell in the air that meant they'd soon be out of school and he'd have summer ahead of him—along with a couple of weeks' pure freedom before the job at the Kresge warehouse.

Damn, what a smell spring has. . . .

He thought about a dozen memories released by that smell. Girls' small boobs and hot grass and the chain-saw rumble of a 350 Chevy engine. And beer. Man, he loved beer. Now as much as then, though he knew there was no taste like the taste of beer when you were a teenager.

Randy Boggs squinted across the gym and could see the loping figure of Severn Washington, two hundred thirty pounds' worth, a broad face in between a scalp of tight cornrows and a neck thick as Boggs's thigh.

Washington had laughed and told Boggs not long af-ter they met that he'd never had a white friend in all of his forty-three years. He'd missed Nam because of his eye-sight and always stayed pretty close to home, which in his family's case had been a Hundred and Thirty-seventh

Street, where there were not many whites at all, let alone any that he'd befriend.

That's why Washington had been uncomfortable when, one day in the yard, Boggs began talking to him, just bullshitting in that soft, shy voice he had. At first, Washington later told him, he had thought Boggs wanted to be his maytag, his loverboy, then Washington decided Boggs was just another white-ass crazy, maybe methed or angel-dusted out. But when Boggs kept it up, talking away, funny, making more sense than most people Inside, Washington and Boggs became friends.

Boggs told him that he'd been through Raleigh and Durham a bunch of times and learned that Washington's family had come from North Carolina, though he'd never been there. Washington wanted to hear all about the state and Boggs was glad to tell him. From there, they talked about Sylvia's, Harlem, Dizzy Gillespie, Dexter Gordon, Eddie Murphy, Denzel Washington (no relation), Class D felonies, beer, traveling around, hitchhiking. . . .

But there was another foundation for the friendship between the two.

One day Washington had sought Boggs out in the yard and said, "Know why you come up and talked to me?"

"Nope, Severn, I sure don't. Why was that?"

"Allah."

"What's that again?" Boggs asked.

The huge man explained that Allah had come to Washington in a dream and told him it was his job to befriend Boggs and eventually convert him.

He told all this to Boggs, who felt himself blushing and said, "Damn, if that's not the craziest thing I ever heard."

"No, man, that's the way it is. Your ass's safe. Me and Allah gonna watch out for you." Which Boggs thought was even crazier, the Allah part at least, but perfectly fine with him.

From the start, though, Washington's job wasn't easy. Boggs was animal feed in Harrison prison. Scrawny, shy, quiet, a loner. He didn't deal, he didn't fuck, he didn't side. Instantly unpopular. The sort that ends up "accidentally" dead—like not paying attention and driving a ¾-inch drill press bit through his neck then bleeding to death before somebody notices the blood.

Or the sort that does it himself. They may take your belt away from you but if you want to get dead in prison you can get yourself dead, no problem.

But Severn Washington did his job. And when it became clear that Boggs was under the wing of one of the most devout Muslims in all of Harrison (who also happened to be one of the largest) when that news made the rounds of the cell blocks, Randy Boggs was left pretty much alone.

"Pretty much," however, didn't mean "completely."

Washington, disposing of the fast Muslin greeting, "Marhaba, sardeek," now frowned as he whispered, "Yo, man, you got trouble."

"What?" Boggs asked, feeling his heart sink.

"Word up they gonna move on you again. Serious, this time. I axed a moneygrip o' mine from the home block and he say he heard it for fucking certain."

Randy Boggs frowned. "Why, man? That's what I don't get. You hear anything?"

Washington shrugged. "Make no sense to me."

"Okay." Boggs's face twisted a little. "Shit."

"I'm putting out some inquiries," Washington said. "We'll find ourselves out what the fuck's going on."

Boggs considered this. He didn't go out of his way to look for trouble. He didn't give steely killer eyes to blacks, he didn't eye anybody's dick in the shower, he didn't get cartons of Marlboros from the guards, didn't look sideways at the Aryan Brotherhood. There was no reason he could think of that somebody'd want to move on him.

"I don't know what I did. I don't think—"

"Hey, be cool, man." Washington grinned. "You walk in what? Twenty-four months. Shouldn't be too hard to keep yo ass intact that long."

"This place, man, I hate it so much. . . ."

Severn Washington laughed the way he always did when somebody expressed the obvious. "Got the antidote. Less play us some ball."

And Randy Boggs said, "Sure." Thinking, as he saw his reflection in a chicken-wire-laced window, that what he was looking at with the red-socketed eyes wasn't his living body at all, but something else—something horrible, lying cold and dead, as his blood fled from the flesh.

Thinking that, despite this huge man's reassurance, the only hope he now had was that slip of girl with the ponytail and the big camera.

chapter 11

THIS CITY WAS A PLAYGROUND YOU NEVER GOT TIRED OF.

Once you took the element of fear out of it (and there wasn't anything Jack Nestor feared) New York was the biggest playground in the world.

He felt the excitement the instant he stepped out of the Port Authority bus terminal. The feeling of electricity. And for a moment he thought: What was he doing wasting his time in piss-ant Florida?

He smelled: fishy river, charcoal smoke from pretzel vendors, shit, exhaust. Then he got a whiff of some gross incense three black guys dressed up like Arabs were selling from a folding table. He'd never seen this before. He walked up to them. There were pictures of men from ancient times, it looked like, dressed the same. The twelve true tribes of Israel. Only they were all black. Black rabbis . . .

What a crazy town this was!

Nestor walked along Forty-second Street, stopped in a couple peep shows. He left and wandered some more, looking at the old movie theaters, the live play theaters, the angry drivers, the suicidal pedestrians. Horns blared like mad, as if everybody driving a car had a wife in labor in the backseat. Already the energy was exhausting him but he knew he'd be up to speed in a day or two.

He stopped and bought a hot dog and ate it in three bites. At the next street corner he bought another one.

This time he asked for onions too. On the third corner he bought two more hot dogs, without onions, and stood eating them and drinking a Sprite, which wasn't a Sprite at all, which he'd asked for, but some brand of lemon-lime soda he'd never heard of. It tasted like medicine. As the vendor split a sausage to fill with sauerkraut, Nestor asked him where there was a hotel in the area.

The man shrugged. "Donoe."

"Huh?"

"Donoe."

"That's a hotel?"

"I donoe."

"Why don't you try learning fucking English?" Nestor walked off. Two blocks later he saw a sign, *King's Court Hotel*. Which was the same name as a motel he'd been to in Miami Beach once and which wasn't a bad place. He remembered it being clean and cheap. It must have been a chain. Nestor walked up to the door, which opened suddenly. He hadn't noticed a tall young man, dressed in black, standing inside. The man said, "Hello, sir, take your bag?"

The Miami branch didn't, Nestor recalled, have a doorman.

"Just wanted to ask the desk guy a question."

She wasn't a guy but a young blonde woman with a French accent and teeth that were absolutely perfect. She smiled at him. "Yessir?"

"Uh . . ." He looked around him. Bizarre. It looked like a warehouse with a low ceiling. Stone and metal furniture everywhere. And a lot of the furniture was wrapped up in white cloth.

"Uh, I was wondering, you have a room?"

"Certainly, sir. How long will you be staying?"

"Uh, how much would that be? For a single?"

A computer was consulted. "Four hundred forty."

For a *week*? Are these people fucking insane?

The question now was how to get out of here without the blonde with the ruler-straight teeth thinking he was a complete asshole.

"I mean by the night."

A moment's pause. "Actually, that *is* the daily rate, sir."

"Sure. I was joking." Nestor grinned, saw no way to salvage the situation and simply walked out.

Only one block away he found the Royalton Arms, which he knew was okay because there were a couple of dirty-looking tourists standing out in front, looking at a Michelin guide to New York City. The desk clerk here didn't even have straight teeth, let alone white ones, and he was behind a Plexiglas bulletproof divider. Nestor checked into a $39.95 room and took the elevator up to the seventh floor. The room was okay. He felt good as soon as he walked inside. It didn't overlook any oceans or expressways or anything else except an air shaft but that didn't bother Nestor. He lowered the window blinds then lay down on the bed and listened to the argument his stomach was having with the hot dogs.

He clicked on the TV and watched some *Miami Vice* rerun for a while, flipped through the channels once then shut off the set. It was irritating not to have a remote control. He stripped down to his boxer shorts and sleeveless T-shirt, brushed his teeth powerfully and got into bed.

He closed his eyes.

Snap. The pictures began.

Nestor often had trouble sleeping. He'd thought, a long time ago, it was something physical. Well, *hoped* more than *thought*. But he knew now that wasn't the case at all.

The reason for his insomnia was the pictures.

The minute his head hit the pillow (unless there was someone next to him, distracting him or at least promising distraction), the minute he was prepared to sleep, the pictures began. He supposed he could call them memories because they really were nothing more than scenes from his past. But memories were different. Memories were like the impressions he had of his family or his childhood. His first car. His first fuck. Maybe they were accurate. Probably not.

But the pictures . . . Man. Every detail perfect.

A Philippine revolutionary he picked off at three hundred yards using an M16 with metal sights, the man just dropping like a sack . . .

A black South African who thought he was safely across the border in Botswana . . .

A coat hanger binding the hands of a Salvadorian, Nestor thinking, Why bother to tie him up? He'll have a bullet in his head in sixty seconds anyway. . . .

Hundreds of others.

They were in black and white, they were in color, they were mute, they were in Dolby stereo sound.

The pictures . . .

They didn't haunt him, of course. He didn't have any emotional response. He wasn't tormented by guilt, he wasn't moved to lust. They just wouldn't go away. The pictures came into his head and they wouldn't let him sleep.

Tonight Nestor—energized by the city and troubled by its fast food—lay in a too-soft bed and fielded the pictures. Pushed one away. Then he did the same with the one that took its place. Then the next. For an hour, then two. He wanted Celine next to him. He thought about her but the pictures pushed *her* away. He thought about what he was in town to do. That kept the pictures away for a while. But they came back.

Finally—it was close to three A.M.—he began to think about the French girl, the one with the straight teeth. With the thought of her, and a little bit of effort on his part (elbow grease was the way he thought of it), Jack Nestor finally began to relax.

•   •   •

IT WAS ENOUGH OF A DATE TO KEEP BRADFORD SIMPSON happy and not enough of one to worry Rune.

They were at an outdoor table at a Mexican restaurant near the West Side Highway, the table filled with red cans of Tecate beer and chips and salsa—and a ton of printed material about Lance Hopper and Randy Boggs.

Bradford *had* wanted to ask her out again, as it happened, but Rune was content to keep the evening mostly professional.

The intern scooted his chair closer to hers and Rune endured a little knee contact while they read through the Hopper files. "Where's Courtney?" Brad asked.

"Let's not go there," Rune said.

"Sure. She's okay?"

Yes, no. Probably not.

"She's fine."

"She's really cute."

Let's not *go* there, she thought and turned back to the files on Lance Hopper that Bradford had found in the archives.

As they read she began to form a clearer picture of the late head of Network News.

Hopper was a difficult man—demanding that everyone at the Network work as hard as he did and not let their personal lives interfere with the job. He was also greedy and jealous and petty and wildly ambitious and several times, when his contract was up, virtually extorted the parent company for stock options that increased his worth by hundreds of millions of dollars.

Yet he was also a man with a heart. For instance, spending as much time with the interns as he did, as Bradford had mentioned. He advocated educational programming for youngsters on the Network, even though shows like those produced far less revenue than after-school cartoons and adventure programs.

Hopper regularly appeared in Washington before the FCC and congressional committees, testifying about the importance of unfettered media. He was often vilified by conservative, family-oriented groups, who thought there should be more censorship on TV.

Hopper also took responsibility for the worst black eye in the history of the Network. Three years ago—just before his death—the Network had run an award-winning story as part of the coverage of a U.N. peacekeeping mission in Lebanon. The story was an exclusive about a village outside of Beirut that appeared to be liberal-minded and pro-Western but was in fact a stronghold for fundamentalist militants.

But when a U.N. force made a sweep of the village to look for suspected terrorists they were so prepared to meet resistance that the operation turned into a bloodbath after a solitary sniper fired one shot near the convoy. A chain re-action of shooting followed. There were twenty-eight deaths, all by friendly fire, including some U.S. soldiers. The "sniper" turned out to be a ten-year-old boy shooting at rocks. The militants, it seemed, were long gone. Some blamed the U.N. for relying on a news story for its intelli-gence but most people thought it was the Network's fault for doing the story in the first place or for not at least fol-lowing up and reporting that the terrorists were no longer there.

Hopper took responsibility for the incident and per-sonally went to Beirut to attend the funerals of the slain villagers.

Bradford and Rune continued to pore over the files and, though a portrait of Hopper as a complex, ambitious and ruthless man appeared, no evident motive for his death emerged.

From there they turned to the transcripts of inter-views Rune had made over the past week as she'd traveled around the East Coast and the South talking to people who knew Randy Boggs.

Yeah, Randy Boggs worked for me for close to two years. He come in and was looking for a job. Good boy. Dependable. He wasn't no killer. He pushed a broom with the best of them. I'm sure it was the sixties. We had the Negro problem then. Course, we still have the Negro problem. 'Bout that, I'd like to say a few words, seeing how you have a camera—

Next . . .

Randy Boggs? Yeah, I knew the Boggs family. Boys I don't remember. Father was a mean motherfucker. Man, the—

Next . . .

Randy? Yeah. We had this lobster business. But—you got the camera rolling? Okay, let me tell you this story. The wife and I were one time over to Portland and we were driving in the Chevy—we always buy American cars, even if they're a pile of you know what. So we were driving along and there were these three lights in the sky, and we knew they weren't planes because they were so bright. Then one of them—

Next . . .

Rune yawned violently.

"You okay?" Bradford asked.

"More or less." She opened another file.

Her life had become an endless circle of long hours by herself, of flying on airplanes and staying in hotels that somebody else paid for, of tense meetings at the Network, of interviews that sometimes careened out of control and sometimes worked, of a lonely houseboat, of a chaotic editing room. (One morning she woke up to find that she'd fallen asleep with the Betacam next to her—which wasn't so scary as the fact that she'd slept with her arm around it all night.) She gave up late-night clubs, she gave up West Village writers' bars. Even gave up seeing Sam Healy much. Piper Sutton would occasionally swoop by Rune's cubicle for a status report, like an eagle grabbing a squirming trout in its talons.

As she and Bradford pored over all this material now,

amid the raucous laughter and boasting and flirting of dozens of young lawyers and businesspeople drunk on tequila and the thrill of life in Manhattan, Rune felt both more and more incensed that such a vital and important man as Lance Hopper had been killed and more and more certain that Randy Boggs hadn't done it.

chapter 12

"COME ON, SAM. PLEASE?" SHE'D TRIED CHARM AND NOW she was pleading.

But Sam Healy was a detective who disposed of bombs for a living; it was tough to talk someone like that into anything he didn't want to do.

They were sitting on the back deck of the boathouse, drinking beer and eating microwave popcorn.

"I just want to look at it. One little file."

"I can't get access to the files in the Twentieth Precinct. I'm Bomb Squad. Why would they even talk to me?"

Rune had spent a lot of time trying to decide if she was in love with this man. She thought she was in a way. But it wasn't like the old days—whenever *they* were—when you were either in love or you weren't. Love was a lot more complicated now. There were degrees, there were *phases* of love. It kicked in and out like a compressor in an air conditioner. She and Healy could talk easily. And laugh. She liked the way he looked like the man in a Marlboro ad. She liked the way his eyes were completely calm and deeper than any man's eyes she'd ever seen. But what she missed was that gut-twist, that weight-losing obsession with the object of your desire that was Rune's favorite kind of love even though it was totally rare.

Also, Healy was married.

Which, oddly, didn't bother Rune that much. At least he was separated and had no problem being bluntly honest about the times he saw Cheryl. Rune looked at his marriage like an air bag in a car—a safety feature. Maybe when she got older, if they were still together, she'd force him to make a decision. But for now his marriage was his business. All she wanted was honesty and a boyfriend who kept you guessing. And no boyfriend kept you guessing like one on the New York City Bomb Squad.

Rune said, "They got the wrong man."

"I know your theory about Boggs."

"I don't need to prowl around the evidence room. I just want to read one file."

"I thought you wanted to be a reporter."

"I *am* a reporter."

"Reporters don't cheat. It'd be unethical to use me to get information."

"Of course it wouldn't. You know about unnamed sources. Come on, you can be my Deep Throat."

"It's a murder investigation. I'd get suspended for leaking information."

"It's a murder *conviction*. It's a closed case."

"The transcript is public record. Why don't you—?"

"I've got the transcript. I need the police report. It's got the names of all the witnesses and the bullet angles and pictures of the exit wounds. All the good stuff. Come on, Sam." She kissed his neck.

"There's nothing I can do. Sorry."

"The man's innocent. He's serving time for something he didn't do. That's terrible."

"You can talk to the public information officer. They'll give you the department's side of the case."

"Bullshit is all he'll tell me."

"*She,*" Healy said. "Not he." He stood up and walked into the galley. "You have anything substantial?"

"Well, first, everybody I've interviewed said that no way in the world could Randy Boggs kill anyone. Then—"

"I mean to eat."

"Oh." She squinted into the galley. "No."

"Don't mope."

"I'm not," she said quickly. "I just don't have anything substantial. Sorry. Maybe some Fruit 'N Fiber cereal."

"Rune . . ."

"A banana. It's pretty old."

"I can't get the report. I'm sorry."

"A can of tuna. That's a pretty icky combination, though, if you mix it with the cereal. Even with the high fiber."

Healy wasn't buying it. "No file. Give it up." He walked back with pretzels and cottage cheese. "So where's your little girl?"

She was hesitating. "I took her to Social Services."

"Oh." He was looking at her, his face blank. Not saying anything, eating the cottage cheese. He offered her a forkful she wasn't interested in.

She said defensively, "They were a really, really good bunch of people there. They were, you know, real professional."

"Uh-huh."

"What they'll do is keep her in a foster home for a while then they'll track down her mother. . . ." She was avoiding his eyes, looking everywhere else. Studying his buttons, the stitching of his shirt seams, the trapezoid of floor between his shoes. "Well, it was a good idea, wasn't it?"

"I don't know. Was it?"

"I had to."

"When I was a portable, walking a beat, we found kids sometimes. If there's any suspicion of neglect or abuse you have to bring them in or get a caseworker out to see them."

Rune said, "Those people are okay, aren't they?"

"I guess so."

She stood up and paced slowly. "What was I supposed to do? I can't take care of a baby."

"I'm not saying—" Healy began.

"Yes, you are. You're saying 'I guess so,' 'I don't know.' "

"You did what you thought was right."

Clench, loosen. Her short, unpolished nails dug into her palm, then relaxed. "You make it sound like I gave her away to the gypsies."

"I'm just a little surprised is all."

"What am I going to do? Keep her with me all the time? It cost five hundred dollars to fix the camera because of her. I had to reshoot eight hours of film. I can't afford a baby-sitter—"

"Rune—"

Volume and indignation rose. "You make it sound like I abandoned her. I'm not her mother. I don't even want her."

Healy smiled. "Don't be so paranoid about it. I'm sure they'll take fine care of her. Have some cottage cheese. What's in here?"

Rune looked. "Apple? Pear? Wait, I think it's a zucchini."

"Should it be that color?"

She said, "It's only until they find Claire."

Healy said, "Just a couple days probably."

Rune stood at the round porthole, looking out over the water, at the way the lights in Hoboken made lines in the waves like runway approach lights. With her eyes she traced them to the land and back again. She watched them for a few minutes, until they were shattered by a passing speedboat. When the colors began to regroup she turned to Healy and said, "I did the right thing, didn't I, Sam?"

"Sure you did." He capped the cottage cheese. "Let's go get something to eat."

PIPER SUTTON SENSED THE POWER SHE HAD OVER HIM and it made her uncomfortable because it was purely the power of sex.

And therefore a power she couldn't exercise. Or, rather, wouldn't *let* herself exercise.

As she looked at the man across the desk from her she crossed her legs and her cream-colored stockings whispered in a reminder of that power. She was sitting in an office exactly two floors above hers—the penthouse of the parent company's monolith.

"We'll have coffee," the man said.

"No, thank you."

"Then I will." Dan Semple was a trim forty-four, compact, with short salt-and-pepper hair curling over his forehead in bangs. He was not—like Piper Sutton or Lee Maisel or his predecessor Lance Hopper—a newsman. He'd sold advertising time for local stations, then for the Network, and eventually he had moved into entertainment and then news programming. The lack of reporting experience was irrelevant; Semple's talent was for money—making it and saving it. No one in the television business was naive enough to believe that high-quality journalism alone was enough to make a network a success. And, with a few exceptions, no one was surprised when Semple was given Hopper's job as director of Network News. The similarities were obvious: Hopper had been a great newsman in the incarnation of a son of a bitch; Dan Semple was a great businessman in the body of a cruel megalomaniac.

Although one thing he wasn't the least bit cold about was Piper Sutton.

She had had affairs with various Network executives in the past—only those men, however, who were on a corporate level equal to hers and only those men whom she desired physically or because she truly enjoyed their company. Sutton didn't give a shit about rumors and gossip but one of her few rules of ethics was that she wouldn't use her body to advance her career; there were plenty of other ways to fuck those you worked for.

The affair with Semple had lasted one year, when they were both on the ascendancy in the Network. But that had been several years ago. Then came Hopper's death, one consequence of which was what Sutton had predicted would happen: Semple was named Hopper's replacement. The day after the board announced the appointment she walked into his office to say how happy she was for him. Sutton had then taken Semple's hand, kissed his cheek and ended the affair.

Since then Semple'd waged an almost adolescent campaign to win her back. Although they saw each other often and dined together and attended benefits and formal functions she'd decided that their intimate days were over. He didn't believe her when she said it was a hard decision for her as well, though it was. She was attracted to him physically and she was attracted to him for his strength and brilliance and decisiveness. Sutton had settled for weak men in the past and had learned her lesson; she had a number of exes to prove it.

This romantic tension was an undercurrent in every conversation she and Semple had. It troubled her that although Semple respected her immensely for her ability he *desired* her only on the most visceral level. The power she had over him was the power of a mistress, not a reigning queen, and that infuriated her—at the same time her continual refusal to resume the affair stung him.

"How was Paris?" she asked.

"*Comme ci, comme ça.* How is it always? The same. Paris never changes."

The coffee arrived. The executive vice presidents had their own dining room, which delivered their requests for food or beverages on Villeroy & Bosch china, carried on parent-company-logoed lacquer trays. Semple poured a cup and sipped it

"Tell me about this story."

Sutton did, quickly, without emotion.

"Her name is Rune? First or last?"

"Some kind of stage name bullshit. She's a cameraman with the O&O here in Manhattan."

"What does Lee think?" Semple asked.

"Slightly more in favor of doing the story than I am. But not much."

"Why are we doing it, then?" he asked coolly. Semple's dark eyes scanned Sutton's blouse. She was glad she'd worn the wool suit jacket over the white silk. But only a part of his eyes was seeing her body. What the other part was considering and what was happening in the brain behind those eyes were a complete mystery to her. It was one of his most magnetic qualities—that she hadn't been able to fathom him. It was also one of his more frightening.

She answered, "The girl said, in effect, that if she didn't produce it for *Current Events* she'd do it independently and sell it elsewhere."

"Blackmail," he snapped.

"Closer to youthful fervor."

"I don't like it," Semple said. "There's no point to the story." He sipped more coffee. Sutton remembered that he liked to sit naked in bed in the morning, a tray resting on his lap, the cup and saucer directly over his penis. Did he like the warmth? she used to wonder.

He asked, "What does she have so far? Anything?"

"Nope. Nothing substantial. Lots of background footage. That's all."

"So you think there's a chance it'll just go away?"

Sutton avoided his eyes. "She's young. I'm keeping a close eye on her. I'm hoping she gets tired of the whole thing."

Semple had the power to make this story go away forever, leaving behind fewer traces than a couple of pixels on a TV monitor. He glanced at Sutton and said, "Keep me informed on what she finds."

"Okay."

"I mean daily." Semple looked out the window for moment. "I dined at a wonderful restaurant. It was off St. Germain."

"Really?"

"I wish you'd been there with me."

"It sounds nice."

"Michelin was wrong. I have to write and urge them to give it another star." And he uncapped a fountain pen and wrote a note on his calendar reminding himself to do just that.

chapter 13

RUNE WAS SLEEPWALKING. AT LEAST, THAT'S WHAT IT felt like.

She'd been sitting at her desk, in the same curvature-of-the-spine pose, for seven hours, looking over tapes. The close air of the studio was filled with the buzz of a dozen yellow jackets, which she'd thought was the video monitor in front of her until she'd shut it off and realized that the buzzing had continued; the sound was originating from somewhere inside her head.

Enough is enough.

She stood up and stretched; a series of pops from her joints momentarily replaced the buzzing. She left Bradford in charge of logging in the recent tapes she'd shot and headed outside. Rune walked through the complicated maze of corridors and into the spring evening. She removed the chrome chain necklace of her ID from around her neck and slipped it in her leopard-skin bag.

Outside a harried woman employee of the Network stood on the sidewalk. Her husband—a young professional—walked up to her with their two young children in tow. It had apparently been his turn to pick up the kids tonight.

The mother gave them perfunctory hugs and then started making weekend plans with her husband. Their daughter, a redhead about Courtney's age, tugged on her mother's Norma Kamali skirt. "Mommy . . ."

"Just a *minute*," the woman said sternly. "I'm speaking to your father." The little girl looked sullenly off.

Rune gave the kid a smile but she didn't respond. The family walked off.

Man, I'm beat, she thought.

But as she walked south she felt the cool, electric-scented city night air waking her up and she saw from the clock on the MONY tower that it was early, only eight P.M. Early? Rune remembered when quitting time had been five. She continued down Broadway, past the pastel carnival of Lincoln Center—pausing, listening for music but not hearing any. Then she continued south, deciding to walk home, a couple miles, to get the blood back in her legs. Thinking of what she needed to do for the story. Getting her hands on the police report of the Hopper case was the number-one item.

Then she'd have to talk to all the witnesses. Get Megler on tape. Maybe interview the judge. Find some jurors. She wondered if there was an old priest who knew Boggs. A Spencer Tracy sort of guy. *Ah, well, now, sure I'd be knowing the boy Randy and I'll tell you, he helped out in soup kitchens and took care of his mother and left half his allowance in the collection plate every Sunday when he was an altar boy. . . .*

A lot to do.

She walked through Hell's Kitchen. Her head swiveled as she went down Ninth Avenue. Disappointed. The developers were doing a number on the area. Boxy high-rises and slick restaurants and co-ops. What she liked best about the neighborhood was that it had been the home of the Gophers, one of the toughest of the nine-teenth-century gangs in New York. Rune had been reading about old gangs lately. Before she got waylaid by the Boggs story she'd been planning a documentary on them. The featured thugs were going to be the Gophers and their sis-ter gang, the Battle Row Ladies' Social and Athletic Club (also known as the Lady Gophers). Not a single producer had been very interested in the subject. The Mafia and Colombians and Jamaicans with machine guns were still the current superstars of crime and there wasn't much demand for stories about people like One-Lung Curran and Sadie the Goat and Stumpy Malarky.

Her feet were aching by the time she got to her neighborhood. She stopped outside the houseboat, looked at the dark windows for a moment. Behind her another family walked past, a mother and father and their child, a cute boy of about five or six. He was asking questions—where does the Hudson River go, what kind of fish are in it—and together the mother and father were making up silly answers for the boy. All three of them were laughing hard. Rune felt an urge to join in but she resisted, realizing that she was an outsider. When they had passed she walked up the gangplank and inside the houseboat. She dropped her bag by the door and stood listening, her head cocked sideways. A car horn, a helicopter, a backfire. All the sounds were distant. None of what she heard was coming from inside the houseboat, nothing except her own heartbeat and the creak of boards beneath her feet.

She reached for the lamp but slowly lowered her hand and instead felt her way to the couch and lay down on it, staring up at the ceiling, at the psychedelic swirls of lights reflecting off the turbulent surface of the Hudson. She lay that way for a long time.

AN HOUR LATER RUNE WAS SITTING IN AN OVERHEATED subway car as it stammered along the tracks. She did an inventory of the tools of the trade in her bag—a claw hammer, a canister of military tear gas, two screwdrivers (Phillips head and straight), masking tape and rubber gloves. Her other accessories included a large bucket, a string mop and a plastic container of Windex.

She was thinking about the law too and wondered if the crime was less if it wasn't breaking *and* entering. If you just entered and didn't break.

It was the kind of question that Sam could've answered real fast but of course he was the last person in the world she would ask that particular question.

She imagined, though, that it was a distinction somebody'd thought of already and just because you didn't jimmy any locks or crack any plate glass the punishment wasn't going to be a hell of a lot less severe. Maybe the judge would sentence her to one year instead of three.

Or ten instead of twenty.

The longer term probably. It wasn't going to help her case that it was government property she had her eyes on.

The building was only a few doors from the subway stop. She climbed out and paused. A cop walked past, his walkie-talkie sputtering with a hiss. She pressed her face against a lamp post, which was covered with layers and layers of paint, and wondered what color it had been in earlier years. Maybe some gang members from the Gophers or Hudson Dusters had paused under this very same post a hundred years ago, scoping out a heist.

The street was empty and she strolled casually into the old government-issue building and up to the night guard, cover story and faked credentials all prepared.

In twenty minutes she was out, having exchanged the mop and pail for the bulky manila folder that rested in her bag.

She paused at a phone stand and pretended to make a call while she flipped through the file. She found the address she was looking for and walked quickly back to the subway. After a ten-minute wait she got on board an old Number Four train heading toward Brooklyn.

Rune liked the outer boroughs, Brooklyn especially. She thought of it as caught in a time warp, a place where the Dodgers were always playing and muscular boys in T-shirts sipped egg creams and flirted with tough girls who snapped gum and answered them back in sexy, lazy drawls. Big immigrant families crammed into narrow shotgun tenements argued and made up and laughed and hugged with hearts full of love and loyalty.

The neighborhood that she now slipped into, along with the crowd exiting the subway, was quiet and residential. She paused, getting her bearings.

She had to walk only three blocks before she found the row house. Red brick with yellow trim, two-story, a narrow moat of anemic lawn. Bursts of red covered the front of the building: Geraniums grew everywhere—they escaped from flowerpots, from terra-cotta statues in the shape of donkeys and fat Mexican peasants, from green plastic window boxes, from milk containers. They bothered her, the flowers. Someone who'd appreciate flowers like this was probably a very nice person. This meant Rune would feel pretty guilty about what she was about to do.

Which didn't stop her, however, from walking onto the front porch, dropping a paper bag on the concrete stoop and setting fire to it.

She rang the doorbell and ran into the alley behind the house and listened to the voices.

"Oh, hell . . . What? . . . Those punks again . . . That's it! This time I call the cops. . . . Don't call the fire department. It's just . . ."

Rune raced up the back stairs and through the open kitchen door. She saw a man leaping forward fiercely and stomping on the burning bag, sparks flying, smoke pouring. A chubby woman held a long-spouted watering can, dousing his feet. Then Rune was past them, unnoticed, taking the carpeted stairs two at a time. Upstairs she found herself in a small hallway.

First room, nobody.

Second, nobody.

Third, chaos. Six children were staring out the window at the excitement below them, squealing and dancing around.

They all turned to the doorway as Rune walked into the room and flipped the light switch on.

One of them cried, "Rune!"

"Hi, honey," she said to Courtney. The little girl ran toward her.

A chubby boy of about ten looked at her. "What'sis? Jailbreak?"

"Shh, don't tell anybody."

"Yeah, right, like I'm a snitch. Got a cigarette?"

Rune gave him five dollars. "Forget you—"

"—saw anything. Right. I know the drill."

Rune said to Courtney, "Come on, let's go home."

She pulled the girl's jacket off a hook and slipped it on her.

"Are we playing a game?" the little girl asked.

"Yeah," Rune said, hustling her out into the corridor, "it's called kidnapping."

THE PRISON YARD WAS SEGREGATED.

Just like the city, Randy Boggs thought, hanging out there at nine the next morning. Just like life. Blacks one side, whites the other, except on the basketball half-court.

The blacks were mostly young. A lot wore do-rags or stockings or they had cornrows. They stood together. Strong, big, sleek.

Yo, homes, quit that noise.

Wassup?

Mah crib. I ever tell you 'bout mah crib?

Hells yeah.

The whites were older, crueler, humorless. They looked bad—it was the longer, unclean hair, the pale skin. They too stood together.

Black, white. Just like the city.

A lot of the men were exercising. There were weights here though the hierarchy didn't allow for democratic use among all prisoners. Still, there were always push-ups and sit-ups. Muscles develop in prison. But Boggs hadn't made a fetish of exercise. Doing that'd be an acknowledgment of where he was. If he didn't stand in line for the thirty-pound dumbbells then maybe he was somewhere else.

"Amazing grace, how sweet thou art. . . ."

An a cappella black gospel group was practicing in the yard. They were really good. Boggs, when he first heard them, wanted to cry. Now he just listened. The group wouldn't be together much longer. They'd walk in two months, four months and thirteen months respectively.

"I once was lost but now I'm found. . . ."

The singers started a second verse and someone nearby yelled, "Yo, shut the fuck up."

He smelled fireplace wood smoke. He tried not to think of the last time he'd sat in front of a fireplace. Thought about that girl from New York. The little girl with the big camera.

He sat quietly. He smoked some though since he'd been inside he'd lost his taste for smoking. He'd lost his taste for a lot of things. He sat for five minutes thinking about the girl, about the story, about prison, about the sky before he realized that the prisoners he'd been sitting with were no longer next to him.

Boggs knew why they'd moved and he felt his skin crackle with fear.

Severn Washington was sick. Got the flu bad, was puking all night, and was in the infirmary. If Boggs knew it everybody knew it.

He looked around the yard and saw the man immediately. Juan Ascipio was back.

He wore a red headband and a fatigue jacket over his jumpsuit. Two other prisoners walked beside him. Ascipio was a newcomer, a dealer who'd been convicted of the assassination of two rivals. He wasn't a big man and he had a face that when it smiled might make children comfortable. A kind face, the sort you want to please. But the eyes, Boggs had noticed, were grinny-mean and chill.

The three of them stopped about fifteen feet from where Boggs sat, next to a tall wall of red brick. Ascipio said, "Yo, man. Here. Now."

Boggs looked at him but didn't get up.

Ascipio pointed to a small shaded area out of sight of the towers. The prisoners called it Lovers' Lane.

Ascipio stepped into the nook and unzipped his fly. "Yo, man, I'm talking to you. You deaf, or what?"

His friend said, "Yo, man, on your fucking knees. Gonna turn you out, man, turn you out. You do that an' you'll live. Big nigger ain' here to save your pretty cheeks."

The other: "Come on, man. Now!"

Boggs looked back at them. He said, "Don't believe I will." He measured the distance to the nearest guard. It was a long, long way. The other inmates were all studying very important things in the opposite direction from Boggs.

This's going to be bad.

Ascipio spit out, "Don't *believe* you will? Motherfucker say he don't believe he will?"

Then Boggs's eyes lowered to his own right hand, which rested on his knee. He glanced down at it. Ascipio followed his gaze.

A long fingernail.

It kept growing. One inch, two, three, four, six. Boggs looked back into their eyes. One by one, his head swiveling.

Severn Washington had given it to him last night, this piece of double-strength glass, a clear stiletto honed on one side so sharp it would shave hair. The handle was taped. Metal-detector-proof. The fingernail could do the most damage glass could ever do. (Boggs had said, "Would Allah, you know, approve of this?" And Washington had reassured him, "Allah say it's okay to fuck up assholes who try to move on you. I heard Him say that personally.")

Ascipio laughed. "Put that 'way, man. Get you pretty white mouth over here, man."

They'd get him on his knees then the other two would hold him and Ascipio would beat him to death and then they'd find the body in the laundry room, where the official word would be he'd died by falling down the stairs.

Boggs shook his head.

Ascipio said, "Three of us, man. More, I want. That"—he nodded at the knife—"that do you shit."

"Man," one of the others growled at the insubordination.

Boggs didn't move. The blade blasted light off its point.

Ascipio walked close. Slowly. And he looked into Boggs's eyes. He stopped. He stood for a long moment as they stared at each other. Finally the Latino smiled and shook his head. "Okay, man. You know, you got balls. I like that."

Boggs didn't move.

"You okay, my friend," Ascipio said, admiration in his voice. "Nobody else ever try that shit with me. You fuckin' all right."

He extended his hand.

Boggs looked down at it.

A bird swooping in.

Boggs half turned as the fist of a fourth man, who'd come up behind him silently, caught him under the ear. A loud *thwock* as knuckles bounced off bone and he felt Ascipio's hand grabbing his right wrist.

The knife fell to the ground and Boggs saw it tumble, appearing and disappearing as it fell.

"No!" The word didn't come out as a shout, though. It was muffled by the meaty forearm of the man who'd hit him.

There were no guards, there were no Aryan Brotherhood protectors, no Severn Washington, there was no one in Lovers' Lane except the five men.

Five men and a glass knife.

Ascipio leaned forward. Boggs smelled garlic on his breath—garlic from his private stocks of food. Tobacco from the endless supply of cigarettes.

"Yo, man, you a stupid motherfucker."

No, Boggs thought in despair. Don't cut me! Not the knife. Not that, please. . . .

As the blade went in, Boggs felt much less pain than he'd expected, but the sense of horror was far worse than he'd thought.

The knife retreated and returned into his body and he felt a terrifying loosening inside him.

Then there were other shouts, from a dozen yards away or a hundred. But Boggs didn't pay any attention; they didn't mean anything to him. All he was aware of was Ascipio's face: the grinny-mean eyes that never flinched or narrowed and the smile, one that might please children.

chapter 14

SHE HEARD THE NEWS ON ANOTHER STATION. NOT EVEN
a network O&O but one of the locals. The one that
broadcast *M*A*S*H* reruns and whose best-seller was a
talk show that did stories about sexual surrogates and dis-
crimination against overweight women.

Rune's own Network News hadn't even thought
Randy Boggs's stabbing was worth mentioning.

Rune sweet-talked Healy into taking Courtney for a
few hours. She figured this was a major abuse of the relationship, but he was so happy she'd gotten the girl back
(she was a little vague about *how* exactly) that he didn't
complain at all.

A half hour later she was on the train to Harrison,
wondering if maybe she should buy a monthly commuta-
tion pass.

The prison infirmary surprised her. She expected it to
be totally grim. More Big House, more Edward G. Robin-
son. But it was just a clean, well-lit hospital ward. A guard
accompanied her, a large black man with a broad chest.
His uniform didn't fit well. The glossy blue collar buttons,
one stamped with a D, one a C, for Department of Corrections, came just to the level of her eyes. He was silent.

Randy Boggs didn't look good at all. He was shell-
white and the spray or cream that he used on his hair
glued it out in all directions. The eyes were what bothered
Rune most though. They were unfocused and still. God,
they were eerie. Corpse eyes.

"It's you, miss." He nodded. "You come all the way up to see me."

"You going to be all right?"

"Got me a pretty nice-looking scar. But the knife missed all the important stuff."

"What happened?"

"Don't rightly know. I was in the yard and I get pulled over backwards and somebody stuck me."

"You must have seen him."

"Nope. Not a glimpse."

"Was it daytime?"

"Yep. This morning."

"How could somebody stab you and you not see it?"

Boggs tried a smile but it didn't take. "People get invisible here."

She said, "But—"

"Look . . ." His eyes came to life for a moment then faded back to lifeless. ". . . this is prison. Not the real world. We got ourselves a whole different set of rules." He lifted his hand to his stomach and touched his belly. He leaned his head back into his pillows and pressed his thin, sinewy forearm over his eyes. "Damn," he whispered.

She watched him in this still pose for a long minute, wishing she'd brought the camera. But then decided that, no, it was better to keep this private. He was the sort of man who'd never want to be seen crying.

"I brought you something."

She opened her bag and removed an old book, flaky and scabbed. She held it out. The pages were edged in gold.

Boggs lowered his arm and looked at it uneasily as if no one had ever given him a present before and he was wondering what would be expected in return.

"It's a book," she said.

"Figured that out." He opened it. "Looks like an old one."

He flipped open to the copyright page. "Nineteen oh

four. Yep, that goes back a ways. Year my grandmother was born. How 'bout that?"

"It's not like it's worth a lot of money or anything."

"What is it, like fairy tales?"

"Greek and Roman myths."

At least his eyes were reviving. He even had a slight smile on his face as he turned the pages, glancing at the pictures, which were protected with tissue.

Rune said, "There's a story I want you to read. One in particular." She flipped through the pages. "Here."

He looked at it. "Prometheus. Wasn't he the guy made the wings out of wax or something?"

"Uh, nope. That was another dude."

Boggs squinted. "Hey, lookit there."

She followed his eyes to the old illustration. "Yeah," she said, laughing and sitting forward. Prometheus chained to a rock, a huge bird swooping down and tearing at his side. "Just like you—getting stabbed. Isn't that crazy wild?"

He closed the book and picked a couple chips of spine off the thin blanket. "So tell me, miss, you a college girl?"

"Me? Nope."

"How come you know this kind of stuff?" He held up the book.

She shrugged. "I just like to read."

"I kind of regretted I never was smart enough to go."

"Naw, I wouldn't feel that way if I was you," she said. "You go to college, get a real job, get married, what happens is you don't ever get a chance to play chicken with life. That's the fun part."

He nodded. "Never could sit still long enough to go to school anyway." He looked at her for a moment, eyes roving up and down. "Tell me 'bout yourself."

"Me?" She was suddenly embarrassed.

"Sure. I told you 'bout me. Remind me what life's like on the Outside. Been a while."

"I don't know. . . ." She thought: So this is what the people I interview feel like.

Boggs asked, "Where you live?"

Houseboats take a lot of explaining. "In Manhattan," she said.

"You can stand it there? It's a crazy place."

"I can't stand it anyplace else."

"Never spent much time there. Never could get a handle on it."

"Why would you want to live somewhere you can get a handle on?" she asked.

"Maybe you've got a point there. But you're talking to somebody who's a little prejudiced. I come to town and what happens? I get myself arrested for murder. . . ." He smiled then looked at her closely. "So, you're a reporter. Is that what you want to do?"

"I have this thing about films. I think I want to make documentaries. Right now I'm working for this TV station. I'll do it for as long as it excites me. The day I wake up and say I'd rather go have a picnic on the top of the Chrysler Building than go to work that's the day I quit and do something else."

Boggs said, "You and me're kind of alike. I've done me a lot of different things too. I keep looking. Always been looking for that nest egg, just to get a leg up."

"Hey, before this job, I spent six months at a bagel restaurant. And before that I was a store-window dresser. Most of my close friends are people I met at the Unemployment office."

"Pretty girl like you I think'd be considering settling down. You have a boyfriend?"

"He's not exactly the marrying kind."

"You're young."

"I'm not in any hurry. I think my mother's got this bridal shop in Shaker Heights on call. In case I tell her I'm engaged she'll be like the Pentagon—you know, Red

Alert. But I have trouble seeing me married. Like some things you can imagine and some you can't. That's one that doesn't compute."

"Where's Shaker Heights?"

"Outside Cleveland."

"You're from Ohio. I spent some time in Indiana." Then he laughed. "Maybe I shouldn't put it that way. Not like I was *doing* time. I lived about a year there, working. A real job. As real as day labor can be. Steel mills in Gary."

"Miss," the guard said, "I let you stay a little longer than you should."

She stood up and said to Boggs, "I'm working really, really hard on the story. I'm going to get you out of here."

Boggs was running his finger along the edge of his book. "I'll keep this." He said this as if it was the best thing he could think of to say to thank her.

As Rune and the guard walked back to the prison exit, the guard, without looking at her, said, "Miss, word been around about what you're trying to do."

She looked up at him. Her eyes didn't get much past the huge biceps.

"About you maybe getting him a new trial."

"Yeah?"

"I like Randy. He keeps to himself and doesn't give us any grief. But there're some people here don't like him much. I'm not supposed to be telling you this and I'm hoping it won't go any further than here. . . ."

"Sure."

"But if you don't get him out soon he's not going to live to parole."

"The people who did that?" She nodded back to the infirmary.

"There's nothing we can do to stop them."

They arrived at the gate and the guard stopped.

"But what did Randy do?"

"What did he do?" The guard didn't understand her.

"I mean, why did somebody stab him?"

The guard's face snapped into a brief frown. "He ended up here, miss. That's what he did."

THE PLACE WAS PRETTY EASY TO GET INTO.

Like water through a sieve, Jack Nestor thought. Then laughed, thinking that probably wasn't the best word to describe a houseboat. The only problem had been there was a parking lot nearby and a booth with a security guard, who'd glance at the boat every so often like he was keeping an eye on it. But Nestor waited until the man made a phone call then walked past him and jogged up the yellow gangplank.

Once he was inside he pulled on brown cotton gloves and started at the back. He took his time. He'd never been on a houseboat before and he was pretty curious about it. He'd done some charters and been on more party boats than he could count and of course he'd done time in military LSTs and landing craft. But this wasn't like anything else he'd ever seen.

The decor sucked, for one thing. It looked like his nutzo stepmother's place. But he admired the pilothouse, if that's what you'd call it, which had beautiful brass fixtures and levers and grainy oak, all yellow with old varnish. Beautiful. All the controls except the wheel were frozen and he guessed the motor was kaput. He resisted a temptation to pull the horn rope.

Downstairs he carefully went through the bookshelves and the cheap, sprung-fiberboard desk that was a sea of papers and pictures (mostly of dragons and knights and fairies, that sort of shit). There were a couple of dozen videocassettes. They were mostly that make-believe stuff too. Fairy stories, dragonslayers, the stuff he never watched. Some dirty films too. *Lusty Cousins*. And something called *Epitaph for a Blue Movie Star*.

So, this chicky had a kinky side to her.

Then he rummaged through the closets and drawers in the bedroom and in the little supply room that had another dresser in it. He went through the kitchen and the refrigerator, which was the first place that most people who thought they were clever hid things and which was the first place most professional thieves looked.

After an hour he was convinced she didn't have anything here that interested—or worried—him.

Which meant the files would be at her office and that was a pain in the ass.

Nestor looked around and sat down on the couch. He had a decision to make. He could wait here until she came back and just waste her. Get it over with, make it look like a robbery. The cops would probably buy that. He was always surprised how people craved to accept the most obvious explanations. Easier all the way around. Robbery and murder.

Or rape and murder.

On the other hand, that might leave a lot of material floating around somewhere, material that shouldn't be floating around.

Still . . .

A car door slammed. He was up fast, glancing out the window. He saw her—not a bad-looking girl if she didn't wear those stupid clothes, like the striped black-and-yellow tights and red miniskirt. It turned him off and made him resent her. . . .

Oh, he knew that emotion. The feeling that he'd get looking at a wiry brown-skinned man in a khaki uniform, looking at him through a telescopic sight, feeling the hatred, working up a wild, spiraling fury (maybe because Nestor was sweating like a steam pipe in the heat or because bugs were digging into his skin or because he had a glossy, star-shaped scar on his belly). Resentment, hate. He needed those feelings—to help him pull the trigger or press the knife in as deeply as he could.

Boots scraped on the asphalt outside.

Nestor felt a low itching and rubbed his scar. He felt the weight of the Steyr automatic in his pocket.

But he left it where it was and climbed out onto the deck.

He watched her open the door, clumsy, tilting against the weight of a movie camera and cassettes and a leather belt of batteries or whatever, which looked like a bandolier of M16 clips. She stacked it all by the door and disappeared into the bedroom. He waited a few minutes to see if he'd get a glimpse of skin but when she came out in a boring work shirt and stretch pants he silently left the boat and disappeared into the West Village.

chapter 15

"*A GENIUS, BUT ALWAYS CONTROVERSIAL . . .*"

Click.

"*A genius, but always controversial, Lance Hopper . . .*"

Click.

Rune hit the rewind button again. It was a good shot of him: Lance Hopper. Or a good shot of his mortal remains, at any rate—the gurney holding his body as it was wheeled out of the deadly courtyard three years before. She wished she could use the footage. Unfortunately, it had been filmed by another station.

"*. . . controversial, Lance Hopper was disliked by co-workers and competitors alike. Although under his leadership the seven P.M. national news program rose to number one in the ratings, he managed to embroil the network in several major scandals. Among them was an uproar caused by numerous firings of staff members, massive and—his critics said—arbitrary budgetary cutbacks and intense scrutiny of the network's news programs and their content.*

"*Perhaps the incident that gave his network the blackest eye, however, was an Equal Employment Opportunity suit brought by five women employees who claimed that Hopper's hiring and promotion practices discriminated against them. Hopper denied the charges and the suit was settled out of court. Associates of the late executive, though, admitted that he preferred men in executive positions and felt that a woman had no business in the higher echelons of network news. His flamboyant personal life belied that reputed prej-*

udice, however, and he was often seen in the company of attractive women from society and the entertainment industry. There were rumors of bisexual behavior and of his having had several young male models as companions. His penchant, however, was for tall blondes. . . ."

Click.

Tall blondes. Why is it always tall blondes?

Rune was at her desk, surrounded by piles of newspapers, magazines, computer printouts, videocassettes and the refuse from a dozen fast-food meals. It was four-thirty in the afternoon and everyone was gearing up for the news at seven. She felt that she was in the eye of a hurricane. Motion everywhere. Frantic, crazed motion.

Rune had also learned that while Hopper's internship program had indeed launched many a career in journalism he himself was maybe a bit more interested in the young people themselves than he should have been. In the archives Rune found a confidential memo in which the network's ethics committee heard complaints from two interns, eighteen and nineteen, that he'd made improper advances toward them. The names weren't given and there seemed to be no follow-up references to the incidents.

She asked Bradford about the reports but he said he knew nothing about them and didn't believe the stories for a minute. Powerful people, he explained, attract rumors. He obviously didn't want his idol to have feet of clay and Rune wondered if it had been purely an oversight that the young man had missed the memo about the investigation when he was digging through the archives for her in search of material on Hopper.

Click.

Rune watched the tape of Hopper's body rolling out into the spring night, the snakes of afterimage etched into the screen by the revolving lights on the EMS vans and police cars, the crowds—pale in the video camera's radiance of light. They looked curious and bored at the same time.

"Rune." A calm voice, a woman's voice.

"Oh, hi." It was Piper Sutton.

Should've cleaned up my desk, she thought. Remembering how neat the anchorwoman's was. And seeing how neat she looked now, standing here in a dark red suit with black velvet tabs on the collar and a white, high-necked blouse and dark fleshy stockings disappearing into the slickest patent-leather shoes Rune'd ever seen. Shoes with high heels and one red stripe along the side.

Shoes that'd put me on my ass, I tried to wear them.

But, man, they looked cool.

"You're busy." Sutton's eyes scanned the desk.

"I was just working on the story."

Rune casually picked up several of the closest paper bags—one Kentucky Fried and two Burger Kings—and dropped them into, well, *onto* an overflowing wastebasket.

"You want to, like, sit down?"

Sutton looked at the ketchup packets that rested on the one unoccupied chair. "No. I don't." She leaned forward and ejected the tape that was in the Sony player, then read the label. "Brand X," she said. "It's from a competitor. You can't use this footage, you know. I'm not putting a super in any of my news programs that says 'Courtesy of another network.'" She handed the tape back to Rune.

"I know. I'm just using it for background."

"Background." Sutton said the word softly. "I want to talk to you. But not here. Are you doing anything for dinner?"

"I was just going to John's for pizza. They're, like, real generous with their anchovies."

Sutton walked away. "No. You'll have dinner with me."

"The thing is, there's this person. Can they come with us?"

"I want to talk to you in private."

"Anything you can say to me, you can say in front of her. She's, you know, discreet."

Sutton shrugged, took one last look at the desk and didn't seem to like what she saw. "Whatever." Then she scanned Rune's pink T-shirt and miniskirt and fishnet stockings and ankle boots and she said, "You do have a dress, don't you?"

Rune said defensively, "I've got two, as a matter of fact."

She wondered what she was missing when Sutton laughed. The anchorwoman wrote out an address and handed it to Rune. "That's between Madison and Fifth. Be there at six-thirty. We'll do the pretheater. Don't want to spend more than we need to, do we?"

"That's okay. My friend likes to eat early."

YOU COULDN'T CALL IT A TIP. IT WAS A BRIBE.

Jacques, the maitre d', took the money Sutton offered him and slipped it into the pocket of his perfectly pressed black tuxedo. However much it was—Rune didn't see— the cash might have bought them access to the dining room but it did nothing to cheer up the poor, sullen man. He sat them at a table off to the side of the main dining room then surveyed Courtney. He said, "Maybe a phone book."

Rune said, "Yellow *and* White Pages."

Jacques pursed his unhappy Gallic lips and went off in search of the best child-seating device New York Telephone could offer.

Rune looked around the room. "This is like really, really amazing. I could get into it. Living this way, I mean."

"Uhm."

The theme of L'Escargot seemed to be flowers and— probably as with the food—excess was in. The center of the room was dominated by a twisty vined centerpiece, sprouting orchids and roses and baby's breath. The walls held huge paintings of flowers. Rune liked them. They were what Monet would have done if he'd used electric-colored

Crayolas instead of oil paint. Rune more or less matched the decor. She'd raced home to change into one of the two dresses, a purple-and-white Laura Ashley floral, which was her spring and summer dress. It was several years old but had very little mileage on it.

On the table in front of them was a bird of paradise in a tall glass vase and some kinky-looking green thing like a pinecone, which, if you were to see it in *National Geographic,* you wouldn't be able to tell whether it was a plant or fish or huge insect. Rune pointed at the bird of paradise. "I love these dudes." She petted it. "I don't think it looks like a bird at all. I think it looks like a dragon."

Courtney said, "I like dragons."

Sutton stared at them blankly. "Dragons?"

The little girl added, "I'm going to be a knight. But I wouldn't kill any dragons. I'd have them for pets. Rune's going to take me to the zoo and we're going to look at dragons."

Through teeth that never separated more than a quarter inch, Sutton said, "How wonderful."

Jacques returned with two bulky phone directories and set them on the third chair at the table. Courtney smiled as he lifted her up and set her on top.

He turned to Sutton. "This really cannot be, uh, *habituel, non?*"

"Jacques, have someone bring the little girl some . . ." She looked at Rune with a raised eyebrow.

"She loves pizza."

"We are a French restaurant, miss."

"She also likes pickles, clam chowder, smoked oysters, rice, anchovies—"

"*Huîtres,*" Jacques said. "They are poached and served with pesto and beurre blanc."

Sutton said, "Fine. Just have somebody cut them up into little pieces. I don't want to watch her mauling food. And have the sommelier bring me a Puligny-Montrachet." She looked at Rune. "Do you drink wine?"

"I'm over twenty-one."

"I'm not asking for a driver's license. I want to know if an eighty-dollar bottle of wine will be wasted on you."

"Maybe a White Russian would be more my speed."

Sutton nodded to the maitre d' and said, "Find me a half bottle, Jacques. A Mersault if there's no Puligny."

"*Oui,* Miss Sutton."

Huge menus appeared. Sutton scanned hers. "I don't think we want anything too adventurous. We'll have scallops to start." She asked Rune, "Do you swell up or turn red when you eat seafood?"

"No, I get fish sticks all the time at this Korean deli. And—"

Sutton waved an abrupt hand. "And then the pigeon."

Rune's eyes went wide. Pigeon?

Jacques said, "*Salades,* after?"

"Please."

Rune's eyes danced around the room then settled on the arsenal of silverware and empty plates in front of her. The procedures here seemed as complicated as Catholic liturgy and the downside if you blew it seemed worse. Be cool, now, she told herself. This's your boss and she already thinks you're damaged. Rune resisted the fierce impulse to scratch under her bra strap.

The first course arrived, along with the little girl's oysters.

"Gross dudes," Courtney said but she began to eat them eagerly. "Can we buy these for breakfast? I like them."

Rune was thankful Courtney was with them; the girl gave her something to do besides feel uncomfortable. Picking spoons up off the floor, wiping oyster off her face, keeping the vase vertical.

Sutton watched them and for the first time since Rune had known her the anchorwoman's face softened. "So that's what it's like."

"What?" Rune asked.

"Kids."

"You don't have children?"

"I do. Only I call them ex-husbands. Three of them."

"I'm sorry."

Sutton blinked and stared at Rune for a minute. "Yes, I believe you are." She laughed. "But that's one thing I regret. Children. I—"

"It's not too late."

"No, I think it is. Maybe in my next life."

"That's the worst phrase ever made."

Sutton continued to study her with curiosity. "You just barge right through life, don't you?"

"Pretty much, I guess."

Sutton's eyes settled on Courtney. Then she reached forward and, with a napkin as big as the girl's dress, wiped her cheek. "Messy little things, aren't they?"

"Yeah, that part's kind of a drag. And she isn't really into being sloppy tonight—I told her to behave. For lunch the other day, okay? We're eating bananas and hamburger, all kind of mixed together and—"

Sutton's hand rose again. "Enough."

Two waiters brought the main courses. Rune blinked. Oh, God. Little birds.

Sutton saw her face and said, "Don't worry. They're not your kind of pigeons."

My kind?

"They're more like quail."

No, what they were like was little hostages with their hands tied behind their backs.

Courtney squealed happily. "Birdies, birdies!" A half-dozen diners turned.

Rune picked up a fork and the least-offensive knife and started in.

They ate in silence for a few moments. The birdies weren't too bad actually. The problem was that they still had the bones in them and using a knife as big as a sword meant there was a lot of meat you couldn't get to. Rune surveyed the room but didn't see a single person sucking on a drumstick.

There was a pause. Sutton looked at her and said, "Where are you with the story?"

Rune had figured this was on the agenda and she'd already planned what she was going to say. The words didn't come out quite as organized as she'd hoped but she kept the "likes" and the "sort-ofs" to a minimum. She told Sutton about the interviews with Megler and with Boggs and with the friends and family members and told her about getting all the background footage. "And," she said, "I've sort of put in a request to get the police file on the case."

Sutton laughed. "You'll never get a police file. No journalist can get a police file."

"It's like a special request."

But Sutton just shook her head. "Won't happen." Then she asked, "Have you found anything that proves he's innocent?"

"Not like real evidence but—"

"Have you or haven't you?"

"No."

"All right." Sutton sat back. Half her food was uneaten but when the busboy appeared she gave him a subtle nod of the head and the plate vanished. "Let me tell you why I asked you here. I need some help."

"From me?"

"Look." Sutton was frowning. "I'll be frank. You're not my first choice. But there just isn't anybody else."

"Like, what are you talking about?"

"I want to offer you a promotion."

Rune poked at a white square of vegetable—some kind she'd never run into before.

Sutton gazed off across the restaurant as she mused, "Sometimes we have to do things for the good of the news. We have to put our own interests aside. When I started out I was a crime reporter. They didn't want women in the newsroom. Food reporting, society, the arts—those were fine but hard news? Nope. Forget it. So the chief gave me the shit jobs." Sutton glanced at Courtney but the girl didn't notice the lapse into adult vocabulary. The anchorwoman continued, "I covered autopsies, I chased ambulances, I did arraignments, I walked through pools of blood at a mass shooting to get pictures when the photographer was kneeling behind the press car puking. I did all of that crap and it worked out for me. But at the time it was a sacrifice."

Something in the matter-of-fact tone of Sutton's voice was thrilling to Rune. This is just what she'd sound like when talking to another executive at the Network, an equal. Sutton and Dan Semple or Lee Maisel would talk this way—in low voices, surrounded by people wearing huge geometric shapes of jewelry, sitting over the tiny bones of hostage birds and drinking eighty-dollar-a-bottle wine.

"Like, you want me to be a crime reporter? I don't—"

Sutton said, "Let me finish."

Rune sat back. Her plate was cleared away, and a young man in a white jacket cleaned the crumbs off the table with a little thing that looked like a miniature carpet sweeper. Most of the mess was on Rune's side.

"I like you, Rune. You've got street smarts and you're tough. That's something I don't see enough of in reporters nowadays. It's one or the other and usually more ego than either of them. Here's my problem: We've just lost the associate producer of the London bureau—he quit to work for Reuters—and they were in the midst of production on three programs. I need someone over there now."

Rune's skin bristled. As if a wave of painless flame had passed over her. "Associate producer?"

"No, you'd be an assistant, not associate. At first at least. The bureaus in London, Paris, Rome, Berlin and Moscow'll feed you leads and you and the executive producer will make your decisions on what you want to go after."

"What does Lee think?"

"He's given me the job of filling the spot. I haven't mentioned you to him but he'll go with whoever I recommend."

"This is pretty wild. I mean, I never thought that's what you were going to say. How long would I be over there?"

"A year minimum. If you like it, something more permanent might be arranged. That would be up to Lee. But usually we like to shift people around. It could be Paris or Rome after that. You'd have to learn the language."

"Oh, I took French in high school. '*Voulez-vous couchez . . .*'"

Sutton said, "I get the idea."

Rune asked a passing waiter for a glass of milk for Courtney. "And a straw? The kind with the bend in them." He didn't grasp the concept and Rune let it drop. She said to Sutton, "I don't want you to think . . . I mean, I'm grateful and all—but what about Randy Boggs?"

"You said yourself you don't have any evidence."

"I still know he's innocent."

No emotion in Sutton's face.

Rune said, "Somebody tried to kill him in prison. They stabbed him. If we don't get him out they'll try again."

Sutton shrugged. "I'll assign a local reporter to pick up for you."

"You would?"

"Uh-huh. So how 'bout it?"

"Uh, would you mind if I thought about it?"

Sutton blinked and seemed about to ask, *What the fuck is there to think about?* But she just nodded and said, "It's a big decision. Maybe you should sleep on it. I won't ask the other people I'm considering until tomorrow."

"Thanks."

Sutton motioned for the last of her wine. A young waiter scurried over and, with alternate glances at her freckled chest and the crystal glass in front of her, emptied the bottle. She looked at her watch. She said, "And the check, please."

OUTSIDE THE RESTAURANT THE THREE OF THEM PAUSED.

"That is one amazing car," Rune said as a glossy midnight-blue stretch Lincoln Town Car turned the corner and slowed. "Don't you wonder who rides in those things?"

Sutton didn't answer.

The car eased to a stop in front of them. The driver hopped out and ran to the door, opened it for the anchorwoman.

Oh.

Sutton said, "You'll give me your answer tomorrow?"

"Sure."

"Piper, we're late," a man's voice called from the limo.

"Good night," the anchorwoman said briskly to Rune and started toward the Lincoln.

The occupant leaned forward to help her in. It was Dan Semple himself, in a beautiful gray double-breasted suit. He glanced at Rune, then kissed Sutton on the cheek. They disappeared into the blackness of the car.

"Thanks—"

The door closed and Rune and Courtney were left looking at their mirrored images for the few seconds it took for the driver to get back inside and speed the limo away from the curb.

"—for dinner."

chapter 16

LONDON WAS THE PROBLEM.

Ever since she'd read *Lord of the Rings* (the first of four times) Rune'd wanted to go to the United Kingdom—the country of pubs and hedgerows and shires and hobbits and dragons. Whoa, and Loch Ness too—

She'd thought about it for a couple of hours and decided that any sane person in the world would accept Piper Sutton's offer in ten seconds flat.

So Rune was a bit curious why she found herself shoving the offer to the back of her mind, dropping Courtney at one of her loyal, expensive baby-sitters and then giving the cabdriver an address on the Upper East Side.

He took her to an old apartment building, dark brick with lion bas-reliefs in dirty limestone trim. She walked into the immaculate lobby, hit the intercom and announced herself. The door opened. She took the elevator to the fourteenth floor. When she stepped into a tiny corridor, she realized there were only four apartments on the whole floor.

Lee Maisel opened the door to one, waved and let her into a rambling, dark-paneled apartment. He didn't shake her hand; he was dripping wet.

She followed, noticing an elephant's foot in the corner; inside were a half-dozen umbrellas and canes. Several of them ended in carved faces: a lion, an old man (Rune thought he was a wizard), some kind of bird.

Maisel had been doing dishes. He was wearing a blue

denim apron, water-stained with Rorschach patterns and taut over his belly.

"When I called . . . Well, I hope I didn't interrupt anything."

"I'd have told you if I didn't want to be interrupted." Maisel returned to the cumulonimbus of suds. "The bar's over there." He nodded. "Food?"

"Uhm, I just ate."

Maisel dove into the dishwater again. Surrounded by implements—scrapers, sponges, metallic scrubbers like tiny steel wigs. A typhoon crashed over the granite countertop. A pan surfaced and beached itself on the Rubbermaid and he examined it carefully. His face was pure contentment. She envied him; cooking and cleaning were loves that Rune knew she would never cultivate.

In the living room, a projection TV set was showing an old movie, the sound low. Bette Davis. Who was the dude? Tyrone Power maybe. What a name, what a face! Men sure looked good back then. She could watch him for hours.

Finally Maisel wiped his hands and said, "Come on."

They walked into the living room.

Rune paused, looking at a framed newspaper article on the wall. From the *Times*. The headline was: "TV Correspondent Wins Pulitzer."

"Excellent," Rune said. "What was it for?"

"A story in Beirut a few years ago."

She asked, "A *Current Events* segment?"

"No. It was before we developed the show." He looked at the article slowly. "What a beautiful city that used to be. That's one of the crimes of the century, what happened there."

Rune skimmed the article. "It says you got an exclusive."

But he was troubled. "It was a mixed victory," he said. "We did what journalists should do—we looked under the surface and reported the truth But some people died because of that."

Rune recalled the incident from the information Bradford had brought her. Remembered too that Lance Hopper had stood up to the criticism and defended his news team.

"Come here," Maisel said, his face brightening. He led Rune down a long corridor, lit by overhead spotlights. It was like an art gallery.

"Hey, this is pretty cool."

There were dozens of framed maps, most of them antique. Maisel paused at each one, told her where he'd found it, how he'd dickered with the booksellers and vendors—and how he'd been taken by some and gypped others. She liked the New York maps best. Maisel pointed to a couple of them, describing what buildings were now on the spots that the maps showed as empty fields or hills.

Her favorite was a map of Greenwich Village in the 1700s. "That is fantastic. I love old New York. Doesn't it just do something to you? Okay, you're out on the street eating a Nedick's with onions—I really love those pickled onions—and you suddenly think, Wow, maybe I'm standing right on the very spot where they rubbed out a gangster or where two hundred years ago there was an Indian war or something."

"I don't eat hot dogs," Maisel said absently and she caught him glancing at his watch. They walked into a low-lit den, filled with leather furniture and more maps and framed photos of Maisel on assignment. They sat. He asked, "So what's up?"

Rune said, "I got an offer for something and I don't know what to do about it."

"Publishers Clearing House?" he asked wryly.

"Better than that." She told him what Piper Sutton had said.

Maisel listened. She got almost all the way through

before she realized that his face was growing a frown. "So she offered *you* the Brit spot, huh?"

"I was kind of surprised."

She could see that he was surprised too. "Rune, I want to be honest. No reflection on you but it's a tough assignment. I had a couple of people more senior in mind. I'm not saying you couldn't get up to speed but your experience is . . ."

"Like, pretty much not there."

Maisel didn't agree or disagree. He said, "You're a good cameraman and you're learning a lot with the Hopper story. But producing involves a lot more than that." He shrugged. "But I asked Piper to fill the spot. It's her call. If she wants you in the job it's yours." He looked across the room. More antique maps. She wondered what country he was focusing on.

"I'm pretty tempted," she said.

"Wonder why," he said wryly. "Couldn't be more than ten, fifteen thousand reporters in the country that'd kill to have that assignment." Maisel stretched his feet out straight. He was wearing bright yellow socks.

"But," he said, "you're worried about the Boggs story."

She nodded. "*That's* the problem."

"How's it coming?"

"Slow. I don't really have any leads. Nothing solid."

"But you still think he's innocent?"

"Yeah, I guess I do. The story'd still get done. Piper said she'd assign someone local to finish it."

"Did she?"

"Yeah, she promised me."

Maisel nodded.

After a moment Rune said, "She doesn't want me to do this story, does she?"

"She's afraid."

"Afraid? Piper Sutton?"

"It's not as funny as it seems. Her job is her whole

life. She's had three disastrous marriages. There's nothing else she can do professionally; nothing she wants to do. If this story goes south she and I, and Dan Semple to some extent, will take the flak. You know how fickle audiences are. Dan and I are worried about news. Piper is too but she's an anchor—she's also got public image to sweat."

"I can't imagine her being afraid of anything. I mean, I'm terrified of her."

"She's not going to have you rubbed out if you tell her you're going to stay and do the story."

"But she's my boss. . . ."

Maisel laughed. "You're too young to know that bosses, like wives, aren't necessarily matched to us in heaven."

"Okay, but she *is* Piper Sutton."

"That's a different issue and I don't envy you having to call her up and tell her that you're declining her offer. But, so what? You're an adult."

Sort of, Rune thought. She said, "I don't know what to do, Lee. What's your totally, totally honest opinion about my story?"

Maisel was considering. A gold clock began pinging off the hours to ten P.M. When it hit eight he said, "I'm not going to do you any favors by being delicate. The Boggs story? You take it way too personally. And that's un-professional. I get the impression that you're on some kind of holy quest. You—"

"But he's innocent, and nobody else—"

"Rune," he said harshly. "You asked my opinion. Let me finish."

"Sorry."

"You're not looking at the whole picture. You've got to understand that journalism has a responsibility to be to-tally unbiased. You're not. With Boggs you're one of the most goddamn biased reporters I've ever worked with."

"True," she said.

"That makes for a noble person maybe but it's not journalism."

"That's sort of what Piper told me too."

"There's government corruption and incompetence everywhere, there're human rights violations in South America, Africa and China, there's homelessness, there's child abuse in day-care centers. . . . There are so many important issues that media has to choose from and so few minutes to talk about them. What you've done is pick a very small story. It's not a bad story; it's just an insignificant one."

She looked off, scanning Maisel's wall absently. She wondered if she'd find an omen—an old map of England, maybe. She didn't.

A minute passed.

He said, "It's got to be your decision. I think the best advice I can give you is, sleep on it."

"You mean, stay up all night tossing and turning and stewing about it."

"That might work too."

THE TWENTIETH PRECINCT, ON THE UPPER WEST SIDE, was considered a plum by a lot of cops.

The Hispanic gangs had been squeezed north, the Black Panthers were nothing more than a bit of nostalgia, and no-man's-land—Central Park—had its very own precinct to take care of the muggings and drug dealers. What you had in the Twentieth mostly were domestic disputes, shopliftings, an occasional rape. The piles of auto glass, like tiny green-blue ice cubes, marked what was maybe the most common crime: stealing Blaupunkts or Panasonics from dashboards. Two yuppies who'd scrunched BMW fenders might get into a shoving match in front of Zabar's. An insider trader might commit suicide occasionally. But things didn't get much worse than that.

There was a lot of traffic in and out of the low, 1960s

decor brick-and-glass precinct station. Community relations was a priority here and more people came through the doors of the Twentieth to attend meetings or just hang out with the cops than to report muggings.

So the desk sergeant—a beefy, moustachioed blond cop—didn't think twice about her, this young, miniskirted mother, about twenty, who had a cute-as-a-button three- or four-year-old in tow on this warm afternoon. She walked right up to him and said she had a complaint about the quality of police protection in the neighborhood.

The cop didn't really care, of course. He liked concerned citizens about as much as he liked his hemorrhoids and he almost felt sorry for the petty street dealers and hangers-out and drunks who got pushed around by these wild-eyed, lecturing, upstanding, taxpaying citizens—the women being the worst. But he'd studied community relations at the Police Academy and so now, though he couldn't bring himself to smile pleasantly at this short woman, he nodded as if he were interested in what she had to say.

"You guys aren't doing a good job patrolling. My little girl and I were out on the street, just taking a walk—"

"Yes, miss. Did someone hassle you?"

She gave him a glare for the interruption. "We were taking a walk and do you know what we found on the street?"

"Nade," the little girl said.

The cop infinitely preferred to talk to the little girl. He may have hated intense, short, concerned citizens but he loved kids. He leaned forward, grinning like a department-store Santa the first day on the job. "Honey, is that your name?"

"Nade."

"Uh-huh, that's a pretty name." Oh, she was so goddamn cute, he couldn't believe it. The way she was digging in her own little patent-leather purse, trying to look grown up. He didn't like the lime-green miniskirt she was wearing and he was thinking maybe the sunglasses around the girl's neck, on that yellow strap, might be dangerous. Her mother oughtn't to be dressing her in that crap. Little girls should be wearing that frilly stuff like his wife bought for their nieces.

The good-citizen mother said, "Show him what we found, baby."

The cop talked the singsongy language that adults think children respond to. "My brother's little girl has a purse like that. What do you have in there, honey? Your dolly?"

It wasn't. It was a U.S. Army–issue fragmentation hand grenade. "Nade," the girl said and held it out in both hands.

"Holy Mary," the cop gasped.

The mother said, "There. Look at that, just laying on the street. We—"

He hit the fire alarm and grabbed the phone, calling NYPD Central and reporting an explosive device.

Then it occurred to him that the fire alarm wasn't such a good idea because the forty or fifty officers in the building could get out only one of three ways—a back exit, a side exit and the front door, and most were choosing the front door, not eight feet from a child with a pound of TNT in her hands.

What happened next was kind of a blur. A couple of detectives got the thing away from the girl and onto the floor in the far corner of the lobby. But then nobody knew exactly what to do. Six cops stood gawking at it. But the pin hadn't been pulled and they got to talking about whether there was a hole drilled in the bottom of the grenade and how if there was that meant it was a dummy like they sold at Army-Navy stores and in ads in the back of *Field and Stream*. But whoever had put the thing in the corner had left it so that you couldn't see the butt end and, since the Bomb Squad got paid extra money to do that sort of thing, they decided just to wait.

But then somebody noticed it was in the sun and they thought that maybe that might set it off. They got into an argument because one of the cops had been in Nam, where it was a hundred and ten degrees in the sun and their grenades never went off but, yeah, this might be an old one and unstable. . . .

And if it did go they'd lose all their windows and the trophy case and somebody was bound to get fragged.

Finally, the desk sergeant had the idea to cover the thing with a half-dozen Kevlar bulletproof vests. And they made a great project out of carefully dropping vests on the grenade one by one, each cop making a run, not knowing whether to cover his eyes or balls with his free hand.

Then there they stood, these large cops, staring at a pile of vests until the Bomb Squad detectives arrived fifteen minutes later.

It was about then that the concerned mother and the little girl, who nobody had noticed walk past the desk sergeant and into the file room of the deserted precinct house, slipped outside through the back door, the mother shoving some papers into her ugly leopard-skin shoulder bag.

Holding her daughter's hand, she walked through the small parking lot full of blue-and-whites and past the cop car gas pump then turned toward Columbus Avenue. A few cops and passersby glanced at them but no one paid her much attention. There was still way too much excitement going on at the station house itself.

chapter 17

RUNE FILLED SAM HEALY'S KITCHEN BASIN WITH WATER and gave Courtney a bath. Then she dried the girl and put on the diaper she wore to bed. By now she'd gotten the routine down pretty well, and, though she wouldn't admit it to anybody, she liked the smell of baby powder.

The little girl asked, "Story?"

Rune said, "I've got a good one we can read. Come on in here."

She checked outside to make sure Healy's Bomb Squad station wagon wasn't back yet. Then they walked into the family room and sat on an old musty couch with tired springs. She sank down into it. Courtney climbed into her lap.

"Can we read about ducks?" Courtney asked. "The duck story is really crucial."

"This is even better," Rune said. "It's a police report."

"Excellent."

The girl nodded as Rune began to read through sheets of paper, stamped "Property of the 20th Precinct." There were some photos of Hopper's dead body but they were totally gross and Rune slipped them to the back before Courtney saw them. She read until her throat ached from keeping her voice in a child-entertaining low register. She'd pause occasionally and watch Courtney's eyes scan the cheap white paper. The meaning of the words was totally lost on the child, of course, but she was fascinated anyway, finding some secret delight in the abstract designs of the black letters.

After twenty minutes Courtney closed her eyes and lay heavily against Rune's shoulder.

The subject of the reading matter apparently didn't matter much to Courtney; ducks and police procedures lulled her to sleep equally quickly. Rune put her into bed, pulled the blankets around her. She looked at the U2 poster that Healy's son, Adam, had bought Healy for his birthday (a great father, the cop had immediately framed and mounted it in a nice prominent location). She decided to sink some money into a Maxfield Parrish or Wyeth reproduction for Courtney's room on the houseboat. That's what kids needed: giants in clouds or magic castles. Maybe one of Rackham's illustrations from *A Midsummer Night's Dream.*

Rune returned to the report.

I'd just come back from Zabars. I walked past my living room window. I see these two men standing there. Then one pulls out this gun. . . . There was a flash and one of the men fell over. I ran to the phone to dial 911, but I'll admit I hesitated—I was worried it might be a Mafia thing. All these witnesses you hear about getting killed. Or a drug shooting. I go back to the window to see if they were just kidding around. Maybe it was young people, you know, but by then there's a police car. . . .

The report contained the names of three people interviewed by the police about Hopper's murder. All three lived on the first floor of the building. The first two hadn't been home. The third was the woman who'd given the report, a clerk at Bloomingdale's, who lived on the first floor of Hopper's building, overlooking the courtyard.

That was all? The cops had talked to only *three* people? And only *one* eyewitness?

At least thirty or forty apartments would open onto the courtyard. Why hadn't they been interviewed?

Cover-up, she thought. Conspiracy. Grassy knolls, the Warren Commission.

She finished the report. There wasn't much else helpful. Rune heard Healy's car pull into the driveway and hid the file. She looked in on Courtney. Kissed her forehead.

The girl woke up and said, "Love you."

Rune blinked and didn't speak for a moment then managed, "Like, sure. Me too." But Courtney seemed to be asleep again by the time she said it.

"FUNNY THING," SAM HEALY WAS SAYING THE NEXT morning.

"Funny?"

"This practice grenade disappeared from the Bomb Squad and, next thing, there's a report of one found on the street near the Twentieth."

"Funny."

He'd just come in from mowing the lawn. She smelled grass and gasoline. It reminded her of her childhood in the suburbs of Cleveland, Saturday morning, when her father would trim the boxwood and mow and spread mulch around the dogwoods.

"Don't think I heard anything about it on the radio," Rune offered.

"The report said a young woman and a baby found it. I seem to remember you stopping by the Bomb Squad yesterday, didn't you? You and Courtney?"

"Sort of, I think. I'm not too clear."

Healy said, "You're sounding like those defendants. 'Yeah, I was standing over the body with the gun but I don't remember how I got there.'"

"You don't think *I* had anything to do with it?"

"Occurred to me."

"You want my solemn word?"

"Will you swear on the Grimm Brothers?"

"Absolutely." She raised her hand.

"Rune . . . Didn't you think it was dangerous for a child to pull a stunt like that?"

"Not that I *did* walk around with a grenade but if I had I would've made sure it was a dummy."

"You could get me fired. And you could get arrested."

She tried to look miserable and contrite and unjustly accused at the same time. He popped open two Pabsts.

He was stern when he said, "Just don't forget: You've got more to think about than yourself."

Which gave her a little thrill, his saying, *Remember me? I'm in your life too.* But he tromped on that pretty fast by nodding toward the bedroom and saying, "Think about her. You don't want her to lose two mothers in one month, do you?"

"No."

They sipped the beers in silence for a minute. Then she said, "Sam, I got a question: You ever do any homicide?"

"Investigations? No. When I was in Emergency Services we ran crime scenes a lot but I never did the legwork. Boring."

"But you know something about them?"

"A little. What's up?"

"Say there's somebody killed, okay?"

"Hypothetically?"

"Yeah, this guy is hypothetically killed. And there's an eyewitness the cops find and he gives a statement. Would the cops just stop there and not interview anybody else?"

"Sure, why not? If it's a solid witness."

"Real solid."

"Sure. Detectives've got more murders than they know what to do with. An eyewitness—which you hardly ever get in a homicide—sure, they'd take the statement and turn 'em over to the prosecutor. Then on to another case."

"I'd think they'd do more."

"An eyewitness, Rune? It doesn't get any better than that."

THE SITES OF TRAGEDY.

It had happened three years ago but as she placed each foot on the worn crest of a cobblestone—slowly, a mourner's hopscotch—Rune felt the macabre, queasy pull of Lance Hopper's killing. It was eight P.M., an overcast, humid evening. She and Courtney stood in the courtyard, at the bottom of the four sides of the building. A square of gray-pink city-lit sky was above them.

Where exactly had Hopper died? she wondered. In the dim triangle of light falling into the courtyard from the leaded-glass lamp by the canopied doorway? Or had it been in the negative space—the shadows?

Had he crawled toward the light?

Rune found that this bothered her, not knowing exactly where the man had lain as he died. She thought there should be some kind of marker, some indication of where that moment had occurred—the instant between life and no life. But there was nothing, no reminder at all.

Hopper would have to be content with whatever his gravestone said. He'd been rich; she was sure it was an eloquent sentiment.

Rune led Courtney into the stuccoed lobby. An entryway of a medieval castle. She expected at least a suit of armor, a collection of pikes and broadswords and maces. But she saw only a bulletin board with a faded sign, *Co-op News*, and a stack of take-out menus from a Chinese restaurant.

She pressed a button.

.   .   .

"WHAT A CUTE LITTLE GIRL. YOU'RE YOUNG TO BE A
mother."

Rune said, "You know how it is."

The woman said, "I had Andrew when I was twenty-
six; Beth when I was twenty-nine. That was old for then.
For that generation. Let me show you the pictures."

The apartment was irritating. It reminded Rune of a
movie she'd seen one time about these laser beams that
crisscrossed the control room in a spaceship and if you
broke one of them you'd set off this alarm. Here, though,
no laser beams, but instead: little china dishes, animal fig-
urines, cups, commemorative plates, a Franklin Mint ceramic thimble collection, vases and a thousand other
artifacts, most of them flowery and ugly, all poised on the
edges of fake teak shelves and tables, just waiting to fall to
the floor and shatter.

Courtney's eyes glinted at these many opportunities
for destruction and Rune kept a death grip on the belt of
the little girl's jumpsuit.

The woman's name was Miss Breckman. She was
handsome. A born salesclerk: reserved, helpful, organized,
polite. Rune remembered she was in her late fifties
though she looked younger. She was stocky, with a double
chin (handsome though it was) and a cylindrical frame.
"Have a seat, please."

They maneuvered through the ceramic land mines
and sat on doily-covered chairs. Rune tamped down her
pride and complimented Miss Breckman on her fine collection of things.

The woman glowed. "I got them mostly from my
mother. We had the same thoughts about decoration. Ge-
netic, I suppose."

From there they talked about children, about
boyfriends and husbands (Miss Breckman's had left her ten
years before; she was, she said, "currently in the market").

Mostly what Miss Breckman wanted to talk about,
though, was the news.

"So you're a real reporter?" Her eyes focused on Rune like a scientist discovering a new kind of bug.

"More of a producer, really. Not like a newspaper reporter. It's different in TV news."

"Oh, I know. I watch every news program on the air. I always try to work the day shift so I can be home in time to watch *Live at Five*. It's a bit gossipy, but aren't we all? I don't care for the six P.M. report—that's mostly business—so I fix my dinner then, and I watch the *World News at Seven* while I eat." She frowned. "I hope you won't be offended if I tell you your network's nightly news isn't all that good. Jim Eustice, the anchorman, I think he's funny-looking and sometimes doesn't pronounce those Polish and Japanese names right. But *Current Events* is simply the best. Do you know Piper Sutton? Sure you do, of course. Is she as charming as she seems? Smart . . . sweet . . ."

If you only knew, lady. . . .

Rune began steering toward the Boggs story, not quite sure how much to say. If Rune was right about Boggs's innocence, of course, she was pretty much calling Ms. Figurine here a liar, and—come to think of it—a perjurer too. She opted for the indirect approach. "I'm doing a follow-up story on the Hopper killing and I'd like to ask you a few questions."

"I'd be happy to help. It was one of the most exciting times of my life. I was in that courtroom and there was this killer right there and he was looking at me." Miss Breckman closed her eyes for a moment. "I was pretty darn scared. But I did my duty. I was kind of hoping that after I came out of the courtroom there'd be all these reporters shoving microphones at me—you know, I love those microphones with the names of the stations on them."

"Uh-huh. Maybe I could set up my equipment?"

While Rune did that, Miss Breckman hoisted Courtney into her lap and rattled on nonstop. Bringing the little girl had been a great idea—she was like a pacifier for adults.

When the portable light clicked on and the red dot on the Ikegami flashed, Miss Breckman's eyes took on an intense shine to a degree Rune figured they would never reach ringing up an American Express charge in Junior Sportswear.

Rune said, "Could you move over there." Nodding at a Queen Anne chair upholstered in forest-green needle-point.

"I'll sit wherever you like, honey." Miss Breckman moved and then composed herself for a moment.

"Now, could you tell me exactly what happened?"

"Sure." She told the camera about the murder. Coming home from shopping, seeing the men argue. The gun appearing. The muffled shot. Hopper falling. Running to the phone. Hesitating. . . .

"You saw him pull the trigger?"

"Well, I saw this flash and the gun was right up against the poor man's body."

"Could you see what kind of gun it was?"

"No, it was too dark."

"And you couldn't hear what they were saying."

"No." Her head turned, eyes gazing into the court-yard. "You can see . . ."

Beautiful shot! Rune zoomed past her and focused on the cobblestones.

". . . it's pretty far away."

Rune dug into her purse and pulled out a piece of paper. She looked at it then said, "The police report said you weren't interviewed until the day after the shooting. Is that right?"

"Uh-huh. The next night, two men showed up. Detectives. But they didn't look like Kojak or anything, though. I was kind of disappointed."

"You didn't contact them right away?"

"No. Like I told you, I was pretty shaken by the whole thing. I was scared. What if it was a drug killing? You know what you see on the news. Practically every day, mothers and children are being murdered because they're witnesses. But the next morning I saw a news report on *Wake Up With the News* that said they'd arrested this drifter. Not a hit man or anything. So when the detectives came to me I didn't hesitate to tell them what I saw."

"It also says that the police asked you if you'd seen anything and you said, 'I'm sorry I didn't talk to you sooner but I *did* see it. I mean, I saw the shooting.' And the detective asked, 'Did you see the man who did it?' And you answered, 'Sure I did. It was Randy Boggs.' Was that pretty much what you said?"

"Nope, not pretty much at all. That's *exactly* what I said."

Rune just smiled and resisted an urge to say, *No further questions.*

SHE SUDDENLY FELT A SHADOW OVER HER AND DIDN'T like the vibrations one bit. Rune looked sideways to see what angel of death was hovering over her in the newsroom and found she was staring into Piper Sutton's eyes.

"Hi," Rune said.

Sutton didn't answer.

Rune's eyes skipped around the room, wondering why exactly the woman was frowning so intensely.

Rune said, "Guess what I've got." She touched the tape. "I talked to the witness and—"

The flash of anger was like a fast shutter on a camera. And so fierce and brutal that Rune gasped. Then Piper Sutton regained control though her eyes were still cold. "You've got a little bit to learn about life." She seemed to swallow something at the end of the sentence, probably: *young lady.*

Rune began, "What did I—?"

Then it hit her—oh, shit. The London assignment.

"Nobody's forcing you to work for a network like ours." Now, the temper was once again on the move—the patented Sutton temper. It was rolling downhill, an avalanche, and Rune was about to get buried. "You have your choice. But if you're going to work here, goddammit, you've got to behave like an adult, or—"

"I was going to tell you about the London job. I'm sorry."

"—you can go pick up paychecks at some fucking restaurant!" The voice dropped threateningly. "I take you out to dinner, where you and that urchin of yours embarrass the hell out of me and I make you a proposition that no one your age has *ever* been offered before!" Now the screeching began. Rune blinked and sat back, her eyes wide. "And do you even give me the courtesy of an answer?"

Heads perked up. Throughout the studio, no one dared look—and no one didn't listen.

"I'm sorry."

But Sutton cranked up a few more decibels. "Do you even show me the respect you'd show a cabdriver? Did you say, 'Thank you, but I've decided not to accept your offer'? Did you say, 'Piper, could you please give me a few days to think about it some more?' No, you goddamn well didn't. What you did was say . . . zip. That's what you said. And then you went on your merry way."

"I'm sorry." Rune heard herself whining and didn't like it. She cleared her throat. "I got caught up in the story. I was going to tell you—"

Sutton waved her hand. "I hate apologies. It's a sign of weakness."

Rune wanted to cry but sat hard on the tears.

Sutton was speaking to the ceiling. "*Everything* about this story has been wrong. I knew it was a mistake. Stupid of me. Stupid, stupid."

Rune swallowed. She touched the file. "Just let me

explain, please. What happened was I talked to the witness."

Sutton smiled coldly and shook her head, exaggerating her lack of comprehension. "What witness?"

"The one who convicted Randy."

"Oh, sure, that explains your behavior." Sutton's sarcasm was thick.

"No. I can prove that she didn't see Randy Boggs."

"How?"

"She's a real, like, newshound."

"A newshound? What the fuck is that?"

"She watches all the news programs every day. She didn't give any description of Boggs until *after* she'd seen him arrested on TV. When the—"

Sutton's hands raised like a martyr's. "What exactly are you getting at?"

"Listen. When the police showed up to interview her she said, 'I saw who did it and it was Randy Boggs.' "

Silence. Pin-resounding silence. Sutton gave a short bark of a laugh. "That's your proof?"

"You can't see into the courtyard clearly from her place—it's too dark. Miss Breckman saw Randy on the *news*. She saw him arrested. *That's* where she got the description—from TV. Otherwise, how would she know his name? She didn't describe him first. She said, right off, 'It was Randy Boggs.' "

Media circus . . .

Sutton considered this with a splinter of interest. But then she laughed. "Keep at it, honey. You've got a long way to go."

"But doesn't this prove that she's a bad witness?"

"A piece in the puzzle. That's all it is. Keep digging."

"I thought—"

"That we'd go with it?"

"I guess."

A brittle nail leveled at Rune's face like a bright red

dagger. "This is the big time. You keep forgetting that. We don't run a story until it's *completely* buttoned up." She walked stridently through the newsroom on her clattering heels while employees moved quickly but unobtrusively as far out of her way as they could.

chapter 18

DOWNSTAIRS, IN THE LOBBY, RUNE SURVEYED THE JOB AND didn't like what she saw.

A directory of residents, containing over a hundred names.

"Help you?" The doorman's accent seemed to be Russian. But then Rune decided she didn't know what a Russian accent sounded like; the man—wearing an old gray uniform shiny on the butt—might have been Czech or Romanian or Yugoslavian or even Greek or Argentine. Whatever his ethnic origin, he was big and snide and unfriendly.

"I was just looking at the directory."

"Who you wanna see?"

"Nobody really. I was just—"

He smiled slyly as if he'd just caught on that three-card monte games were rigged. "I know. They done that before."

"I'm a student."

"Yeah, student." He worked a spot on the inside of his mouth with his tongue.

"How long you worked here?" she asked.

"Six months. I just came over here. This country. Lived with my cousin for a while."

"Who worked here before you?"

He shrugged. "I dunno. How would I know? You make good money doing it? You know what I'm saying?"

"What do you mean? I'm a student."

"I've heard it all. You think I haven't heard it?"

"I'm an art student. Architecture. I—?"

"Yeah." The smile was staying put. The tongue foraged. "What you make?"

"Make?" Rune asked.

"How much you sell them for?"

"What?"

"The names." He nodded. "You sell them to companies send everybody that junk mail. No junk mail in my country. Here! It's everywhere."

"What I'm doing is I'd like to talk to some people who live here. About the design of their apartments."

A nod joined the smile.

There was nothing worse than being accused of something you hadn't done—even if you were doing something you shouldn't've been doing.

She rummaged for a minute in the dark recesses of her bag until she came up with a stiff bill. A twenty. Hot out of the ATM. She handed it to him.

Zip. It vanished into his pocket.

"How much you make?"

Another twenty joined its friend.

"Ah." He walked off, pressing his hand to the pocket that held the crisp, non-reimbursable bills and Rune turned back to her task.

The smart thing would have been to find out which rows of apartments looked out over the courtyard where Lance Hopper had been shot but she didn't know how soon the Slavic-Ruskie South American capitalist would be back to suck up another bribe. So she started at the top left of the directory. From Myron Zuckerman in 1B she speed wrote straight down to Mr., or Ms., L. Peters in 8K.

Twenty minutes later, the doorman returned, just as she finished.

"Still studying?" he asked snidely.

"I just finished."

"So tell me, yeah, which company you with? One of the big ones? Am I right?"

"It's a big one," Rune said.

"Is in Jersey, right?"

"How'd you guess?"

"I've been around. I seen a lot. You can't fool me."

"I wouldn't even try."

SCORCHING PAIN ROAMED AROUND IN HER BACK. THE IN-side of her ear was sweating. Her voice had gone from low soprano to throaty alto and she'd have to clear her wind-pipe with a stinging snap every few minutes. Rune had been sitting in her cubicle at the studio, speaking into a phone, for nearly eight hours straight.

Hello I'm a producer for Current Events *the news pro-gram Mr. Zuckerman Norris Williams Roth Gelinker we're doing a segment about the Lance Hopper killing you proba-bly remember the man killed in the courtyard of your build-ing several years ago I'm hoping you can help me what I'm looking for is . . .*

It was late, after eight o'clock. Past bedtime for Courtney. The little girl sat at Rune's feet, tearing sched-uling sheets into the shape of Easter bunnies.

. . . How long have you lived in apartment 3B, 3C, 3D, 3E, 3F . . . ?

"Rune, bunny."

Whispering, hand over mouthpiece: "Beautiful, honey. I'm on the phone. Make a momma Easter bunny now."

"That *is* the mommy."

"Then make a daddy."

Rune's poll of the tenants so far:

One was Miss Breckman. Eight had unlisted num-bers. Twenty weren't home when she called. Thirty-three had moved into their apartments after Hopper's death. Eighteen hadn't been home the night of the killing (or said they hadn't). Nineteen were home but didn't see anything related to the murder (or said they didn't).

That left twelve on her list.

A bad number. If there'd been only three she would've called them. Twenty, she'd have given up and gone home to sleep. But twelve . . .

Rune sighed and stretched, hearing some remote bone protest with a pop.

Courtney yawned and tore a bunny in half with fidgety glee.

Quitting time, Rune thought. I'm going home. Then she thought of Sutton's raspy, bitchy voice and fuming eyes and she picked up the phone.

Which was fortunate because when she asked Mr. Frost, 6B, if he knew anything about the Lance Hopper killing he paused for only a moment then responded, "Actually . . . I saw it happen."

"YOU PUT THAT IN A BOTTLE AND YOU'VE GOT YOURSELF something," she said.

Rune had walked into the apartment, right past the elderly man who'd opened the door, and stepped up to a glass case. Inside was an elaborate model of a ship—not a rigged clipper ship or man-of-war but a modern cargo ship. It was four feet long. She said, "Audacious."

"Thank you. I've never made ships in bottles. To tell you the truth, I don't like hobbies."

She introduced herself.

"Bennett Frost," he said. He was about seventy-five years old. He wore a cardigan sweater with a moth hole on the shoulder and cheap gray pants. He was balding and had dark moles on his face and head. He leaned forward, a vestigial bow, as he shook her hand. He held it for a moment longer than one normally would have and looked at her closely. The touch and the examination, though, were not sexual. He was appraising her. When he was done he released her hand and nodded at the glass case.

"The *Minnesota Princess*. Odd name, don't you think, for a ship that spent most of her time in the Mediterranean and the Atlantic? My very first ship. No, I shouldn't say that. My very first *profitable* ship. Which is, I suppose, better than my first ship. I named her *Minnesota* because I was born there."

He walked into the large apartment. Rune followed him. In the cluttered living room she noticed suitcases.

"You going on a trip?"

"I have a place in Bermuda. Haiti was my favorite. The Oloffson—what a hotel that was. Not true any longer, of course. I never used to go to British colonies but you know how things are elsewhere." He looked at her with slits of eyes, a shared secret. She nodded.

His eyes fell on her camera.

"You have a press pass or something?"

She showed him her Network ID. He scanned her up and down again, a CAT scan of her soul. "You're young."

"Younger than some. Older than others."

He gave that a curly smile and said, "*I* was young when I got started in business."

"What did you do?"

He gazed at the model. "That was my contribution to the shipping industry and the aesthetics of the sea. She isn't beautiful; she isn't a stately ship."

"I think she looks pretty nifty."

Frost said, " 'And the stately ships go on/To their haven under the hill/But O for the touch of a vanished hand/And the sound of a voice that is still.' Tennyson. Nobody knows poetry anymore."

Rune knew some nursery rhymes and some Shakespeare but she remained silent.

He continued, "But that ship made money hand over fist for a lot of people." He lifted a heavy decanter and started pouring two glasses of purple liquor, as he asked, "Would you like some port?"

She accepted the glass and sipped. It was cloying as honey and tasted like cough medicine.

"I started out as a ship's chandler. Do you know what that is?"

"A candle maker?" Rune shrugged.

"No, a provisioner. A supplier. Anything a captain wanted, from a ratchet to a side of beef, I would get it. I started when I was seventeen, rowing out to the ships as soon as they dropped anchor, even before the agents arrived or they'd started off-loading. I gave them cut prices, demanded half as a deposit, gave them fancy-looking receipts for the cash and always returned with what they wanted or a substitute that was better or cheaper."

"I was wondering, sir—" she began.

Frost held up a hand. "Listen. This is important. During the thirties I moved into the shipping side of the business."

Rune didn't see what was important but she let him talk.

And talk he did. Fifteen minutes later she'd learned about his growing fortune in the shipping business. He was talking about ship propellers he'd designed himself. "They called them Frost Efficiency Screws. I got such a kick out of that! Efficiency Screws! So my ships could make the run from the Strait of Hormuz around the horn to the Ambrose Light in thirty-three days. I had the fastest oil carriers in the world. Thirty-three days."

Rune said, "If I could ask you a few questions. About the Hopper killing."

"There's a point I'm trying to make."

"Sorry."

"I got out of shipping. I could see what would happen to oil. I could see the balance of trade shift. I didn't want to leave my ships; oh, that hurt me. But you have to think ahead. Did you hear about the buggy-whip manufacturers who went out of business when autos were developed? You know what their problem was? They didn't think of themselves as being in the *accelerator* business. Ha!" He loved the story, had probably told it a thousand times. "So what did I go into?"

"Airlines?"

Frost laughed derisively. "*Public* transportation? Regulations ad nauseam. I thought about it but I knew that it would take one Democrat, two at the most, to ruin the industry. No, I diversified—financial services, mining, manufacturing. And I became the fourth-richest man in the world . . . You're skeptical. I can see that. You've never heard of me. Some old crackpot, you're thinking, who's lured me in here for who knows what nefarious prospects. But it's true. In the seventies I had three billion dollars." He paused. "And those were the days when a billion meant something."

He sat forward and Rune sensed he was getting to his long-awaited point.

"But what could I do with money like that? Provide for my wife and children. Buy comfortable shoes, a good set of golf clubs, a warm coat, an apartment where the plumbing worked. I don't smoke; rich food makes me ill. Mistresses? I was contentedly married for forty-one years. I put my children through school, set up trust funds for the grandchildren, though not very fat ones, and . . ." He smiled, significantly. ". . . I gave most of the rest away. Hence, you."

"Me? What exactly does all that have to do with the Lance Hopper killing?"

Frost considered this for a moment. "I'm confessing." She blinked.

"But," he said, "you have to understand. It didn't make any difference, you know."

"Uh, like, how exactly do you mean?"

"They had the other witness. You can't blame me really."

"Could you explain please."

"At the time, when he was killed, I had my fortune. I was giving money away. I had people who worked for me who depended on me for their livelihood. Their families . . . You people in the media—a man never has any privacy around you." He pronounced it with a short i, privacy. Like "privileged."

He continued. "I was simply scared back them. I was afraid to tell the police that I'd seen Hopper killed. I'd be on news programs. I'd be in court. There'd be stories about my wealth. Kidnappers might come after my family or me. Do-gooders would start hounding me for money for their causes. I felt guilty at first but then I heard that that Breckman woman downstairs saw the whole thing and told the police about the killer. It took the pressure off me."

"But now you don't mind telling me what you saw? What's different now?"

Frost walked to the window and looked into the gloomy courtyard. "I have a different attitude toward life."

Oh, please, Rune was praying, do it now. Tell me what you saw. And, please, make it good. "May I?" She gestured toward the camera.

A pause. Then he nodded.

The lights clicked on. The camera hummed. She aimed it at Frost's long face.

"It's odd," he said wistfully, "what giving away your fortune does. It's a marvelous thing. I don't know why it hasn't caught on." He looked at her seriously. "Let me ask you, you know anybody else giving away a billion dollars?"

"None of *my* friends," Rune said. "Unfortunately."

chapter 19

RUNE AND PIPER SUTTON SAT IN FRONT OF THE ANCHOR-woman's desk, watching the monitor. Out of it came two tinny voices.

"*Mr. Frost, did you see the shooting?*"

"*Plain as the nose on my face. Or your face—however that expression goes. It was horrible. I saw this man come up to Mr. Hopper and pull out this little gun and shoot him, just push the pistol at him. It reminded me of the pictures of Ruby, you know, Jack Ruby, when he shot Oswald. Mr. Hopper held his hands out like he was trying to catch the bullet. . . .*"

Sutton stirred but didn't say anything.

"*Could you describe him?*"

"*He was a fat man. Not fat all over but with a beer belly. Like a timpani.*"

"*A what?*"

"*A drum. Dark blondish hair. A moustache . . . What's that? Sure, I'm positive about the moustache. And side-burns. A light jacket. Powder-blue.*"

Rune said to Sutton, "That's Jimmy. The man who picked up Randy and drove him to New York."

Sutton frowned and waved her silent.

"*Why didn't you go to the police?*"

"*I told you.*"

"*If you could tell me again. Please.*"

"*I was afraid—of retaliation. Of publicity. I was very*

wealthy. I was scared for me and my family. Anyway the killer was caught and identified. That woman downstairs identified the man, and I read that the police caught him practically red-handed. Why would they need me?"

"I'm going to show you a picture of someone. . . . Could you tell me if this is the man you saw in the courtyard?"

"Who? This skinny fellow? No, that wasn't him at all."

"You'd swear to it?"

"Sure I would."

Click.

Rune kept staring at the monitor, a proud schoolkid waiting for the teacher's praise.

But Sutton's only comment was a breathy "Damn."

Rune tried not to smile with pleasure and unadulterated pride.

Sutton looked at her watch, then added, "I'm late for a meeting with Lee. Did you make a dupe of that tape?"

"Sure," Rune said. "I always make dupes. It's locked in my credenza."

Sutton said, "We've got a story conference on Friday. Bring your proposed script. You'll present to both of us and be prepared to defend every goddamn line. Got it?"

"You bet."

Sutton started to leave the office. She paused and said in a soft voice, "I'm not very good at praise. Just let me say that there aren't many people who would've stuck with it long enough to do what you did." Then she frowned and the old Sutton returned. "Now get some sleep. You look awful."

"THIS IS THE STORY OF A MAN CONVICTED OF A CRIME HE *didn't commit unjustly. . . ."*

Uh, no.

"*. . . of a man unjustly convicted of a crime he didn't commit . . .*"

Well, sure, if he didn't commit it it's unjust.

"... *the story of a man convicted of a crime he didn't commit ...*"

Words were definitely the hard part.

Rune spun around in her desk chair and let out a soft, anguished scream of frustration. Words—she hated words. Rune *saw* things and she *liked* seeing things. She remembered things she saw and forgot things she was told. Words were real tricky little dudes.

"*This is the story of a man convicted of a crime he didn't commit, a man who lost two years of his life because ...*"

Why? Why?

"... *because the system of justice in this country is like a big dog ...*"

A dog? Justice is like a *dog*? Are you insane? "Crap!" She shouted. "Crap, crap, crap!" Half the newsroom looked at her.

What is Lee Maisel going to say when he reads this stuff? What's Piper going to say?

"... *because the system of, no, because the justice system in this country, no, because the American justice system is like a bird with an injured wing ...*"

Crap, crap, crap!

FRED MEGLER WAS AS ENTHUSIASTIC AS COULD BE EX-pected, considering that his lunch was two hot dogs (with kraut and limp onions) and a Diet Pepsi and considering too that his view while he was eating was the Criminal Courts Building—the darkest, grimiest courthouse in all of Manhattan.

And considering finally that one of his clients, he explained to Rune, was about to be sentenced on a three-count conviction for murder two.

"Stupid shmuck. He fucking put himself away. What can I say?"

Megler, still skinny, still gray, was chewing, drinking

and talking simultaneously. Rune stood back, out of the trajectory of flecks of hot dog that occasionally catapulted from behind his thick, wet lips. He was impressed with her story about Frost even as he tried not to be. He said, "Yeah, sounds like Boggs might have a shot at it. Not enough to reverse the conviction, probably. But the judge might go for a new trial. I'm not saying yes, I'm not saying no. There's new evidence, then there's new *evidence*. What you're telling me, this was evidence that could have been discovered at the time of the trial."

"I was sort of wondering about that. How come *you* didn't find Frost?"

"Hey, I was making minimum wage on that case. I don't have an expense account like you newspeople do. I don't sit around at five o'clock drinking manhattans in the Algonquin."

"What's a manhattan?"

"A drink. You know, rye and vermouth and bitters. Look, the Boggs trial, I did what I could. I had limited re-sources. That was his problem. He didn't have any money."

The tail of the last hot dog disappeared. Rune had an image of a big fish eating a small fish.

"Doesn't sound like justice to me."

"Justice?" Megler asked. "You want to know what justice is?"

Rune sure did and as she pressed the record button on the little JVC camcorder hidden from his view in her leopard-skin bag, Megler—who could probably have cited all kinds of laws on being taped surreptitiously—was po-lite enough to finish chewing and to take on a reflective expression before he spoke again. "Justice in this country is luck and fate and circumstances and expedience. And as long as that's true, people like Randy Boggs're going to serve time they shouldn't."

"Will you handle the case?"

"We had a conversation about my fee. . . ."

"Come on. He's innocent. Don't you want to help him out?"

"Not particularly. I don't give money to homeless people. Why should I be more generous with my time?"

"I don't believe you." Rune's voice went high. "You—"

"Would your network pay my bill?"

Something sounded wrong about it. She said, "I don't think that'd be ethical."

"What, ethical? I wouldn't get into hot water for that."

"I meant journalists' ethics."

"Oh, *your* ethics." He swilled the last of the Pepsi, glanced down and noticed a spot on his navy-blue tie. He took a pen from his pocket and scribbled back and forth on the tie until the smudge was obscured. "Well, that's the net-net. I work, I get paid. That's carved in stone. But you got some options. There's Legal Aid. Or ACLU—those dips get orgasmic, they get a case like this. One of those three-piece do-gooders from Yale or Columbia or Hahvahd might get wind of it and pick up the case. So you run your story—I'll guarantee you, some scrawny little NYU graduate'll be banging on your door begging to get Boggs's phone number."

"But that could take months. He's got to get out now. His life's in danger."

"Look, I've got to walk back to that hellhole in twenty minutes and stand next to a man who—it is alleged—machine-gunned three rival gang members while he told Polack jokes to one of his mistresses. I have to stand there and listen to the judge explain to him that he's going to spend at least fifteen years in a ten-by-twenty cell. When he came to me he said, 'Fred, I hear good things 'boutchu. You get me off. You do that? You get me off.'"

He laughed and slapped his chest. "Hey, I *didn't* get him off. He's not happy and he and his friends are killers. What I'm saying is, Boggs's in danger, *I'm* in danger. Think about it. You're in danger too. *You're* the one saying the cops, the prosecutor and your own Network're a bunch of dickheads. *Life* is dangerous. What can I say?"

Megler looked at his watch. "Time to do my bit to beautify America and get some more garbage off the street."

"I've got an offer," Rune said.

The lawyer looked over his shoulder. "Make it fast. You don't keep drug lords waiting."

She said, "You know how many people watch *Current Events?*"

"No and I don't know the average annual rainfall in the Amazon either. Do I care?" He started up the stairs.

"Depends on whether or not you want ten million people to see your name and face and hear what kind of incredible work you do."

Fred Megler stopped.

Rune repeated, "Ten million."

Megler glanced at the courthouse door. He muttered something to himself and walked back down the steps.

"ME, OKAY. I WAS BORN IN ATLANTA, AND WE LIVED THERE for ten years before our daddy decided he was going to the land of greater opportunity, which was the way he put it, and I can still remember him saying that. . . ."

From inside a thirteen-inch Japanese television monitor, the color unbalanced, too heavy in red, Randy Boggs was telling his life story.

"Greater opportunity. I was scared because I thought we were going to die—because I got 'land of greater opportunity' confused with 'Promised Land,' which I remembered from Day of the Ascension Baptist Church meant heaven. At the time I was close to eleven and religious. Okay, I got myself into some pretty fair scrapes at school. Somebody, some older kid'd cuss, 'Jesus Christ,' and I'd get madder 'n a damp cat and make him say he was sorry and what happened was I got the hell beat out of me more times'n I can recall or care to."

Editing videotape was a hundred times easier than

film. It was an electronic, not mechanical, process and Rune thought that this represented some incredible advancement in civilization—going from things that you could see how they worked to things that you couldn't see what made them tick. She liked this because it was similar to magic, which she believed in, the only difference being that with magic you didn't need batteries. The ease of editing, though, didn't solve her problem: that she had so much good tape. Thousands and thousands of feet. This particular footage was from the first time she'd interviewed Boggs and it was all so pithy that she had no idea what to cut.

"*. . . Anyway, it wasn't heaven we ended up in but Miami and some opportunity that turned out to be . . . Man, that was just like Daddy. This was right after Batista and the place was lousy with Cubans. For years I didn't like, you know, Spanish people. But that was stupid 'cause a few years ago I went down to Central America—the only time I was ever out of the country—and I loved it. Anyway, I was talking about before, when I was a kid, and I saw these wealthy Cubans who were no longer wealthy, and that's the saddest kind of man there is. You can see that loss in his walk, and the way he looks at the car he's driving now, which isn't nearly so nice as the kind he used to have. But what happened was they begun sucking up the jobs us white folks oughta've been having. Not that I mean it in a racial way. But these Cubans worked for next to nothing. They had to, just to get work and feed their families. Which were huge. I've never seen so many little shitters in one family. I thought my daddy was bad. He'd practically roll over on Momma and bang, she was carrying. Home, I had six sisters and two brothers and I lost a brother in Nam, and a sister to ovarian cancer. . . .*

"*Daddy had a head for mechanics but he never applied himself. I'm just the opposite. You pay me and I'll sweat for you. I like the feel of working. My muscles get all nervous when I don't work. But I have problems with calculating.*

My daddy was out of work many days running. My eldest brother signed up, marines, and I was coming up on sixteen so naturally I considered doing the same but started working instead."

The careers of Randy Boggs: warehouse picker, then carny hawker, then ride operator, then sweeper at a Piggly Wiggly, then selling hot dogs on the highway near Cape Kennedy (where he saw the Apollo moon launching and thought he might like to be a pilot), then a stock boy, then fisherman, then janitor, then cook.

Then thief.

"I was to Clearwater once with Boonie, that was my brother, what I called him and a friend from the service. And we went to this drive-in and they were talking about the money they were making and how Boonie was going to buy himself a Bulltaco motorcycle, the kind with the low handlebars, and here I was—oh, heavens—I was nineteen and my brother had to pay my way into the theater? I was pretty embarrassed by that. So that night they went to a, well, you know, whorehouse—which wasn't all that easy to find in Clearwater—and they let me keep the car for a couple hours. What I did, I was feeling so bad about being busted flat, I drove back to the drive-in, which was just closing up, and I did this distraction—set fire to some brush near the screen—and when everybody ran out to see what was going on I ran into the booth and was going to grab the money. Only what happened was there was no money. It'd been packed up and taken somewhere already, probably the night deposit at the bank. I run out, right into one of the owners. I'm a thin man now and I was a thin boy then and he saw what was happening and laid me right out.

". . . You know what they got me for? I have to laugh now. They couldn't arrest me for stealing and they couldn't arrest me for burglary. They arrested me for arson. For burning a plant that wasn't more'n a weed. You believe that?"

The tapes went on and on and on, endlessly.

The format of the *Current Events* stories made Rune's

job tough. Piper Sutton insisted that she herself be on camera for a good portion of each segment. Most of the story would be the interviews Rune was now editing. But every three minutes or so there would be a cut back to Sutton, who would continue with the story, reading off a TelePrompTer. Then, back to more tapes—the crime scene, atmosphere footage, interviews. The Bennett Frost revelation. Coordinating everything—the voice-over and the dialogue on the tape segments, and Piper Sutton's script—was overwhelming.

("And," Lee Maisel had warned her, "if you put a mixed metaphor or string of sibilants into her mouth, not even God can help you.")

But so what if it was tough? Rune was ecstatic. Here she was—three in the morning, Courtney (and a stuffed bear) dozing near her feet—editing tape into what was going to be a sensational news story on the number-one-rated prime-time newsmagazine on network television. Best of all, the story would get seen by ten million people, who unless they made a snack or john run immediately after the Fade Out would also see her name.

And, she considered for a moment, the best part of all: She'd be responsible for getting an innocent man released from prison—a man whose muscles got nervous when he couldn't move.

Prometheus, about to be unbound.

chapter 20

THE CONFERENCE ROOM.

The legendary conference room on the fortieth floor of the Network's skyscraper.

It was here that the executives and senior newsmen planned the special coverage for Martin Luther King's assassination and Bobby Kennedy's and Nixon's resignation and the taking of the hostages in Iran and the *Challenger* explosion. It didn't look very impressive—yellow-painted walls, a chipped and stained oval table and ten swivel chairs whose upholstery had faded to baby-blue from the parent company cerulean. But the shabbiness didn't detract from the fact that history had been chronicled—and sometimes even made—in this room.

Rune paused outside the teak door. Bradford Simpson, who hadn't been invited to the meeting, handed her the files he'd helped carry from her desk. "Break a leg," he said and gave her a kiss on the cheek—one that lasted a bit longer than your standard good-luck buss, she thought. He disappeared back to the lowly newsroom.

Rune looked inside. Lee Maisel and Piper Sutton sat at the table. Behind them was a map of the world with red stickers showing where the Network had permanent bureaus. No more than a couple inches of space separated any of the red dots, except in the oceans and at the North and South Poles.

This was a room Rune never thought she'd be in. When she'd applied at the Network for a job as assistant cameraman they'd told her there was no chance to move into news, producing stories herself; those slots were all reserved for newsmen with experience or star journalism school students.

But here she was, a line producer working for Lee Maisel, and holding in her nervous hands a draft script, one she'd actually written for Piper Sutton.

Rune fought down the assault of anxiety.

She shifted the huge stacks of notes and tapes from one arm to the other. Her heart was beating wildly and her palms left sweaty stains on the black cassettes she held. Sutton noticed her and nodded her in. "Come on," she said abruptly. "What're you waiting for?"

Maisel gave Rune a fast distracted glance.

"Let's get on with it," Sutton said. "Let's see the script. Come on."

Rune distributed the sheets and they both read in silence, except for the tapping of Piper Sutton's gold Cross pen, impatient, on the table. Stone-faced, they skimmed the sixteen pages. First Sutton, then Maisel, slid the sheets into the center of the table.

"All right," Sutton said. "Why is it so important that you do this story?"

This was right out of left field. Rune hadn't expected a question like that. She swallowed, looked at Maisel but he didn't offer anything. She thought for a moment and began to speak. She *knew* better than she could *say* (words, goddamn words again). As she responded to Sutton a lot of "uhms" and "what I means" slipped in. She corrected herself, said the same things twice. She sounded defensive. She tried to look into Sutton's eyes as she spoke but that just turned her mind to jam. Words came out, about justice and journalism's responsibility.

Which was all true but Rune didn't, of course, tell Sutton one piece of the answer: She never once said, *Why am I dying to do this story? Because part of me wants to be you. I want to be tall and have crisp blonde hair that stays where I put it, and walk on high heels and not look like a klutz. I want presidents of networks and corporations to look at me with envy and lust. I want a mind that's as cool and sharp as a black belt's body. I want to try your kind of power, not mine. Not like magic in fairy stories but the power to cast the strongest kind of spells—the ones that make it seem like you know exactly what to do every minute, exactly what to say. . . .*

But she talked about the press, about innocence, about Boggs. When she'd finished, she sat back. Sutton must have been satisfied with the response. She said, "All right, let me ask you a few specific questions."

These were even worse, though, because they were about things Rune should have thought of herself. *Did you interview the original crime scene team?* (Good idea; never occurred to her.) *Did you talk to any of Boggs's earlier lawyers?* (Rune didn't know he'd had any.) *Did he ever see a shrink about his criminal tendencies?* (She never asked.)

The three of them debated for ten minutes and in the end both Maisel and Sutton nodded and said that the program should go forward as long as the show didn't claim Boggs was innocent—only that there were some serious questions about his guilt.

That left only the question of when the story should air.

They asked her opinion.

Rune cleared her throat, shuffled papers, then said, "Next week's show."

Maisel said, "No, seriously."

And the battle began.

"The thing is," Rune said, "he's got to get out of prison as soon as possible. They don't like him in there. They've already tried to kill him. I told you that."

Sutton said, "'They'? Who's 'they'?"

"Other prisoners."

Maisel asked, "Why?"

"I don't know. A guard told me he isn't popular. He's a loner. He—"

"Today's Friday," Maisel barked. "Rune, to air next Tuesday, the whole program should have been shot and edited by now. It has to be in the computer by Monday. That just can't be done."

"I don't think he'll last another week. They tried to kill him once and they'll try again."

Sutton and Maisel looked at each other. Sutton looked back to her and said, "Our job is to report the news, not save anybody's ass. Boggs gets killed the story's still valid. We could—"

"That's a horrible thing to say!"

"Oh, come off it," Sutton said.

Maisel said, "Piper's right, Rune. The story is the important thing, not springing a prisoner. And I don't see how we can do it. There just isn't time."

"The script's all written," she said. "And I've spent the last three nights editing. I've got everything timed to the second."

"The second," Sutton said in a tired sigh.

Maisel said, "Piper'd have to tape on Sunday night or Monday morning."

In a soft, spiny voice, Rune said, "I want the story to air next week." She folded her hands and put them in her lap.

They both looked at her.

Rune continued. "What's going to happen if somebody finds out that we could have saved his life and we just didn't get around to doing the story in time?"

Silence, as Sutton and Maisel exchanged glances. Maisel broke the tension, asking the anchorwoman, "What do you think?"

Rune felt her teeth squeeze together with tension. Sutton responded by asking, "What else was scheduled for that show?"

"The Arabs in Queens," Maisel said. "It's half edited."

"I never liked that story," Rune offered.

Sutton shrugged. "It's soft news. I hate soft news." She was frowning, apparently because she found herself agreeing with Rune.

"My story isn't," Rune said. "It's hard news."

Sutton said, "I suppose you'll want a credit."

For ten million people to see.

"You bet I do."

The anchorwoman continued, "But that name of yours. You'll have to change it."

"Not to worry," Rune said. "I have a professional name."

"A professional name?" Maisel was fighting to keep down the smile.

"Irene Dodd Simons."

"Is that your real name?" the anchorwoman asked.

"Sort of."

Sutton said, "Sort of." And shook her head then added, "At least it sounds like the name of somebody who knows what she's doing." She pulled her personal calendar out of her purse; the scents of perfume and suede followed it. "Okay, honey, first we'll get together and do a script—"

"A script?" Rune blinked. "But it's all finished." She nodded at the sheets in front of them.

Sutton laughed. "No, babes, I mean a *real* script. We'll meet at six-thirty tomorrow morning in the *Current Events* newsroom."

Rune's first thought was: Shit, a baby-sitter. Where'm I going to get a sitter? She smiled and said, "Six, if you want."

"Six-thirty'll be fine."

YOU DON'T HAVE A RIGHT TO TALK ON THE PHONE BUT they usually let you. *A privilege, not a right.* (One day, Boggs'd heard some prisoner yelling, "Gimme the phone!

We got rights." A guard had answered, pretty politely under the circumstances, "You got what we give you, asshole.")

But maybe because Boggs had been knifed or maybe because he wasn't a punk or just maybe because it was a nice warm day, the guard in charge of the mail and telephone room sent somebody to find him so he could take the call.

"Randy, how you feeling?" Rune asked.

"That you, miss?"

"You out of the infirmary?"

"Kicked my butt out yesterday. No pain to speak of, unless I stretch. I read that story. In the book you give me. I like it. Don't think I look much like him, though, and if I ever stole fire from the gods I sure don't know a fence who'd handle it. . . ." He paused and she laughed, like she knew she was supposed to, figuring he'd probably spent a good amount of time thinking up the joke. Which he had.

"Guess what?" she asked.

"Don't know."

"I found a new witness."

"New witness?"

"Sure did."

"Well, my, tell me about it."

She did, from start to finish, all about Bennett Frost, and Randy Boggs didn't utter a single word the entire time she was speaking. In fact, not a single syllable or grunt or even a breath.

When she was through there was silence for a long moment.

"Well," she said, "you're not saying anything."

"I'm grinning, though, I'll tell you that. Damn, I can't believe it. You done yourself something, miss."

"What's going to happen now is I'm going to try to get the program on the air next week. Megler said that if he gets his name and picture on the story he'll do the motion for a new trial for free."

"Mr. Megler said that?"

"It hurt him to. I could see the pain but he said he would. He said if the judge buys it, and grants the motion, you could be out right away."

"The judge might not grant it, though, I suppose."

"Fred said that having the program on *Current Events* would really help. The judge'd be like more inclined to release you, especially if he was up for reelection."

"Well, damn. Goddamn. What do I do now?"

"You just take care of yourself for the next week. Don't go getting knifed anymore."

"No, ma'am . . . One thing . . . What you did . . . ?"

Silence.

"I guess I'm trying to say thank you."

"I guess you just did."

After they hung up, Randy Boggs, the grin still on his face, left the administration building to go find Severn Washington and tell him the news.

AS BOGGS LEFT THE BUILDING, ANOTHER PRISONER, A short Colombian, followed, then overtook him. Prisoners like this were what used to be called trusties in the prisons of the forties and fifties and were now generally known as pricks or assholes or scum. He'd just had a short conversation with the guard he worked for, the guard who randomly monitored prisoners' phone conversations. The prisoner smiled at Boggs, said, *"Buenas dias,"* and walked ahead, not hearing what Boggs said in reply. He didn't particularly care what the response was. He was in a hurry. He wanted to get to Juan Ascipio as soon as he could.

chapter 21

RUNE DECIDED SHE'D FOUND A GREAT NEW DRUG, ONE
that was completely legal and cheap. It was called
"awake," and you didn't even take it. All you did was not
sleep for thirty hours straight and it sent you right on the
most excellent psychedelic trip you could imagine.

Gremlins climbed out of the Sony, dragons swooped
down from Redhead lights and trolls had abandoned
bridges and were fox-trotting on the misty dance floor of
her desk. Weird amoeba were floating everywhere.

It was six P.M. on Tuesday and the reason for the hallucinations—and sleeplessness—was a small plastic cassette containing a one-inch videotape master of a news
story to be shown in a few hours on that night's *Current
Events* program. The story was called, "Easy Justice." The
voice-overs were mixed, the leads and countdown added,
the "live" portions of Piper Sutton's commentary inserted.

The tape, which ran the exact time allocated for the
segment, rested somewhere in the bowels of the Network's
computer system, which acted like a brilliant, never-sleep-
ing stage manager, and would start the segment rolling exactly on time, at 8:04:36 P.M. The system would then
automatically broadcast the Randy Boggs story for its pre-
cise length of eleven minutes, fourteen seconds, which
was the Network's version of a quarter hour—a bit shorter
than in Edward R. Murrow's time, but back then each ad-
ditional minute of advertising didn't mean another half-
million dollars in revenue the way it did today.

Rune squinted away a few apparitions and sat back in her chair.

The last few days had been a nightmare.

Piper Sutton had been satisfaction-proof. "What's this? What do you call this?" she'd shouted, pacing back and forth behind Rune, who sat terrified, willing her hands not to shake as she typed. "Is this supposed to be fucking *poetry*? Is it supposed to be *art*?"

Sutton would walk another ten feet, leaving behind a wake of cigarette smoke and Chanel No. 5.

Nothing she'd write could please Sutton. "Is that a fact? Is it supported? Who's your attribution? . . . What the fuck is this? A figure of speech? 'Justice is like a lumbering bear'? Sure, I know a *lot* of lumbering bears. Our audience is really going to relate to lumbering bears. Just look out on Broadway, Rune, you see many bears? Come on, babes . . ."

Rune would write some more then Sutton would lean over and look at the word processor screen, focusing on the words like a sniper.

"Here, let me . . . ," Sutton would say and practically elbow Rune aside.

Tap, tap, tap . . . The delete code would chop another dozen sentences. Sutton's nails never chipped. They were like red Kevlar.

But finally the story had been finished.

Sutton and Maisel approved the completed script Monday night (the twenty-eighth draft). Sutton had recorded her on-camera portions and sent those to editing, along with the clips from Rune's interviews and atmosphere footage. As she was leaving the studio Tuesday morning at one A.M. Rune asked her, "You, like, always spend this kind of time with producers?"

"No, I don't, *like*, spend this kind of time. Most producers can spell."

"Oh."

Now, though, Rune had nothing to do but try to stay

awake and watch the show itself while she fought the sensation that she was levitating. There were a couple options. Her first choice: She wanted to be home watching it with Healy. But he'd gone to investigate a package sitting in front of an abortion clinic in Brooklyn. Another possibility: There was a bar not far from the houseboat—Rune was a regular there—and everybody there would be glad to watch her program (fortunately this was Tuesday so no Monday night sports programs would create difficult choices for some of the regulars).

But that involved standing up and walking somewhere. Which at the moment was a feat Rune believed she was incapable of.

So, she sat where she was—at her desk. There was a nice color monitor in front of her and maybe—just maybe—Piper and Lee would come and join her. They'd all watch the show together and they'd tell her what a good job she'd done then take her out for a drink at some fancy bar afterwards.

Her thoughts shifted and she found she was thinking of Randy Boggs. She hoped the guards were letting him watch *Current Events*. That thought sounded funny—*letting* him watch, like when she was a kid and she'd begged her parents to let her stay up to read more fairy stories or watch TV.

"Hey, Rune."

She looked up, thinking the hallucinations were getting stranger: Some heavyset guy was disattaching himself from a camera and coming toward her. How did he do that? Like the monster in *Alien*, climbing out of the pipes to eat Sigourney Weaver.

"Rune," he said again. She squinted. It was Morrie Weinberg, the chief engineer of the show. He wore engineer clothes—blue jeans and a black shirt and a tweed jacket.

"Morrie," she said. He was frowning—the first time she'd ever seen him do this. Engineers are usually Rolaidspoppers but Morrie didn't understand the concept of stress. She had an image of him as a lumbering bear and that made her want to laugh out loud.

"What's up?"

"Your segment."

She giggled. "Uh-huh."

"What happened?" His voice fluttered.

The humor was leaving quickly. "Happened?"

"Jesus, how come you didn't get your segment in? 'Easy Justice.' It should've gone into the computer by three. It was already a day late. We *had* to have it there by three. You know that."

Her eyes swept around the studio. Was he saying what she was hearing? "I did. I gave it to Charlie around four. But he said that was all right."

Morrie looked at a clipboard. "This is a problem. It ain't in there now. We got eleven minutes of blank airtime starting at eight-oh-four-thirty-six."

"Check again." Her voice was edged with panic.

"I just did check. Five minutes ago."

"Check again, check again!" No laughing, no lumbering bears, no amoebae. Adrenaline had wakened her completely.

Morrie shrugged and made a call. He held his hand over the mouthpiece and said to her, "Zip."

"How did it happen?"

"The way it usually happens is the producer doesn't get the tape in on time."

"But I *got* it in." She ran through her vague memory. She didn't think she'd screwed up. It was too major a mistake even for her. It was like the pilot forgetting to lower the airplane's wheels before landing.

Anyway, there were other tapes. She had a dupe of the final cut. This was an inconvenience, not a tragedy.

Her hands were shaking. Morrie listened into the phone again. He looked up and said to her, "All right, your butt is safe so far. Charlie says he remembers you delivering it. He put it in the computer but somehow it's vanished. You have a dupe?"

"Sure."

He said into the phone, "We'll get another one up to you in five minutes." He hung up. "This's never happened before. Thank you, dear Lord, for dupes."

The gratitude was premature. The dupe was missing too. Rune's voice was shrill in panic. "I put it there. On my desk." She pointed frantically to an empty corner.

"Oh, man."

"I put it right *there*."

He stared skeptically at the bald spot.

She said, "I'm not making this up."

"Rough cuts?" Morrie was looking at his watch. "Shit, we don't have time. But we maybe—"

She opened a drawer. "Oh, no," she muttered breathlessly.

He said, "They're gone too?"

Rune was nodding. She couldn't speak.

"Oh, boy. Oh, shit. Eleven minutes of blank air. This's never happened before. This's never happened."

Then she thought of something else and ripped open her credenza.

The *original* tape she'd done of Bennett Frost, the new witness, and the dupe of *that* were also gone. All that remained of the story about Randy Boggs were scripts and notes and background interview tapes.

"We've been robbed," Rune whispered. She looked around in panic, feeling a terrible sense of violation. "Who was it?" She looked at Morrie. "Who'd you see on the set today?"

"Who'd I see?" he echoed shrilly. "A dozen reporters, a hundred staffers. That intern kid with the blond hair who was helping you with the story. Piper was here, Jim Eustice, Dan Semple. . . . I mean, half the Network walked through here today." Morrie's eyes strayed uneasily toward the phone and she knew what he was thinking:

Somebody had to call Piper Sutton. The large quartz wall clock—timed, for all Rune knew, to the pulse of the universe—showed that they had forty-four minutes until *Current Events* was going to air. Forty-four minutes until it became the first prime-time television program in history to air eleven minutes and fourteen seconds of blank space.

THE ONLY THING THAT KEPT PIPER SUTTON FROM EX-ploding through the double doors into the newsroom was the live broadcast of *Nighttime News With Jim Eustice,* the Network's flagship world news show, now on-air thirty feet behind Rune.

But still she stormed ferociously toward Rune's desk. During the broadcast the veteran anchorman was so damn reassuring and smooth that even the crew enjoyed watching him. Tonight, though, only the head engineer and the producer kept their eyes on his craggy, square face. Everyone else in the huge studio gazed at Sutton and Maisel, as they hurried toward the *Current Events* desks like surgeons answering a code blue.

"What the fuck happened?" Sutton asked in a shrill whisper.

"I don't know." Rune felt the tears start. She dug her short nails into her palms furiously; with the pain the urge to cry lessened. "Somebody robbed me. They took everything."

Maisel looked at the clock above the control booth. "We don't have *anything*? Nothing at all?"

"I don't know what happened. I turned the tape in—"

Morrie said delicately, "She did. Charlie got it. He programmed it in. Sometime after four it disappeared."

"Son of a bitch. How long was that segment?"

Morrie consulted his clipboard but Rune answered from memory. "Eleven minutes, fourteen."

Sutton whispered furiously, "You should always make backups, you should—"

"I did! *They* were stolen too. Everything. Even the original tapes . . ."

"Fuck," Sutton spat out. Then she turned to Maisel, whose mind must have been in the same place and known what she was thinking. There were three other stories programmed for *Current Events* that evening. But Maisel said they had nothing else finished that could be used as a replacement for "Easy Justice." He said, "We'll have to cancel the show."

"Can we go with Arabs in Queens?" she asked.

He said, "We never finished editing. We stopped all postpro for the Boggs story."

"What about the former-mayor profile?"

"Mostly unshot and a lot of unattributed quotes. It's legally hot."

"The Guardian Angels piece?" she snapped.

"We've got footage but there's no script."

"It's outlined?"

"Well, in general. But—"

"I know the story." She waved her hand. "We'll do that."

"What do you mean?" Maisel asked, frowning. "Do what?"

"We do the original three stories plus the Guardian Angels."

Maisel's voice rasped, "Piper, we'll have to cancel. We can slot a rerun." He turned to Morrie and started to say something. But she said, "Lee, a rerun of a news show? We'll go with the Angels."

"I don't understand what you're saying, Piper. We don't have a script. We don't have footage of you. We—"

"We'll go live," she said.

"Live?"

"Yep."

Maisel looked at Morrie. "It's too late, isn't it?"

He answered calmly. "We can't do half and half. We can shut off the computer and queue up the other stories by hand, using a stopwatch. Like in the old days. You'll have to be live in all of your on-camera commentary. Hell, we'll have to manually roll the commercials too and you know how many fifteen-second buys there are during *Current Events*? It'll be a nightmare."

"Then it'll be a nightmare." the anchorwoman said.

"But, Piper," Maisel said, "we can slot something else."

She said evenly, "Lee, every TV guide, cable guide and newspaper in America shows that we're running a new *Current Events* tonight. You know what kind of questions it'll raise about the program if we go to a rerun or slip in something from syndication?"

"We'll say technical difficulties."

"There are no technical difficulties on my show."

"Piper—" Rune began.

But Sutton didn't even hear her. She and Maisel hurried off and Rune stayed behind, in her cubicle. She curled up in her chair, the way Courtney did sometimes, drawing her legs up. She thought of all the work she'd have to do over again. She felt numbed, stunned, like somebody had died.

Uh-uh, she thought. Like someone was *about* to die.

Randy Boggs.

AT 7:58 P.M. LEE MAISEL WAS SITTING IN THE HUGE CONtrol booth overlooking the *Current Events* set. The booth was filled with three times its normal staff (most of whom were from the Jim Eustice crew and had experience with the rare and demanding art of live production).

Maisel hadn't done live producing for years and he sat forward, sweating and uneasy, like the captain of a torpedoed ship still doing battle with an enemy destroyer. He was holding an expensive digital stopwatch in his hand, gripping it tightly.

Maisel and Sutton had managed to write half the

Guardian Angels piece and get it, handwritten, into the TelePrompTer, but at 7:56 they'd had to break off. So Sutton had said, "I'll ad-lib."

Maisel called over the loudspeaker, "You got a ten-second countdown and a five-second cheat. . . ."

Sutton, in full makeup, under the hot lights, gave him a fast nod and sat down in the black leather chair behind the desk bearing the *Current Events* logo. A technician clipped the lavaliere mike onto her lapel and inserted the small earphone into her left ear, the one hidden under the flop of hair (where it was less visible and no one would absently think she was wearing a hearing aid).

Maisel called, "All right, this is it."

She gave another nod and fixed her eyes on the TelePrompTer that a floor producer pointed at.

In the control booth Lee Maisel shut off the loud speaker and began talking into the microphone that would carry his words to Sutton's and the rest of the crew's earphones. He glanced at the big clock on the control room wall and began counting down. "Seven, six, five, four, three, two, one . . . Graphics up now . . . Theme running. . . ."

Exactly four seconds later, he said, "Graphics dissolve, camera one fade in . . . Theme down . . . Okay, Piper, you're . . . on."

chapter 22

PIPER SUTTON'S EYES LOCKED DIRECTLY INTO THOSE OF ten million people. She gave a sincere smile and said in the low comforting voice that so many people had come to trust more than that of their own spouses, parents, children and friends, "Good evening. Welcome to *Current Events* for Tuesday, April twentieth. I'm Piper Sutton. . . ."

The program began.

Exactly fifty-six minutes later, the credits rolling at a breakneck pace, viewers around the country stood or stretched, arguing about some of the stories or critiquing Piper Sutton's fashion selection of the week or wondering which sitcom to turn to now, all unaware that they'd just seen TV history.

Morrie Weinberg oversaw the passing of the scepter back to the computer and the fifty-million-dollar system began sending the spurious art of television advertising into American households.

As soon as the studio mikes were shut off, the newsroom applauded. Sutton was far too diplomatic to ignore it and she gave a brief smile and offered a bow—not a curtsy—to her audience.

Maisel left the booth and walked straight up to her, hugging her and kissing her on the cheek.

Both Dan Semple and Jim Eustice had been watching from the control booth. They now joined her. Eustice shook her hand formally and complimented her then left with Maisel. Semple kissed Sutton quickly and the two of them walked into the corridor.

Not a single one of them glanced at Rune, who sat in her desk chair and stared at the monitor where her program would have run.

THE NEXT MORNING, COURTNEY WOKE HER UP BY CLIMBing into bed.

"Can we go to the zoo?"

Rune had collected the girl just after the program was over the night before. They'd gone home, had tuna sandwiches for dinner and Raisin Bran for dessert. They both went to bed at ten.

Rune rolled over and sat up. "The what?"

"The zoo."

"First, coffee, then we'll think about the zoo."

"I want some juice. Coffee's icky."

Rune was feeling better now that she'd gotten some sleep. The horror of last night had faded. True, the tapes had been stolen but there were some upsides to what'd happened. For one thing, it was clear proof that somebody else had killed Hopper. Randy obviously hadn't stolen the tapes; the real killer must have. Also, there was now another dimension to the story: Somebody's breaking into a major television network studio and stealing a news program—that was a story in itself.

Anyway, it turned out that the damage wasn't as bad as she'd thought. All that was missing was the master tape and the dupes and the tape of Bennett Frost. Bradford, bless his heart, had managed to find copies of almost everything else. The program could be remixed from that material although she'd have to retape Bennett Frost.

What worried her most was that Randy was still in danger. But then she wondered if maybe the story didn't have to run to get his release process started. True, the impact wouldn't be so neat—her story actually getting him released. But what had her goal been anyway? To get him out.

No, *Current Events* could easily redo the story after he was released. That might be a nice touch. She'd add footage of him wandering around New York, a free man. Maybe reuniting with his brother or sisters.

In the galley, Rune poured cranberry juice for Courtney and made her some instant oatmeal.

"I want to go to the zoo."

"Okay, honey, we'll try. But there's something I have to do first. We're going to go visit somebody. A man."

"Who is he? Is he a nice man?"

"Not really," Rune said and looked up Fred Megler's address in her book.

"POKER," MEGLER SAID. "I THOUGHT THERE WAS THAT show running last night. What happened? I missed poker to stay home. I really hate to miss poker." He lifted up a series of soda cans, looking for one that was full.

"It got stolen."

"Stolen? Somebody stole a TV show?"

"The tape. It got lifted.

"No shit?" Then he winced and glanced at Courtney.

"Shit," the little girl said.

Rune said, "I'm going to do the story over again. But I was thinking maybe you could start the—the what do you call it? To get Randy out?"

"The motion papers."

"Right. I thought you could get Mr. Frost to go into court and . . ." She paused.

Megler's face was blank for a moment. "You didn't hear?"

"Hear what?"

"The accident?" His voice, thin as his body, rose, sounding as if everybody in the city were supposed to know.

Oh, no. Rune closed her eyes. "What happened?"

"Frost slipped in the bathtub. He drowned."

"What? Oh, God . . . When did it happen?"

"A couple days ago." Megler found a nearly full can of Diet Pepsi. His face brightened at the discovery. "Sure is a good thing you made that tape of him. Otherwise we'd be up . . ." He glanced at Courtney. ". . . you know which creek without a paddle."

chapter 23

ALLAH TELLS US:

Those who do good will find the best reward in heaven, and more. Neither dust nor ignominy touch their faces. Such are the rightful owners of the Garden, and they will abide therein.

Late Thursday morning, Severn Washington was waiting for Randy Boggs to come out of the library. He sat on a concrete step and read the Koran. He frequently did this. Like praying five times a day and ritual washing and forsaking liquor and pork, reading the holy book gave him great personal satisfaction. He kept it with him at all times.

The typeface of the copy he owned was dense. Under the repeated touch of his huge, nubby fingers the delicate onionskin paper of the small volume had become even more translucent than when it was new. He liked that. He had an image of Allah reaching down and making the book more and more invisible every time Washington read it. Eventually it would become transparent, would become just a spirit—vanished and gone to heaven.

And then Washington would follow and his sins—all of them (the liquor store shooting in particular)—would be forgiven; his new life would begin.

Washington didn't want to go too fast, however. There were certain aspects of his present life that he'd come to enjoy. Even here, in Harrison. Prison life wasn't much different from that in his prior residence. Instead of a brick project, he had a stone cell block to live in (a building that wasn't graffitied and didn't smell of shit). Instead of his common-law wife's bland macaroni and chicken and potatoes, he had the Department of Corrections's bland macaroni and hamburger and potatoes. Instead of hanging out on the street and doing occasional construction work, he hung out in the yard and worked in the machine shop. Instead of getting dissed and threatened by dealers and gangs, who had MAC-10s, he got dissed and theatened by the Aryan Brotherhood, who had clubs and shivs.

On the whole, it was *better* inside. Maybe you didn't get paychecks but you didn't *need* paychecks like when you were doing straight time.

He had friends, like Randy Boggs.

He had his Koran.

No, couldn't complain. He looked down at his holy book once more.

. . . If Allah afflict thee with some hurt, there is none who can remove it save Him; if He desireth good for thee, there is none who can repel His bounty. He—

The sentiment in that passage was the last thought Severn Washington ever had.

And the last sound he ever heard was the hiss of the steel barbell pole that swung into the back of his head.

He didn't even live long enough to hear the delicate flutter of his Koran as it pitched from his convulsing fingers and lay open on dirt, the book which it turned out wasn't going to precede Washington into heaven after all.

THE CONVERSATION WAS HUSHED.

"Whatever you thinking, man, fuck it," said Juan Ascipio. "We had to do the nigger. I told you . . ." He was talking rapidly to one of his Hispanic brothers in the area beside the library where they'd just dragged Washington's body. ". . . we move on Boggs, put the bar in his hand and knife in the nigger's. Looks like the nigger wanted to fuck Boggs and Boggs moved on him, and then the nigger did Boggs."

"I know, man," the second man said. "Hey, I'm not saying nothing."

"You don't look happy, man, but it had to be that way."

"Yeah. It's just, man, they *know* it's us."

"Fuck," Ascipio spat out. "What they know ain't what they can prove."

"After the first time, man. They know it's us. He coulda talked."

"Motherfucker didn't talk. He coulda said who it was did him. He didn't say nothing." Ascipio laughed.

"Yeah."

A third man loped back to them. "Boggs—he's in there by hisself."

Ascipio laughed again.

RANDY BOGGS LIKED THE LIBRARY.

Reading was one of those things you don't think anything of until you actually did it. When he was Outside there were some things he'd do for the peace of it. Like sitting with a quart of beer for the evening, listening to cicadas and owls and the surf of leaves and the click of branches. That was something he could do practically forever. Which seemed like doing nothing but was actually one of the most important ways a man could spend time.

That was how he now looked at reading.

Most of the books here were pretty bad. Somebody— a school, he guessed—had donated a lot of textbooks. Sociology and psychology and statistics and economics. Boring as dry toast. If that was what people learned in college no wonder nobody seemed to have any smarts.

And some of the novels were a bit much. The older ones—and the library here seemed to have mostly 1920s and '30s books—were pretty dense. Man, he couldn't make heads or tails out of them. He had to slug his way through, just like the way he'd clean a floor: scrape, then sweep, then mop, then rinse. Inch by inch. Then he found some newer ones. *Catch-22,* which he thought was really okay. He grinned for five minutes straight after finishing that one. Then somebody mentioned Kurt Vonnegut and although there were none of his books in the prison library a guard he'd become friendly with gave him a copy of *Cat's Cradle* and a couple others as well. Whenever he saw the guard he'd wink and say, "So it goes." Boggs loved Paul Theroux's travel writing. He also tried John Cheever. He didn't like the short stories but the novel about prison really struck home. Sure, it was about prison but it was about something *more* than prison. That seemed to be the sign of a good book. To be about something but about something more too, even if you didn't know exactly what.

The book that girl reporter had given him wasn't so good, he'd decided. The writing was old-fashioned and he had to read some sentences three, four times in order to figure out what was going on. But he kept at it and would pull it out occasionally and read some more. He wanted to finish it but the reason was so he could talk about it with Rune.

That got him thinking about that girl again and he wondered why her program hadn't run on Tuesday. Rune hadn't called to say anything about it. But then he wasn't sure what day she'd said. Maybe she'd meant a week from Tuesday. She'd probably said "next" Tuesday, instead of "this" Tuesday; Boggs always got confused with "next" and "this."

Damn, that girl was something else. Here, he'd spent months and months trying to figure out how to get out of prison, thinking of escaping, thinking of getting sick, thinking of appealing, and then here she comes and does it for him and it doesn't cost him anything in grief or money.

He—

And that was when he heard the noise and felt the first hum of fear.

The prison itself was old but the library was a newer addition, away from the cell blocks. It looked and smelled like a suburban school. There was only one door in and out. He looked around. The library was completely deserted. And he understood that the Word had gone around. No other prisoners, no guards. No clerk behind the desk. He'd been reading away and hadn't noticed everybody else leaving.

Oh, hell . . . Boggs heard the slow footsteps of several men coming up the corridor toward that one door.

He knew Severn Washington was outside and he knew too that the big black man was as loyal as a friend could be in prison.

But that was a big qualifier. *In prison.*

Inside, anybody can be bought.

And, when it comes right down to it, anybody can be killed.

Boggs still had no idea why Ascipio wanted to move on him. But it was clear he was marked. No doubt in his mind. And right now, hearing footsteps come closer to the door, he knew—not a premonition or anything like that— he *knew* something was going down.

He stood up instinctively. The possibilities for weapons were: a book or a chair.

Well, now, neither of them's much help at all.

Oh, he didn't want the knife again. That terrible feeling of the glass blade. Terrible . . .

He looked at the chair. He couldn't pull it apart. And when he tried to lift it, a searing pain from the first knifing swept through his back and side.

He tried again and managed to get the chair off the ground, holding it in both hands.

Then part of his mind said, Why bother?

They'd burst in, they'd circle around him, they'd take him. He'd die. What could he do? Swing a chair at them? Knock one of them off balance while the others easily stepped behind him?

So Randall Boggs, failed son of a failed father, simply sat down in the chair, in front of a fiberboard table in a shoddy prison library, and began thinking for some reason, suddenly and obsessively, about Atlanta and the Sunday dinner menu of his childhood.

From his pocket he took out the book the reporter girl had given him and put his hands on it as if it were a Bible then he thought that was funny because probably to the old-time people, the old Greeks or Romans, or whatever, this myth book probably *was* a bible.

Prometheus got freed.

But it didn't seem like this was going to be a replay of that story. Not here, not now.

The footsteps stopped and he heard mumbled voices.

Randy Boggs swallowed and tried to remember a prayer. He couldn't so he just swallowed again and tried not to think about the pain.

The door swung open.

"Hey, Boggs."

He blinked, staring.

"Boggs, come on. Haul ass."

He stood up and walked toward the guard. He opened his mouth to say something but nothing came out, which was just as well because he didn't know what to say anyway.

"Let's move it along, Boggs."

"What's up?"

The guard had drowsy eyes and a voice to match. "The warden wants to see you. Hustle it."

•　　•　　•

"YOU GOT YOURSELF A PRETTY LITTLE GIRL," FRED MEG-
ler said to Randy Boggs.

The lawyer was trooping around the office. He
couldn't sit still and was on some kind of energy trip.

Randy Boggs was sitting forward in a chair in
Megler's office, his hands pressed tightly together as if
they'd been manacled. He wore blue jeans and a blue
denim work shirt, clothing he'd worn when he'd entered
the prison three years before. Rune, sitting nearby,
smelled mothballs.

"Little girl, yessir." Boggs was nodding a lot, agreeing
with what everybody said. But at the little girl part he
looked questioningly at Rune, who launched Courtney toward him. Boggs's hands reached out and she gave him a
shy hug.

"Daddy," she said and looked at Rune to see if she'd
gotten the line right. Rune nodded at her, smiling, then
said to Boggs, "Mr. Megler didn't know that you had a little girl. That was one of the reasons he was so nice to help
you even though the program hasn't run yet."

"Yeah," Boggs said, squinting to see if that helped him
understand things any better. It didn't seem to. "Sure appreciate it."

Megler paced. His polyester tie with the Bic repair
job flopped up and down on the baggy shirt where his
belly would have been if he weighed forty pounds more.
His hair jutted out behind his thin skull as if he were facing into a gale. He said, "So, here's the deal: The young
lady here found some pretty good evidence that would've
gotten you out but it seems some asshole . . ." He looked
at Courtney but she was playing with daddy's shoelaces
and missed the word. ". . . some *person* got into the studio
and stole it. That was strike one. Then—"

"Oh, you should've seen it!" Rune interrupted. "It was
a really great story, Randy. It would've gotten you out in a
minute. I did the fades just perfect. The sound was mixed

like a symphony. And I had a really, really super shot of your mother—"

"Mom? You did?" He grinned. "What kind of stuff'd she say?"

"Didn't make a lot of sense, I have to tell you. But she looked real motherish."

"Yeah, that's one thing she does good."

Megler said, "You guys mind?" Courtney pointed her tiny index finger at him like a pistol and fired. It was a game she'd decided they should play. He smiled grudgingly at her and shot back. She clutched her chest and fell to the floor. Megler seemed to hope she'd play dead for a long time.

Rune preempted the lawyer. "You know who did it? You know who the killer was?"

"Uhm. If I knew that . . ." Boggs shrugged.

"It was the guy who picked you up who did it. Jimmy."

Boggs was shaking his head. "I don't know about that."

"Wait, wait, wait," Rune's legs bounced in the chair. "I'll tell you why I know in a minute. But, see, everything got stolen by Jimmy—he somehow found out about the story. I kind of told a reporter about it and there was this newspaper story so I think he read it and came to town to stop the program. . . ."

Courtney revived and climbed up into her lap.

"Anyway, I came here to tell Fred that the evidence had been stolen. We felt awful, didn't we, Court?"

"Awful, yeah," the little girl said.

Megler said, "And I told this young lady that not having the tape or the second witness—"

Rune interrupted to explain about Bennett Frost's death.

Boggs was frowning. "Got himself killed?"

"Medical examiner says it was an accident, but who knows?" Megler said, wanting to take the stage again. "Anyway, with him dead, it wasn't looking too good. But what with you having a cute little girl you have to support—"

Megler missed the glance Boggs shot Rune and the sweep of her eyes across the grimed ceiling.

"—I thought we could make a good case in court. I got a deposition from the first witness, Ms. Breckman, who admitted that most of her ID was based on seeing you on TV *after* you'd been arrested. Then . . ." He paused dramatically. "I got a special ex parte hearing and presented my new secret witness."

Boggs cocked his head. "You found yourself *another* witness?"

Rune bowed. "Me!"

"I put Rune on the stand for Frost's testimony. Frost told her what he saw, about this other guy killing Hopper. Normally, that's hearsay and wouldn't be admissible but since Frost is dead she can testify about what Frost said."

She said, "Oh, I was great. 'Do you solemnly swear . . .' "

Megler said, "I also let slip the fact that she was a reporter for *Current Events*. I mean, justice is one thing but media? Forget about it. . . . The judge practically made sure she had the correct spelling of his name."

Rune said, "And, poof, he released you."

"From the bench," Megler said solemnly. "Don't happen too often that way."

"I'm free?"

"Pending the prosecutor's decision on a new trial. They'll probably just let it drop. But you have to stay in New York City until they decide. You can travel if you tell the DA's office but you can't leave the state."

"My dear Lord," Boggs said. "I don't know what to say." He leaned forward and shyly kissed Rune's cheek. Then he stood up and walked to the window.

Megler said, "You've earned yourself the right to walk through the slime of New York just like anybody else. . . . Now, you got any money?"

"They give me some when I came out. Not a lot."

Megler was opening up his wallet. A wad of twenties appeared. A couple hundred bucks' worth. He aimed it toward Boggs, who shook his head. "No, sir, thank you anyway."

"It's a loan is all it is. Come on. Pay me back when you can. Ha, you don't, I'll sue your butt."

Boggs was blushing as he took the money and he put it into his pocket as quickly as possible.

Megler was giving him advice about getting jobs, what sort of work to look for.

Boggs looked solemn for a moment. "Something I'd like to do. A friend of mine got himself killed in prison. I'd like to go see his family. Up in Harlem."

"You look like you're asking permission," Megler said. "You want to go, just go."

"Yeah, I could, I guess. Sure. I wasn't thinking."

Then Boggs was saying he had to look for a hotel room. . . . No, first some food then a room. No, first he wanted to walk down . . . what was that street there? Boggs pointed out the window.

"Over there? Broadway," Megler answered.

"I want to walk down Broadway."

Rune corrected, "Actually, you'd probably be walking *up* Broadway from here."

"Up Broadway, and I want to stop and go into some of those stores."

"Plenty to choose from," the lawyer offered. "Shitty merchandise, overpriced."

"Shitty," Courtney echoed.

"And check out some other streets too. And nobody's going to tell me not to."

"Not a soul in the world."

Boggs was grinning.

Rune said, "I've got some tapes left but I'll have to interview you again. I want to start as soon as possible."

Boggs laughed. "Well, you don't hardly have to even ask. There's only one thing I'd ask first."

"Sure."

"You think we might rustle up some beer? It's been a while, and I've really got me a taste."

chapter 24

THE PLASTIC BAG RANG LIKE SLEIGH BELLS. IT CON-tained: a Heineken, a Moosehead, a Grolsch, two Bud-weisers ("Not the best by a long shot but it was my first—mind if I get a couple for, you know, sentimental reasons?"), a Tecate and a six-pack of Corona. Rune had also bought some Amstel but Randy Boggs had never drunk light beer in his life. "Don't believe I'd like to cele-brate my freedom with something like that."

They turned onto Christopher Street and aimed themselves at the Hudson, waiting for the stoplight to change. When it did they crossed the wide West Side Highway, Courtney holding tight to Rune's hand and look-ing left and right the way she'd taught the little girl.

Boggs asked, "Uh, where'd we be going?" He looked uncertainly toward the deserted waterfront.

Rune felt Southern when she was with Boggs and she answered, "Yonder."

He looked at where she was nodding and laughed. "There?"

They walked up the yellow gangplank to the house-boat, Boggs grinning and looking around him. "You don't need me to say anything 'bout it, I suppose. You live on one of these, you musta heard all kindsa comments by now."

Inside, Boggs walked from room to room, shyly in-specting. He'd carefully touch the stuffed animals, the scraps of lace Rune draped over lamps, the rose and blue magic crystals, her books. He'd laugh occasionally as he

tried to figure out something—an eyelash curler or a broken antique apple parer that Rune bought because she
thought it was a medieval weapon.

In the kitchen she put the beers away and fixed the
food they'd bought—crispy-fried Chee-tos and cans of re-
fried bean dip and little shrimp cocktails in jars with pry-
off lids. "I love these things. And you can use the jars for
juice glasses later."

"Juice," said Courtney. Rune poured Ocean Spray for
the girl then filled a Winnie-the-Pooh dish with bean dip
and handed her a spoon.

"This is ugly," the girl said, looking into it. "Yes, it is."
But she took the utensil and began to pick up bits of dip
and wad it onto the spoon.

"She's showing off for guests," Rune said to Boggs.
"Court—you know how," she added sternly.

"Ugly food." She scrunched her nose up but began to
eat properly.

"Napkin," Rune reminded her and Courtney picked a
paper napkin out of a stack in the center of the table and
placed it on her lap. She resumed eating.

Boggs watched them. "You're kinda young to be a
mother. Who's the father?" He laughed. "Other than me, I
mean."

"Long story." She then said, "What kind of beer you
like to start with?"

"Believe I'll start with a Bud. 'Buy American.' When I
went Inside, three years ago, that's what everybody was
saying. 'Buy American.' But nobody makes beer like Mexi-
cans. I'll save that Corona for dessert."

"Come on over here." Rune led him out to the deck,
where they could have some privacy but she could still
watch Courtney.

"I didn't want to say anything in there. In front of
her." She told him how Claire had abandoned the girl.

Boggs shook his head. "I don't think I ever met anybody who'd do something like that."

"Claire's totally immature."

"I never had me any kids." He grinned. "Not that I know of, anyway. Not so there was a paternity suit."

Rune said, "Me with a kid." She shook her head. "You don't know me that well but it's definitely role reversal."

"Looks to me like you two get along pretty good, though."

Rune's eyes were dancing. "Oh, she's the best. I always thought kids were, like, completely obnoxious. You know, they go through this phase where they can't talk—they have to screech. And they don't eat; they just barf. But what it is—I've figured this out—they're just like adults. Some days they're in good moods, some days they're in bitchy moods. And can we talk! We walk all over the place and I tell her things. She understands. Our minds kind of work alike." Rune glanced at Courtney. "She's going to be just like me when she grows up."

"I know natural *mothers* who don't sound that happy with their kids."

Boggs was tasting the Bud like it was vintage wine. Rune offered him the bag of Chee-tos. He shook his head. He said, "Must be nice having someone to live with. I had me a couple girlfriends, various times, but I was never married. I don't know, it'd be pretty strange for me, I think. Living with somebody when you don't have to. Inside, you don't have any choice, of course."

"Inside?"

"In prison."

"Oh, sure . . . Well, I usually have roommates. They're sort of a necessary evil in New York, with what rents go for. But I've lived by myself a lot. I've gotten used to it. It's like a skill you work on."

"Don't get lonely, huh?"

"Sure. I remember some nights I'd be sitting there, watching *Gilligan's Island* reruns on this black-and-white TV—you know, the kind with a coat hanger for an antenna? And I'd be watching this show and I'd hear a piece of paper slide under the door. And I'd start to get up and see what it was but then I wouldn't. Because I knew it was only a menu from a Chinese restaurant a delivery guy was slipping under all the doors in the building. But if I *didn't* go see then maybe it'd be a note from someone. Maybe it would say, 'There's a party, in three-G. Plenty of men. Come in costume.' Or maybe it would be mysterious. 'Meet me on the corner of Avenue A and Ninth Street at midnight on the night of the full moon.' "

Boggs was looking at her, trying to figure this all out.

"But, naw, it was always just a menu. And I'd go back to sitcoms and commercials. But ups and downs—that's what makes life what it is." She thumped her chest. "I'm from Ohio peasant stock."

Boggs said, "There's one thing I'd like to say. . . ."

Rune had been wondering if he'd bring up the sleeping arrangements, which is what this sounded like it was going to be about. But just then Courtney called, "I want juice."

"Say 'please.' "

"I want please."

"Very funny." Rune called, "One minute, honey." To Boggs, she said, "I'm hungry for some real food. I've got a couple leftover Whoppers in the fridge. You interested?"

"Sure. Heat me one up too."

Rune started into the houseboat. Suddenly Boggs stopped. He turned and twisted his head, like a dog hearing an ultrasonic whistle. He lifted his face to the sky. His nostrils flared wide as he inhaled. "How 'bout that?"

"What?"

"The smells," he said.

"Yeah, we aren't exactly talking perfume in New York."

"No, I don't mean that. What I mean is there're a bunch of them. A thousand smells."

She sniffed then shook her head. "I can't make out too many."

Boggs inhaled again. "When you're Inside there are only a couple smells you smell. Disinfectant. Onions or grease from the kitchen. Sweat. Spring air. Summer air. . . . It's like you get used to them. But here—What do I smell?"

"Rotten fish and dog doo and garbage and car exhaust."

"Nope. What I smell is freedom."

ONE POTATO, TWO POTATO, THREE POTATO, FOUR . . .

Jack Nestor, walking slowly along the old docks on the Hudson River, was thinking: In Florida people *ought* to be on boats. Especially in south Florida, close to the 'Glades, you realize that even on land there's water everywhere and it's a part of your life. Houses are raised up on stilts and everybody's got a boat of some kind in the yard.

But in New York, it seemed pretty weird to live on a boat.

Five potato, six potato, seven potato, more . . .

Nestor had parked on Tenth Street not far from the river. He'd rented the car, which he didn't like doing because that left a record. But he knew that after what was about to happen there was a pretty good chance his description would go out citywide, including to the Port Authority police at the airports and bus and train stations. But nobody could ever stop you from *driving* out of New York.

The sun was down by now and the sky was a shade of blue it never was in Florida. It was a gray-blue, metal-blue, junkyard blue. Nestor was thirsty but didn't want to look for a deli—that many more people to see him. So he sat on a bench facing the city and waited for more darkness to fall. He stubbed out his cigarette, after taking one long final drag, deciding that the menthol made him less thirsty.

Eight potato, nine potato, no cops anymore . . .

The blue-and-white that had been parked on the highway near the houseboat, the cops eating sandwiches, drinking coffee, pulled away, made a lazy U-turn, then headed north.

Time to go to work. He pulled out his gun and eased slowly toward the houseboat.

"I LEARNED A LOT OF LAW FOR ONE THING. THEY HAD A mess of law books Inside. Some of the fellows write their own appeals. They do pretty good at it."

Rune nodded. Boggs was working on his Corona—he still wasn't drunk, or even tired, it seemed—and Rune was sipping herbal tea and eating Twinkies. She'd wanted to tape him and ask him more questions about what life was like in prison. But he'd begged off. He was tired. To-morrow, he said. Shoot me all you want tomorrow.

Courtney had gotten cranky; it was a little early for bed but she'd had a busy day helping get prisoners re-leased from jail and playing the role of a convict's daugh-ter so Rune gave her a bath then put her to bed. She fell asleep almost at once. Rune bounded back into the living room portion of the cabin and saw Boggs sitting on the couch, looking uneasy, nervous.

He cleared his throat and looked at her for a long mo-ment, then away.

Something was on his mind and she wondered if this was the moment when he was going to bring up sleeping arrangements again or even make a move.

As in, a man and a woman alone together.

As in, a man who's been behind bars for three years suddenly alone with a woman.

But no propositions were forthcoming. Boggs got an-other beer and kept up a nervous chatter. They talked about life in the city for a few minutes, about Atlanta, about pol-itics and Washington (he seemed to know a surprising number of facts for someone who appeared so redneck).

Rune, expecting the line at any minute: *You know, I was thinking I might have me some trouble getting a room. . . .* But just as that was going through her head Boggs yawned and looked at his watch. He said, "I ought to be finding a room for the night."

And she surprised herself by saying, "You want, you can sleep in the living room. Courtney's got the futon but we could fix up something."

But he was shaking his head. "No, it's funny, I can't explain it but I'd really be inclined to spend the night by myself, you know?"

"Sure." Not understanding at all, but feeling relieved that he wanted to do this. "Let me pack up the rest of the beers. And I'll give you some pizza for breakfast."

"Uh, no thanks. I'm pretty partial to oatmeal."

"I got some packets of instant," she said. "You want a couple?"

Which was a question that never got answered.

With a huge crack, the front door burst open, hitting a table and knocking over a pile of Rune's books.

She looked at the fat man rushing into the houseboat, saw the big gun in his hand and instinctively leapt in front of the storeroom where Courtney was asleep. Rune pulled the door shut, standing defiantly in front of it. Staring back at the man she knew without a bit of doubt had killed Lance Hopper and Bennett Frost.

This was Jimmy.

Boggs stood up fast, knocking over the beer, which chugged onto the floor.

The big man stopped then closed the front door slowly, calmly, as if he'd been invited in.

He stood with his arms hanging awkwardly at his side. Cautious, but confident, squinting, checking out the room and its inhabitants. Nothing he saw scared him.

Randy Boggs, his eyes wide with shock, faced the man. The way Boggs stood made him look like a soldier. No, more like a boxer—one foot forward, turned sideways. Which was crazy because even without the gun, no way could he have taken this fat guy, who outweighed him by a hundred pounds and looked like a ball-kicker and eye-gouger. A dirty fighter.

"What do you want?" Rune whispered.

He ignored her and stepped right up to Boggs. Five seconds of complete silence passed as the men seemed locked in a staring contest.

No one moved.

It was Randy Boggs who grinned first, then said, "Jack Nestor, you son of a bitch! Wasn't expecting you for a couple of days or so."

The fat man laughed and let out a whoop. He slipped the gun into his belt and the two men embraced like long-lost cossack brothers suddenly reunited.

chapter 25

THE ONE QUESTION ON HER MIND: COULD COURTNEY swim?

Rune could—about as well as any Midwest girl who never saw a body of water with waves until she was ten.

Hell, she could just hold on to Courtney—picturing her now, screaming and waving her arms in panic—and kick to the far pier. How many yards was that? Maybe thirty or forty?

And, God, the Hudson was gross and yucky. . . .

But that didn't matter. If they didn't get out now they'd be dead in three minutes.

She tore the door to the storeroom open and lunged, vaguely aware of a sudden rush of activity behind her in the living room. Footsteps, voices. She slammed the door and turned the skeleton key lock. "Court, wake up."

The little girl didn't stir.

Rune pressed her back against the thick wood and began to untie her boots, which were laced up tight through dozens of eyelets. She knew she'd drown if she didn't get them off. She shouted, "Courtney."

"Juice," a weak voice said.

"Wake up!"

Maybe some of the toys would float. There was an anemic balloon tied onto the wall. Rune grabbed it and looped it around the girl's wrist. "I'm sleepy," Courtney said.

Rune had one boot off. She started on the second.

With a huge snap of cracking wood the door crashed inward, catching Rune on the shoulder. She flew into the far wall and lay still. Jack Nestor stepped into the room, narrowing his eyes against the darkness. He looked around and walked toward Rune.

When he got to her she sprang.

It wasn't much of an assault. The only damage: Her shoulder caught him in the cheek and he jerked back, blinking in surprise, as a tooth cut into his tongue or the flesh of his mouth. "Little shit!" he muttered. She pounded him with her hands, knotted into small fists. But he was resilient as hard rubber. And strong too. He just picked her up, stuffed her under his arm and carried her out into the living room.

She screamed and twisted and kicked.

Nestor was laughing hard. "Whoa, this one's a hell-cat." He dropped her into a wrought-iron butterfly chair. She kicked him in the thigh. Flinching, he said angrily, "Settle down."

"You son of a bitch!" She leapt out of the chair, making for Boggs. Nestor roared, "Settle down!" He grabbed her like a receiver snagging a sixty-yard bomb and tossed her into the chair again. She bounced once, the breath knocked out of her. She wiped at her tears. "You bastard." Looking into Randy Boggs's evasive eyes.

Boggs said to Nestor, "You got yourself wheels?"

"Sure do. Some kind of Hertz shit. But it'll do. Damn, you look good, for somebody who ain't seen but prison sunlight for three years."

Boggs said, "You look ugly as you ever did."

Nestor laughed and the men did a little good-natured sparring. Boggs landed a left hook on Nestor's chest and the fat man said, "You prick, you always were fast. You hit like a pussy but you're fast."

"You'll see a bruise the shape of my knuckles there, come morning."

Nestor looked around. "We gotta blow this joint."

"I'll vote for that."

Rune said to Boggs, "You did it? You really did it?"

Nestor was speaking to Boggs. "Let's take care of business and get on our way." He pulled the gun out of his waistband and glanced at Rune.

The smile left Boggs's face. "Whatcha aiming to do?"

Nestor shrugged. "Pretty clear, wouldn't you say? Don't see we have much choice."

Boggs was looking down, avoiding both their eyes. "Well, Jack, you know, I wouldn't be too happy, you did that."

Rune stared at the gun, afraid to look into Nestor's face. He seemed to be the sort who would kill you sooner if you looked him in the eye.

"Randy, we gotta. She knows everything."

"I know, but, hell, I wouldn't want that to happen. It just wouldn't be right, you know?"

" 'Right'?"

Her hands were shaking. Sweat popped out on her forehead, and she felt a trickle run from under her arms to her waist.

Boggs said, "The thing is, she's got a kid. A little girl."

Nestor's face darkened. "A baby?"

"This little kid."

"In there?" Nestor looked at the storeroom. "I didn't see her."

"You can't do the kid, Jack. I won't let you do that."

Meaning it's okay if he shoots *me*? Rune began to cry more seriously. Nestor was saying, "I wouldn't do a kid anyway. You know me better than that, Randy. After all we've been through, I hope you do."

"And what's the kid going to do without a mother? She'd starve to death, or something."

"She's pretty young to be a mother."

From somewhere Rune found the voice to say, "Please, don't hurt her. If you . . . do anything to me, please call the police or somebody and tell her that she's here. Please."

Nestor was debating.

Boggs said, "I really gotta ask this one, Jack. I really gotta ask you to let her be."

Nestor sighed. He nodded and put the gun into his belt. "Shit, that's the way it is, that's the way it is. Okay. I'll do it for you, Randy. I don't think it's a good idea, I just want to go on the record and say that but I'll do it. But . . ." He walked to the chair and took Rune's face in his onion-scented fingers. "You listen up good. I know who you are and where you live. If you say anything to anybody about us I'll come back. I get to New York all the time. I'll come back and I'll kill you."

Rune nodded. She was crying—in pure fear, in pure relief.

And from the worst pain of all—betrayal.

You *believe* him? Piper Sutton had asked Rune such a long time ago, as if she were talking to a child. You *believe* him when he says he's innocent?

Nestor said brutally, "You hear me?"

She couldn't speak. She nodded her head.

They used lamp cord and tied her into the chair and gagged her with an old wool scarf.

Boggs knelt down and tested the wires. He smiled shyly. "I suspect you're right upset and I don't blame you. You helped me out and I repay you this way. But sometimes in life you've gotta do things just for yourself. You know, for your own survival. I'm sorry it worked out this way but you saved my life. I'll always be thankful for that."

She wanted to say *Fuck you!* or *Go to hell!* or *Judas!* A thousand other things. But the gag was tight and, besides, no words could convey the undiluted anger she was feeling for this man. So she stared into his eyes, not blinking, not wavering a millimeter, forcing him to see how much hate welled up and overflowed between them. How she wished Prometheus was still chained to rock, being eaten by birds.

Boggs squinted for an instant. He swallowed and finally looked away.

"Lessgo, boy," Nestor called. "We got a date with the road."

Then they were gone.

MAN, MAN, MAN, THERE'S NOTHING LIKE DRIVING, RANDY Boggs was thinking.

There's not a goddamn thing in the world like it. The way the tires make that hissing sound on asphalt. The way the car dances over beat-up pavement. The way you know the road'll always be there and that you can drive forever and never once cover the same spot twice, you don't want to.

The Ford Tempo, Jack Nestor driving, had left Jersey and Pennsylvania way behind and was cruising down the highway through Maryland. Heading south.

Motion is like smooth whisky. Motion, like a drug. Randy Boggs kept up his meditation.

And the best part of all—when you're driving, you're a moving target. You're the safest you can ever be. Nothing can hurt you. Not bad love, not a job, not your kin, not the devil himself . . .

"Crabs," Nestor said. "Keep an eye out for a crab place."

They couldn't find any and instead got cheeseburgers at McDonald's, which Boggs preferred to crabs anyway and Nestor said was better for him because he was on a diet.

They drank beer out of tall Double-Arches waxed cups they'd emptied of soft drink. They drove the speed limit but at Boggs's request had rolled down all the windows; it seemed like they were racing at a hundred miles an hour.

Randy Boggs lowered the passenger seat and sat back, sucking the beer through a straw, and ate a double cheeseburger and thought again about freedom and moving and realized that was why prison had been so hard for him. That there are people who have to stay put and people who have to move and he was a mover.

These were thoughts he had and that he believed were true in some universal way. But they were thoughts that he didn't tell to Jack Nestor. Not that Jack was a stupid man. No, he'd probably understand but he was somebody Boggs didn't want to share much with.

"So," Jack Nestor asked, "how's it feel?"

"Feels good. Feels real good."

"How 'bout that little girl back there. She's a pistol. You get any?"

"Naw, wasn't that way."

"Didn't seem to have any tits to speak of."

"She was more like a friend, you know. Wish I could've leveled with her."

"Did what you had to though."

"I understand that. Couldn't've stayed Inside for any longer, Jack. I gave it my best. But I had to get out. Somebody was moving on me."

"Spades?"

"Nope. Was an asshole from, I don't know, Colombia or someplace. Venezuela. For some reason he didn't take to me. Got cut."

"Cut, huh?"

"Two weeks ago. Hardly hurts anymore."

"Yeah, I was cut once. I didn't like it. Better to get shot. Kind of more numb."

"Prefer to avoid either."

"That's a good way to think," Nestor offered. He was in a good mood. He was talking about restaurants down in Florida and fishing for tarpon and the quality of the pot they had down there and this Cuban woman with big tits and a tattoo somebody'd given her with his teeth and a

Parker pen. Talking about the heat. About a house he was buying and how he had to live in a fucking hotel until the place was ready.

"How long to Atlanta?" Boggs asked.

"Tomorrow. Then I'm going on to Florida. You interested in coming with me, you'd be welcome. You like spic women?"

"Never had me one."

"Don't know what you're missing."

"That a fact?"

"Yessir. One I's telling you 'bout? Man, she could probably do both of us at once."

Boggs thought he'd pass on that. "I don't know."

"Well, just keep 'er in mind. So you gonna pick up that money?"

"Yessir."

"You got the passbook with you?"

"Got her good and safe."

Nestor said, "Funny about how that works. You just let some money sit in the bank and there she be, earning interest every day. They just throw a few more dollars into the till. And you don't do nothing."

"Yeah."

"Bet you made yourself another ten thousand dollars."

"You think, no foolin'?"

"For sure. I think that account earns maybe five, six percent."

Boggs felt a warm feeling. He hadn't remembered about interest. He'd never had a savings account to speak of.

"You know, there's something you ought to think about. You hear about all those bank failures?"

"What's that?"

"A lot of savings and loans went under. People lost money."

"Hell you say."

"Happens a lot. Last couple of years. Didn't you watch the news Inside?"

"Usually was cartoons and the game we were watching." Boggs was tired. He put the seat way back. The last car he'd owned was a big '76 Pontiac with a bench seat that didn't recline. He liked this car. He thought he was going to buy himself a car, a new one. He lay back, closed his eyes and tried not to think about Rune.

"So," Nestor said, "you might want to think about investing that money."

"I'll do that."

"You have any idea what?"

"Nope. Not yet. I'm going to keep my eyes peeled for the right thing. You got money, people listen to you."

"Money talks, shit walks," Nestor said.

"That's the truth," Randy Boggs said.

THREE HOURS LATER COURTNEY WOKE UP AND WANTED some juice.

The little girl sat up slowly and unwound herself from the cocoon of a blanket that had twisted around her as she slept. She eased forward and climbed over the edge of the rolled-up futon like Edmund Hillary taking the last step down from Everest and then sat on the floor to put her shoes on. Laces were too much of a challenge but the shoes didn't look right with the white dangling strings, so after staring at them for five minutes she bent down and stuffed the plastic ends into her shoes.

She climbed carefully down the stairs, sideways, crablike, then walked up to Rune, who was tied into the butterfly chair. She looked at the cords, at Rune's red face. She heard hoarse, wordless sounds coming from behind the scarf.

"You're funny, Rune," Courtney said then went into the galley.

The refrigerator was pretty easy to open and she found a cardboard carton of apple juice on the second shelf. The problem was that she couldn't figure out how to open it. She looked at Rune, who was staring into the kitchen and still making those funny noises, and held up the carton in both hands then she turned it upside down to look for the spout.

The carton, which, it turned out, had been open after all, emptied itself onto the floor in a sticky surf. "Oh-oh." She looked at Rune guiltily then set the empty container on top of the stove and went back to the refrigerator.

No more juice. A lot of cold pizza, which she was tired of, but there were dozens of Twinkies, which she loved. She started working on one and then wandered around the small kitchen to see what she could find to play with.

Not a lot. There was, however, a large filleting knife on the counter that intrigued her. She picked it up and pretended it was a sword, like in one of Rune's books, stabbing the refrigerator a few times.

Rune, watching this, was making more noise, and started jiggling around, rocking and swaying back and forth.

The girl then looked into drawers and opened up some pretty-much-unused cookbooks, looking for pictures of ducks, dragons or princesses. The books contained only photos of soups and casseroles and cakes and after five minutes she gave up on them and started playing with the knobs on the stove. They were old and heavy, glistening chrome and trimmed with red paint. Courtney reached up and turned one all the way to the right. Way above her head was a *pop*. She couldn't see the top of the stove and she didn't know what the sound came from but she liked it. *Pop*.

She turned the second knob. *Pop*.

Rune's voice was louder now though the little girl still couldn't understand a word of it.

With the third *pop* she got tired of the stove game. That was because something else happened. There was suddenly a red glare from above her head, a hissing sputter, then flames.

Courtney stepped back and watched the juice carton burn. The flaming wax shot off the side of the carton like miniature fireworks. One piece of burning cardboard fell onto the table and set a week-old *New York Post* on fire. A cookbook *(A Hundred Glorious Jell-O Desserts)* went next.

Courtney loved the flames and watched them creep slowly along the table. They reminded her of something . . . A movie about a baby animal? A deer? A big fire in a forest? She squinted and tried to remember but soon lost the association and stood back to watch.

She thought it was great when the flames quickly peeled away the Breeds-of-Dog contact paper Rune had painstakingly mounted on the walls with rubber cement.

Then they spread up to the ceiling and the back wall of the houseboat.

When the fire became too hot Courtney moved back a little farther but she was in no hurry to leave. This was wonderful. She remembered another movie. She thought for a minute. Yeah, it was like the scene where Wizardoz was yelling at Dorothy and her little dog. All the smoke and flames . . . Everybody falling on the floor while the big face puffed and shouted . . . But this was better than that. This was better than Peter Rabbit. It was even better than Saturday morning TV.

chapter 26

THE TOURISTS COINCIDENTALLY WERE FROM OHIO, RUNE'S home state.

They were a middle-aged couple, driving a Winnebago from Cleveland to Maine because the wife had always wanted to see the Maine coast and because they both loved lobster. The itinerary would take them through New York, up to Newport, then on to Boston, Salem and finally into Kennebunkport, which had been featured in *Parade* magazine a year before.

But they made an unplanned stop in Manhattan and that was to report a serious fire on the Hudson River.

Cruising up from the Holland Tunnel, they noticed a column of black smoke off to their left, coming, it seemed, right out of the river. They slowed, like almost everybody else was doing, and saw an old houseboat burning furiously. Traffic was at a crawl and they eased forward, listening for the sirens. The husband looked around to find a place to pull off to get out of the way of the fire trucks when they arrived.

But none did.

They waited four, five minutes. Six.

She asked, "You'd think somebody'd've called by now, wouldn't you, dear?"

"You'd think."

They were astonished because easily a hundred cars had gone by but it seemed that nobody had bothered to call 911. Maybe figuring somebody else had. Or not figuring anything at all, just watching the houseboat burn.

The husband, an ex-marine and head of his local Chamber of Commerce, a man with no aversion to getting involved, drove the Winnebago up over the curb onto the sidewalk. He braked to a fast halt in front of the pier where the flames roared. He took the big JCPenney triple-class fire extinguisher from the rack beside his seat and rushed outside.

The wife ran to a pay phone while he kicked in the front door of the houseboat. The smoke wasn't too bad inside; the hole in the rear ceiling of the houseboat acted like a chimney and was sucking most of it out. He stopped cold in the doorway, blinking in surprise at what he saw: two girls. One, a young girl, was laughing like Nero as she watched the back half of the houseboat turn into charcoal. The other, a girl wearing a yellow miniskirt, two sleeveless men's T-shirts and low boots dotted with chrome studs, was tied in a chair! Who'd do such a thing? He'd read about Greenwich Village but this seemed too sick even for a Sodom like that.

He pulled the pin of the fire extinguisher and emptied the contents at the advancing line of flames, but it had no effect on the fire. He carried the little girl outside to his wife and then returned to the inferno, opening his Case pocketknife as he ran. He cut the wires holding the older girl. He had to help her walk outside; her legs had fallen asleep.

Inside the couple's Winnebago the little girl saw the older one's tears and decided it was time to start crying herself. Three minutes later the fire department arrived. They had the fire out in twenty. The police and fire department investigators knocked on the campers' door. The girls stood up and went outside and the couple followed.

A huge black cloud hung over the pier. The air smelled of sour wood and burnt rubber—from the tires that had dangled off the side of the boat to cushion it against the pier. The vessel hadn't sunk but much of the structure on the deck had been destroyed.

One of the detectives asked the older girl, "Could you tell me what happened?"

She paced in a tight circle. "That goddamn son of a bitch he tricked me he lied to me I'm going to find him and have his ass thrown back in jail so goddamn fast. . . . Shit. Hell. Shit!"

"Shit," Courtney said, and the husband and wife looked at each other.

The police asked questions for almost a half hour. The girl was telling a story about a man who was convicted wrongly of murder then got released, only now it was clear he'd done it after all and there was a big fat man named Jack Nestor, who had a gun and wanted to kill them and he was involved in the first killing. The couple lost a lot of the details—just like the cops must have too—but they didn't really need to hear any more. They had enough of the facts for a good traveling story, which they'd tell to friends and to themselves and to anybody they happened to meet on the way to Maine and which unlike a lot of the stories they'd told didn't need much embellishment at all. Finally a tall, balding man in a plaid shirt and blue jeans and with a badge on his belt arrived and the girl fell into his arms, though she wasn't sobbing anymore or hysterical. Then she pushed him away and went into one of her tirades again.

"Goodness," the wife said.

When the girl calmed down she told the cop the couple had saved her life and he introduced himself to them and said thank you. They talked about Ohio for a few minutes. Then the cop said that the girls could go to the Bomb Squad and stay there until he was off duty and the little girl said, "Can we get another hand grenade? Please?"

And that was when the couple decided not to do what had crossed their Midwestern minds—ask the girls if they would like to stay with them in the camper that night—and figured it would probably be best if they pressed on to the alternate destination of Mystic, Connecticut, which came highly recommended in their guidebook.

AT ELEVEN THAT NIGHT, JACK NESTOR SAID HE NEEDED A real drink and pulled off the highway at a motel somewhere in Virginia.

"I could use some real *food,* too," Randy Boggs said. He wanted a steak burnt on the outside and red inside. He'd spent a lot of time thinking about steaks when he first went Inside. Then—as with most of the things he enjoyed—he forgot about good meat. Or it was more that those things became distant. Like facts in a history book. He understood them, he remembered them, but they had no meaning for him.

Now, though, he was out and he wanted a steak. And the way Nestor had said *real drink,* Boggs was now thinking that he'd like his first shot of whisky in three years.

They parked the car and went into the motel office. Nestor gave a fake name and car license then asked for a room in the back, explaining to the young night clerk that he didn't sleep well; highway noise bothered him. The young man nodded apathetically, took the cash and gave him the key. Boggs was impressed at how smoothly Nestor had handled things. Boggs himself would have been more careless, leaving the car in front. But Nestor was right. The girl had probably gotten free by now and might've turned them in. Or maybe someone in New York had seen the license plate. He was glad he was with somebody like Nestor, somebody who could teach him to think Outside again.

Nestor lugged his duffel bag into the room and Boggs followed with the paper bag that was his suitcase. He was relieved to see there were two large beds. He hadn't wanted to spend his first night of freedom in bed with another man. Without commenting on the room, Nestor dropped his luggage onto the bed nearest the door and said, "Food."

Boggs said, "Hold up. I want to wash." He disappeared into the bathroom, amused and feeling almost heartsick with joy at how clean it was. At all the sweet smells. At the soap and wrapped glasses and a john behind a door that closed and locked. He ran the water cold, then hot, then cold again, then hot and washed his face and hands as the steam rose up and filled the room.

"I'm hungry," Nestor bellowed over the sound of the running water.

"Minute," Boggs shouted back and dried himself with luxurious towels that seemed thick as down comforters.

The bar-restaurant near the hotel was a local hangout, done up in prefab Tudor—dark beams, plastic windows mimicking stained glass, beige stucco walls. The place was half filled—mostly around the bar—with contractors and plumbers and truck drivers and their girlfriends. The men were in jeans and plaid shirts. A lot of beards. The women were in slacks, high heels and simple blouses. Almost everyone smoked. *The Honeymooners* was showing on a cockeyed TV above one end of the bar.

Nestor and Boggs sat down at a rickety table. Boggs stared at his place mat, which was printed with puzzles and word games. He could figure out the visual ones— "What's Wrong With This Picture?"—but he had trouble unscrambling letters to make words. He turned the place mat over and looked at the women at the bar.

The waitress came by and told them the kitchen was

closing in ten minutes. They ordered four Black Jacks, neat, Bud chasers, and steaks and fries.

"That girl," Nestor said. "Too bad you didn't fuck her."

"Who?"

"The one sprung you."

"Naw, I told you, we was mostly friends."

Nestor asked, "So?"

"Well, I only got out a few hours before you showed up."

"It was me, the first thing I woulda done was get me some poontang."

Boggs felt he was on the spot. He said, "Well, she had the baby there."

The drinks arrived and they poured the shots down without saying anything because neither of them could think of a toast. Boggs wheezed and Nestor laughed. The big guy did his second shot right after.

"Don't get any of that Inside, do you?" Nestor asked him.

"There was stuff you could get, depending on what you were willing to do or how much money you had. It was shit, though. Me, I didn't get any care packages, so I had to settle. Sometimes I'd get me some watered vodka or a joint or two. Mostly I didn't get nothing."

"When I was Inside we had it easy. Fucking country club. A lot of dealers from L.A. There was so much shit."

Boggs, dizzy from the liquor, asked, "You did time?"

"Fuck yeah, I was in. Did eighteen months in Obispo. Was fanfuckingtastic. You wanted blow, you got blow. You wanted sess, you got sess. You wanted fucking wine, you could get a good bottle of wine. . . ."

Boggs was feeling the liquor sting his lips. They must've gotten windburned from the drive. "When were you in Obispo?"

"Four, five years ago about."

"I didn't know you'd done time."

Nestor looked at him, surprised. "Hey, there's probably a thing or two we don't know about each other. Like I don't know how long your dick is."

Boggs said, "Long enough to keep a grin on *her* face for an hour or two." His eyes slipped to the bar, where a round-faced young woman, with two-tone hair—blonde returning to black—sat with her elbow on the bar and her hand up, a cigarette aimed at the ceiling like a sixth finger. In front of her was a no-nonsense martini. The way she stared vacantly at the TV he figured the drink was the descendant of a long line of the same.

Nestor said, "You can have her. She don't have tits."

"Sure she does. She's sitting hunched over."

The food arrived and took both men's attention. Boggs was eating but he'd found his appetite was gone. Maybe the steak was too rich. Maybe the burgers had filled him up or the alcohol had burned out his taste buds. He thought about Rune, about the little girl. He ate mechanically. He looked at the woman, who caught his eye and held it for a minute before she looked back at the TV. He thought a bit more then decided to finish eating. Maybe food would sober him up.

Boggs finished while Nestor was still halfway through.

"Man," Boggs said, "that was a meal."

Nestor looked at Boggs's thin stomach. "You eat that way, how come you ain't fat?"

"Dunno. I just never gain any. Not *my* doing." Boggs's voice faded as he stared again at the girl at the bar. This time she gave him a bit of a smile.

Nestor caught it. "Oh-oh." He smiled. "Prison-boy gonna get laid."

Boggs finished his beer. "You mind if I take the room for about an hour?"

"Shit, boy, it'll take you five minutes, unless you jerked off every night inside the slammer."

"Well, gimme an hour anyway. Maybe we'll wanta do it twice."

"Okeydokey," Nestor said. "But get her butt out by one. I'm tired and I need some sleep."

Boggs stood up and walked slowly toward the bar, trying to remember how to be cool and slick, trying to remember how to talk to women, trying to remember a lot of things.

chapter 27

BOGGS AND THE GIRL HAD BEEN GONE A HALF HOUR when Jack Nestor finished the lousy apple pie and sucked the ice cream off his fork. He took the last swallow of coffee and called for the check.

The bar was pretty empty now and, aside from the waitress, there was nobody who saw him stand and go out to the parking lot. He looked up and saw the light on in his and Boggs's room. He opened the trunk of the car and took out his pistol. He hid the gun under his jacket and climbed the stairs to the second floor then moved slowly along the open walkway to the room. He'd thought about getting another key from the desk but that would have given the clerk another look at him. He'd decided to just knock on the door and when Boggs opened it shoot him in the gut—his I-dunno-I-just-eat-and-don't-get-fat gut. Then do the girl if she was still there.

He paused. What was the noise? The TV? They were fucking and the TV was on? Maybe she was a screamer and Boggs kept the sound up so other guests wouldn't hear. That was good. Maybe it was a cop show and there'd be gunshots, which would help cover up the sound of the Steyr.

Nestor walked closer to the door. He pulled the slide back on the gun. He saw something flashing.

That putz . . .

Boggs was so horny he'd left the key in the door,

which wasn't even fully closed. All Nestor had to do was push inside. He made sure the safety was off, slipped his finger into the trigger guard and swung into the room.

Empty.

The bedclothes weren't even turned down.

The bathroom was dark but he walked inside anyway, thinking that maybe they were fucking in the tub. But no, that was empty too. The only motion in the room was the flicker of the TV screen, on which several *Hill Street Blues* cops were looking solemn. Nestor shut off the set.

Then he noticed that Boggs's bag was gone. Shit.

He picked up the note, which rested on the pillow. Shit.

> *Jack, Lynda—that's her name—and me went back to her house. Seems she is going to Atlanta tomorrow, that's a coinsidence, huh, so we're going to be driving together for a spell, her and me, I mean. I will meet you at your place in Florida in a couple days. Sorry, but you don't have legs like her.*

Son of a bitch.

Motherfucker!

Nestor kicked the bed furiously. The mattress bounced off the springs and came to rest at an angle. He slammed the door shut violently, which brought a sleepy protesting pounding from the next room over. Nestor hoped the guest would come over because he had an incredible desire to beat the living hell out of someone.

He sat down on the bed, picturing Boggs balling the scrawny bitch while the passbook sat in a crumpled paper bag probably five feet away from them. The anger seeped away slowly, as he decided what to do.

Well, it wasn't the end of the world. It was a change of plans was all. He had to kill the girl anyway—the one on the houseboat. He might as well do that now then get down to Atlanta or Florida and take care of Boggs. It didn't really matter who he did first.

Six of one, half a dozen of another.

THE WAY PIPER SUTTON FOUND OUT WAS THE *POST* HEAD-line: "TV Scoop Becomes Oops." Which she wouldn't have paid any attention to, except that on the front page was a picture of Rune talking to a couple of men in suits. They didn't look happy. Rune didn't either, and now Piper Sutton joined the club.

Standing on the street corner near her apartment, she stared at the story. She'd bought the *Post* and then a *Daily News* and a *Times*. Ripping open each furiously, skirt and hair tousled by the wind as she stared at the smudged type. Thank God for a big assault in Central America that buried the *Daily News* story inside. The *Times* had simply reported, "Houseboat Burns in Hudson," with a reference to a possible convict's escape.

But the *Times* would be on the story today. How the Fit-to-Print paper loved to take potshots at the competition, especially TV.

Sutton flagged down a cab, giving up her usual mile walk to the office, and sat with the newspapers on her lap, staring out the window at people on their way to work. But not seeing a single one of them.

At her office Sutton found her secretary juggling two calls.

"Oh, Ms. Sutton, Mr. Semple has called several times, there're calls from all the local TV stations, and somebody from the *Village Voice*."

The fucking *Voice*?

"And a Mr. Miller, with the Attorney General's Of-fice, then—"

"Hold all the calls," Sutton hissed. "Ask Lee Maisel to come over. "Get me the legal department. I want Tim

Krueger here in fifteen minutes. If any other reporters call tell them we'll have a statement by noon. If any of them say they have an earlier deadline take his or her name and let me know immediately." Sutton pulled her coat off. "And I want *her*. Now."

"Who, Miss Sutton?"

"You know who," Sutton replied in a whisper. "Now."

RUNE HAD BEEN FIRED WORSE BUT THE SAD THING WAS that the other times she didn't really care.

She'd screwed up often in the past, sure, but there's a big difference between getting fired from a video store or restaurant and getting fired from a real job, one you cared about.

Usually she'd say, "Eh, happens," or "Them's the breaks."

This was different.

She'd wanted to do this story. Badly. She'd *lived* for this story. She'd breathed it and tasted it. And now not only was she getting axed but she was getting fired because the whole thing had been a complete lie. The very core, the most very basic fact was false. The worst. It was like reading a fairy tale and then the writer telling you, *Oh, yeah, by the way, I was just kidding. There's no such thing as a demon.*

Although she had proof there was such a thing. And his name was Randy Boggs.

Rune now stood in front of Piper Sutton's desk. Also in the room was a tall, thin, middle-aged man in a gray suit and white shirt. His name was Krueger. Lee Maisel leaned against the wall behind Sutton, reading the *Post* account. "Jesus Christ," he muttered. He looked at Rune with dark, impenetrable eyes and went back to the paper.

"Tell me exactly what happened," Sutton said. "Don't embellish, don't minimize, don't edit."

Rune explained about the fat man and Boggs and what happened on the houseboat. She added what Sam Healy had found out—that the police could find no leads to a Jack Nestor.

"So Boggs did it, after all," Maisel said. "There was another killer but they were partners. Jesus."

"Sort of looks like it." Rune wasn't counting *"likes,"* *"sort-ofs"* and *"kind-ofs."* "When I saw them there, kind of hugging each other, I totally freaked. I mean . . ." Her voice faded.

Sutton closed her eyes and shook her head slowly, then asked the gray-suited man, "What's the legal assessment, Tim?"

The lawyer said calmly, "I don't think we have any liability. We didn't fabricate evidence and the court decision was legitimate. I wish she"—not looking at Rune—"hadn't gotten him released without telling anybody here. That adds another dimension."

For the first time since she'd known him Maisel turned angry eyes on Rune. "Why didn't you tell me you were going to get Boggs sprung?"

"I was worried about him. I—"

Sutton couldn't keep cool any longer. "I've told you from the beginning that our job isn't to get people out of jail. It's to report the truth! That's the *only* job."

"I just didn't think. I didn't think it would matter."

"Didn't . . . think." Sutton stretched the words out for a vast second.

"I'm really—"

Sutton turned to Maisel. "So, what's the next step?"

"Nighttime News."

The lawyer winced. "It's a New York story. Can't we justify keeping it local?"

Maisel said, "No way. *Time* and *Newsweek*'ll cover it. You know what the other nets are going to do and forget about the *Times.* They'll crucify us. It'll be understated but it'll still be a crucifixion."

"We'll have to preempt them," Sutton said. "Put it on the *News at Noon,* then do a piece at five and have Eustice do it at seven. We tell all. We confess. Not a single word of excuse or backpedaling."

Krueger said, "God, that'll hurt."

Maisel sighed.

The lawyer asked Rune, "You have any idea where Boggs went?"

"All I know is like he came from the South. Atlanta was where he was born and he lived in Florida and North Carolina but other than that . . ." She ended in a shrug.

The lawyer said, "I'm going over to our law firm and brief the litigators, just in case." With a fast, curious glance at Rune he left the office. Sutton stared at the *Daily News*. Lee Maisel played with his pipe and sat in a slump. He was uncomfortable. Rune looked into his eyes, though his darted away quickly. The disappointment she saw hurt her more than the hatred she felt gushing from Sutton.

Oh, how could I do it?

He believed in me and I let him down.

Sutton looked at Rune. "Don't talk to the press about what happened. You've already blabbed your mouth off, I see." Waving her arm at the newspaper.

Rune said, "I didn't say anything. The police must've told the reporters."

"Well, all I'll say is, the Network is going to be in deep shit for this and heads are probably going to roll. If you make things worse for everybody because you can't keep your mouth shut, then you'll be opening yourself up to a big fat fucking lawsuit. You understand me?"

Rune nodded.

There was a long pause, broken by Sutton's saying, "Well, I guess that's it. You're out of here."

Rune stared at her, blinked. "Just like that? Today?"

"Sorry, Rune," Maisel said. "Today, yes. Now."

Sutton added, "And don't take any files or cassettes with you. That's our property."

"Do you mean I should go back to my job at the O&O?"

Sutton looked at her with a disbelieving smile.

Rune said, "You mean, I'm like totally fired."

Sutton said, "Like totally."

SAM HEALY WOKE UP AT EIGHT THE NEXT MORNING when Courtney emptied a box of Raisin Bran in their bed.

The noisy cascade didn't wake Rune up.

"Jesus Christ," Healy muttered and shook her arm. He rolled over. Rune opened her eyes and said, "What's that noise? That crunching?"

Courtney stood in front of the bed and looked down at the flakes, frowning.

Rune swung her feet over the side of the bed, her legs covered with cereal. "Courtney, what did you do?"

"I'm sorry," the little girl said. "Spilled."

Healy, who'd gotten home two hours before from duty watch, said, "I'm going into Adam's room." He vanished.

Rune scooped the cereal up and brushed it off her legs, then put it back into the box. "You know better than that. Come on."

"I know better."

"Don't look so damn cute when I'm yelling at you."

"Damn cute," Courtney said.

"Come on." Rune trudged into the kitchen. She poured juice and bowls of cereal, made coffee. "Can we go to the zoo?" Courtney asked.

"Tomorrow. I've got some errands to do first. You wanta come?"

"Yeah, I wanta come." She held up her hand. "Five-high."

Rune sighed then held up her hand. The little girl slapped it.

chapter 28

A HALF HOUR LATER RUNE AND COURTNEY GOT OFF THE E train at West Fourth and started walking down Christopher Street to the water. Rune paused at the West Side Highway, took a deep breath for courage then plunged around the corner to survey the damage to her late home.

The houseboat still floated but it looked like a load of charred wood had been dumped onto the deck; irregular, glistening slabs of fluted charcoal rose from it. A haze of smoke still hung around the pier and made everything— the houseboat, the debris, the trash cans, the chain-link—appear out of focus. The front of the pier was cordoned off with yellow police tape, fifty feet in front of where the boat bobbed like a man-o'-war that had lost a sea battle. Rune remembered her excitement at seeing the houseboat for the first time, riding in the Hudson, fifty miles north of here.

And now, a Viking burial.

She sighed, then waved to the patrolman in the front seat of a blue-and-white. He was a friend of Healy's from the Sixth Precinct, the station where the Bomb Squad was housed.

"Look at this," she called.

"Sorry about it, honey. Some of us'll drive by once in a while, check up on things, just till you get your stuff moved out."

"Yeah, if there's anything left."

There was, but the stink and smoke damage were so

bad she didn't have the heart to go through it. Anyway, Courtney was restless and kept climbing on the pilings.

Rune took her by the hand and led her back up Christopher Street.

"What's that?" Courtney asked, pointing at a storefront sign encouraging safe sex. It showed a condom.

"Balloon," said Rune.

"I want one."

"When you're older," Rune answered. The words came automatically and she decided she was really getting into this kid bit. They continued on Christopher then along the tail end of Greenwich and finally onto Eighth Street. It had become a lot shabbier in the past year. More graffiti, more garbage, more obnoxious kids. But, God, the shoe stores—more places to buy cheap shoes than anywhere else in the world.

They walked down to University Place, past dozens of chic, black-clad NYU students. Rune made a detour. She stopped in front of an empty storefront. Above the door was a sign, *Washington Square Video*.

"I used to work there," she told Courtney. The little girl peered inside.

In the window was another sign, on yellow cardboard: *For Rent Net Lease*.

Just like my life, she thought. For rent net lease.

They walked to Washington Square Park and bought hot dogs then kept walking south through SoHo and into Chinatown.

"Hey," Rune said suddenly, "want to see something neat?"

"Yeah, neat."

"Let's go look at some octopuses."

"Yeah!"

Rune led her across the street to a huge outdoor fish market on Canal Street. "It's like the zoo, only the thing is the animals don't move so much."

Courtney didn't buy it, though. "Pukey," she said

about the octopus then got yelled at by the owner of the stand when she poked a grouper.

Rune looked around and said, "Oh, hey, I know where we are. Come on—I'll show you something totally excellent. I'll teach you some history and when you start school you can blow everybody away with how much you already know."

"Yeah. I like history."

They walked down Centre Street past the black Family Court Building. (Rune, glancing across the square at the Criminal Courts Building and thinking of Randy Boggs. She felt the anger sear her and looked away quickly.) In a few minutes they were in front of the New York Supreme Court at 60 Centre Street.

"This is it," Rune announced.

"Yeah." Courtney looked around.

"This used to be called Five Points. A hundred years ago it was the worst area in all of Manhattan. This is where the Whyos hung out."

"What's a Whyo?"

"A gang, the worst gang that ever was. I'll read you a bedtime story about them some night."

"Yeah!"

Rune remembered, though, that her present copy of *New York Gangs* was now just a cinder and wondered where she could get a new one. She said, "The Whyos were really tough. You couldn't join them unless you were a murderer. They even printed up a price list—you know, like a menu, for how much it cost to stab somebody or shoot him in the leg or kill him."

"Yuck," said Courtney.

"You hear all about Al Capone and Dutch Schultz, right?"

Courtney said agreeably, "Uh-huh."

"But they weren't anything compared with the Whyos. Danny Driscoll was the leader. There's this great story about him. He was in love with a girl named Beezy

Garrity—isn't that a great name? I'd like to be named Beezy."

"Beezy."

"And this rival gang dude, Johnny somebody or another, fell in love with her too. Danny and him had this duel in a dance hall up the street. They pulled out guns and blasted away." Rune fired a couple shots with her finger. "Blam, blam! And guess who got shot?"

"Beezy."

Rune was impressed. "You got it." Then she frowned. "Danny was pretty bummed by that, I'd guess, but it got worse because they hanged *him* for killing his girlfriend. Right over there," Rune pointed. "That's where the Tombs were. The old criminal building. Hanged him right up."

Well, now she'd have plenty of time to do her documentary about old-time gangs. She wished she'd done that story in the first place. *They* wouldn't have lied to her. Nope, Slops Connolly would no way have betrayed her. They were creeps and scum but, she bet, back then thugs were honorable.

"Come on, honey," Rune said, starting toward Mulberry Street. "I'll show you where English Charley started the last big fight the Whyos were ever in. You want to see?"

"Oh, yeah."

Rune stopped suddenly and bent down and hugged the girl. Courtney hugged back, squeezing with just the right amount of strength that Rune needed just then. The little girl broke away and ran to the corner. A woman in a business suit, maybe a lawyer on break from court, crouched down and said to Courtney, "Aren't you a cute one?" Rune joined them and the woman looked up and said, "She's yours?"

And as Rune started to say she was just looking after her Courtney said, "Uh-huh, this is my mommy."

•　　•　　•

RANDY BOGGS LAUGHED OUT LOUD. THE MAN SITTING IN the seat next to him, on the Atlanta-bound Greyhound bus, glanced his way but must have been a seasoned traveler and didn't say anything. He probably knew not to engage in conversation with people who laughed to themselves. Not on a bus, not in north Georgia.

What Boggs was laughing at was the memory of Lynda's astonished face as they walked out of the restaurant and he handed her fifty dollars, telling her to get on home and not go back in that bar if Tom Cruise himself was in there offering to take her to Bermuda. "Uh-huh," she said suspiciously. "Why?"

"Because," Boggs answered and kissed her forehead.

"You mean you don't wannta?" Nodding toward the room.

"I'd love to, 'specially with a pretty thing like you but there's someplace I gotta be."

He collected his bag and she gave him a drive to the Charlottesville bus station, which was a ways away but not so far that fifty dollars didn't buy the trip. He thanked her and trotted off to wait at the terminal for the bus that would eventually get him to Atlanta.

What had tipped him off had been the Men's Colony comment—the California State Men's Colony at San Luis Obispo.

Seemed pretty strange that Jack Nestor—knowing that Boggs was Inside and knowing intimately *why* Boggs was Inside—he had never before mentioned he'd served time himself. It'd be natural for him to tell Boggs what it was like. Maybe brag a little. Ex-cons always did that.

But what was stranger still was that Nestor had been in the same prison, at the same time, as Juan Ascipio.

Okay, it could have been a coincidence. But if Nestor wanted something to happen to Boggs in Harrison, Ascipio would have been a good choice to start that accident happening.

The accident that killed Severn Washington and came close to killing Boggs.

A lot of strange things happening. The Obispo thing. And the way the witness, Bennett Frost, had died. And then the tape of Rune's story disappearing.

Beneath his lazy smile and easy manner Randy Boggs was spitting mad. Here he'd done right by Nestor, never said a goddamn word at trial or the entire time he was Inside. Boggs was a stand-up guy. And look what happened: betrayed.

The bus rocked around a turn fast and he felt less angry. Boggs smiled. It wasn't as good as a car but it was still movement. Movement taking him away from Harrison and toward a pile of money.

He laughed again and said to the man beside him. "I love buses, don't you?"

"Be all right, I guess."

"Be *damn* all right," Boggs said.

WHOA, A FIRE.

Jack Nestor, back on Christopher Street, looked at the charred wreckage of the houseboat. He leaned against a brick building next to the highway and wondered what this meant. He thought about it some. Okay, if she'd been inside, still tied up, when it happened she'd be dead and, fuck it, he could leave. But it was also pretty likely that somebody would've seen the fire and come to help her before she got toasted.

Or maybe she'd moved and some asshole just torched the place.

A lot of questions, no answers.

So Boggs the prick was gone. And now the girl was gone too.

Damn. Jack Nestor lit a cigarette and leaned up against the brick, wondering what to do next.

The answer, he decided, was to wait.

He hadn't slept well the night before. A lot of driving.
The pictures again too. They'd wakened him and he'd lain
in bed, thinking that now he was going to kill Randy
Boggs he needed to find something to resent about him.
There wasn't much. He wasn't a nigger, a fag, a spic. He
didn't insult you. He didn't go after your woman.

Nestor's hand went to his stomach and he squeezed
the glossy scar. The imaginary itching crawled around in
his belly somewhere. Then he decided that Boggs's sin
was that he was a Loser, capital L. Nestor smiled. That
was plenty of reason to hunt the shit down and kill him.

Good. That was taken care of.

It was a mild April night and the sky was lit by this eerie
glow you couldn't tell where it came from. All the streetlights, probably. And headlights from cars and taxis and office buildings and stores . . . This made him think about all
the buildings in the city, which of course included restaurants. Which reminded him that he was starving.

And then, just as he was about to go get a burger,
there was the girl! She was walking slowly up the dock to
the houseboat, looking at the smoldering mess. She was
dressed in those weird clothes of hers—black miniskirt,
boots, a couple of T-shirts, one bright red, the other yellow. Over her shoulder was a large bag but she was nice
enough to set that down and stand with her hands on her
hips, looking at the boat. She walked forward to look at
some of the burnt junk on the pier and kicked it absently.
She walked to the yellow police *Do Not Cross* tape and
stood with her hands on it, looking down as if she was
praying.

Nestor took the gun from his jacket pocket and
looked around. Cars zipped past and there were people
strolling along the riverfront but no one was near him.
The sun was going down fast, a huge wad of orange fire,
sinking directly in front of him. He could see it disappearing, inch by inch into Hoboken behind the charred skeleton of the houseboat.

Nestor aimed. He kept both eyes open; he didn't squint. It was a seventy-five-yard shot and he wished he had a stock and butt piece but he didn't so he leaned hard into the brick wall for support, crooked his arm and set the pistol in the V between his biceps and forearm. He aligned the sights and lifted it a millimeter to compensate for the distance. There was no wind.

He held his breath.

Complete stillness.

Then: The last streak of sun slipped under the horizon.

A car sped past and honked.

The girl turned.

Jack Nestor fired two fast shots, whose sharp cracks spread across the water, echoed briefly then faded.

He'd aimed for her back first then her head. Both slugs hit her. The first one struck her shoulder high. The second caught her in motion as she spun around. He saw a puff of blood, like smoke, on her cheek.

She dropped to the ground like a puppet with cut strings.

Nestor walked quickly back to the car. On the way he changed his mind. A burger would no longer do the trick. He decided to go looking for the biggest steak he could find in this goddamn town.

chapter 29

AT FIRST, RANDY BOGGS THOUGHT HE'D BEEN CHEATED by the bank.

He'd never had a good relationship with financial institutions. Although he'd never robbed any, several Georgia and Florida savings and loans (with the word "Trust" in their names, no less) had foreclosed on his family's houses after his father had missed various numbers of mortgage payments.

He was therefore predisposed to be suspicious.

So now, when the pretty girl behind the window handed him eleven tiny piles of cash so thin that they looked like a kid's building blocks, he thought in panic they'd kept most of the money for a fee or something.

She looked at his expression and asked, "Is everything all right?"

"That's one hundred ten thousand?"

"Yessir. They just look small 'cause they're new bills. I counted 'em once and our machine there counted 'em twice—you want me to do it again?"

"No, ma'am." Looked right at Ben Franklin, who stared back at him with that weird smile as if it was as natural for Boggs as for anyone else to be holding a fortune. A hundred ten thousand and some change—the extra being thanks to the interest Jack Nestor had mentioned.

"Kind of thought a hundred thousand'd be a bigger pile."

"You got it in nickels and dahms, it'd be pretty sizable then."

"Yes, ma'am."

"Y'all want an escort? Lahk a guahd or anything?"

"No, ma'am."

Boggs loaded the money in his paper bag and left. Then he wandered around downtown Atlanta for an hour. He was astonished at the changes. It was clean and landscaped. He laughed at the number of streets with "Peachtree" in them—laughed because he remembered his daddy saying most people thought that referred to peaches when in fact the name came from "pitch tree," like tar. He passed the street named Boulevard and laughed again.

This was a town where it seemed you could laugh at something like that and nobody would think you were crazy—as long as you eventually stopped laughing and went about your business. Boggs went into a luggage store and bought an expensive black-nylon backpack because he'd always wanted one, something made for long-distance carrying. He slipped the money and his change of shirt into the bag, which put him in mind of clothes.

He passed a fancy men's store but felt intimidated by the weird, headless mannequins. He walked on until he found an old-time store, where the fabrics were mostly polyester and the colors mostly brown and beige. He bought a tan off-the-rack suit and a yellow shirt, two pairs of black-and-red argyle socks and a striped tie. He thought this might be too formal for a lot of places so he also bought a pair of double-knit brown slacks and two blue short-sleeve sport shirts. He thought about wearing the new clothes and having the clerk bag his jeans and work shirt. But they'd think that was odd and they might remember him.

Which probably wouldn't matter at all. So *what* if they remembered him? He hadn't done anything illegal here. And so *what* if they thought he was odd? If he'd been a rich Buckhead businessman who'd decided on a whim to buy some clothes and wear them home nobody'd think twice.

But he wasn't a businessman. He was a former convict. Who wasn't supposed to leave New York. And so he paid fast and left.

He walked into a Hyatt and strolled past the fountains. Boggs had always loved hotels. They were places of adventure, where nothing was permanent, where you could always leave and go elsewhere if you weren't happy. He liked the meeting rooms, where every day there was a new group of people, learning things for their jobs or maybe learning a new skill, like real estate investing or how to become Mary Kay pink-Buick saleswomen.

Every guest in a hotel stayed there because they were traveling.

And a traveling person, Randy Boggs knew, was a happy person.

He went into the washroom on one of the banquet room levels and, in a spotless stall, changed into his suit. He realized then that he was still wearing his beat-up loafers with the 1943 steel penny in the slit on the top. That afternoon he'd get some new shoes. Something fancy. Maybe alligator skin or snakeskin. He looked at himself in the mirror and decided he needed more color; he was pretty pale. And he didn't like his hair—very few men wore it slicked back the way he did nowadays. They wore it bushier and drier. So, after lunch: a haircut too.

He walked out of the john and into the coffee shop. He was seated and the waitress brought him an iced tea without his saying a word. He'd forgotten about this Southern custom. He ordered his second steak since he'd been Outside—a sandwich on garlic bread—and this one, along with the Michelob that went with it, was much better than the first. Boggs considered this his first real meal of freedom.

By three he'd bought new shoes and a new hairstyle

and was thinking of taking the MARTA train out to the airport. But he liked the hotel so much he decided to stay the night.

He checked in and asked for a room close to the ground.

"Yessir. Not a problem, sir."

He tried out the room and the bed and felt comforted by the closeness of the walls. He realized only then that he was uncomfortable in the spaciousness of Atlanta. With their tall, dark canyons of buildings, the streets of New York had made him feel less vulnerable. In Atlanta, he felt exposed. He took a nap in the darkened room and then went out for dinner. He saw an airline ticket office and went inside.

He walked up to the United counter. He asked the pretty ticket agent what was nice.

"Nice?"

"A nice place to go."

"Uh—"

"Outside of the country."

"Paris'd be beautiful. April in Paris, you know."

Randy Boggs shook his head. "Don't speak the language. Might be a problem."

"Interested in a vacation? We have a vacation service. Lots of good packages."

"Actually I was thinking about moving." He saw a poster. Silver sand, exquisite blue water crashing onto it. "What's the Caribbean like?"

"I love it. I was to St. Martin last year. Me and my girlfriends had us a fine time."

Man, that sand looked nice. He liked the idea. But then he frowned. "You know, my passport expired. Do you need a passport to go to any of those places?"

"Some countries you do. Some all you need is a birth certificate."

"How would I tell?"

"Maybe what you could do is buy a guidebook. There's a bookstore up the street. You make a right at the corner and it's right there."

"Now there's an idea."

"You might want to think about Hawaii. They got beaches there that're just as nice as the Islands."

"Hawaii." Boggs nodded. That was a good thought. He could just buy a ticket and go and sit on the beach for as long as he wanted.

"Find out what those tickets cost, wouldya?"

As she typed information into her computer he hesitated for a moment then quickly asked, "You be interested in having dinner with me?"

She blushed and consulted her computer terminal. Immediately he wanted to retract his words. He'd stepped over some line, something that people on the Outside—people who stay in Hyatt hotels and buy airline tickets—instinctively knew not to do.

She looked up shyly. "The thing is, I sort of have a boyfriend."

"Sure, yeah." He was as red as a schoolboy's back in August. "I'm sorry."

She seemed startled by his apology. Then she smiled. "Hey, nothing's harmed. Nobody ever died from being asked out." As she looked back to her terminal Randy Boggs thought, This being out in the real world . . . it's going to take a little time to get used to.

SAM HEALY, SITTING ON HIS COUCH, LOOKED OVER HIS lawn as he hung up from the phone call that had delivered the terrible news. He told himself to stand up but his legs didn't respond. He stayed where he was and watched Courtney playing with a set of plastic blocks. He took a deep breath. When Healy was a kid blocks were made of varnished hardwood and they came in a heavy corrugated cardboard box. The ones the little girl was making a castle out of were made of something like Styrofoam. They came in a big clear plastic jar.

Castles. What else would Rune's child build?

Magic castles.

Sam Healy stared at the colored squares and circles and columns, wondering not so much about the toys of his childhood as about the human capacity for violence.

People'd think a Bomb Squad detective would have a pretty tough skin when it came to things like shootings. Hell, especially in the NYPD, the constabulary for a city with close to two thousand homicides a year. But, Healy'd be fast to tell them, it wasn't so. One thing about bombs: You dealt with mechanics, not with people. Mostly the work was render-safe procedures or postblast investigations and by the time you got called in the victims were long gone and the next of kin notified by somebody else.

But he wasn't on the job now and he could no longer avoid what he had to do.

He stood up and heard a pop in his shoulder—a familiar reminder of a black-powder pipe bomb he'd gotten a little intimate with a couple of years back. He paused, glancing at the little girl again, and walked to the TV. Some old Western was playing. Bad color, bad acting. He shut off the set.

"Hey, that dude was about to draw on three bad guys. Sam, you're a cop. *You* should watch this stuff. It's like continuing education for you."

He sat down on the ratty green couch and took Rune's hand.

She said, "Oh-oh, what's this? The-wife's-coming-back-to-roost speech? I can deal with it, Sam."

He glanced into the living room to check on Courtney. After he saw she was contentedly playing he kept his eyes turned away as he said, "I got a call from the ops coordinator at the Sixth Precinct. It seems there was a shooting on the pier where your boat was docked."

"Shooting?"

"A girl about your age. Shot twice. Her name was Claire Weisman."

"Claire came back?" Rune asked in a whisper. "Oh, my God, no. Is she dead?" Rune's eyes were on Courtney.

"Critical condition. St. Vincent's."

"Oh, God." Rune was crying softly. Then, her voice fading, she said, "Somebody thought it was me, didn't they?"

"There are no suspects."

She said, "You know who did it, don't you?"

"Boggs and the other guy, the fat one. Jack Nestor."

"It has to be them. They came back to kill me." Her eyes were red and miserable. "I—" Her hands closed on her mouth. "I never thought Claire'd come back." Rune's gaze settled on Courtney.

Healy held her then said, "I'll call it in to the detectives. About Boggs and Nestor. For a shooting they'll do a citywide search."

"Please," she whispered, "please, please . . ."

"Claire's mother's on her way. She's flying down from Boston."

"I've got to go see her."

"Come on, I'll drive you there."

"I'M SO SORRY," RUNE SAID.

The woman must've been in her early fifties. She didn't know how to respond to the grief and did the only thing she could think of—put her arm around Rune's shoulders and told her that they all had to be brave.

Claire's mother was heavy, wearing a concealing blue-satin dress. Her hair was a mix of pure black strands and pure white, which made it look disorganized even though it was sprayed perfectly into place. She held what Rune thought was a crushed bouquet but what turned out to be a thin white handkerchief, the kind Rune's grandmother called a hankie.

Rune looked at the bed. It was hard to see Claire. The lights were very dim, as if the doctors were afraid that too much brightness would give her life a chance to get away. Rune leaned forward. Claire's left shoulder and arm were in a huge cast, and the left side of her face was a mass of bandages. There were tubes in her nose and several others led from a dressing on her neck into jars on the floor. A monitor above her head gave its alarming messages about heartbeats or pulses or breaths or who knew what. The lines were erratic. Rune wished the monitor faced the other way.

Mrs. Weisman kept her eyes on her daughter and said, "Where's Courtney? Claire said she was staying with you."

"I left her with the nurse outside. I didn't think it was a good idea for her to see Claire like this."

There was the dense silence of two people who have nothing in common except grief.

After a few minutes Rune asked, "Do you have a place to stay?"

The woman wasn't listening. She stared at Claire then a moment later asked Rune, "Do you have any children?"

"Other than Courtney, no."

Mrs. Weisman turned her head toward Rune at this answer. "Did you tell her anything? Courtney, I mean. About what happened."

"I said her mommy was sick and she was going to see her grandmother. She's okay. But she should get some sleep pretty soon."

Mrs. Weisman said, "I'll keep her with me."

Rune hesitated. "Sure."

"Does she have her things with her?"

The clothes *I* bought, she's got. The toys *I* gave her. Rune said, "Claire didn't leave her with much."

Mrs. Weisman didn't respond.

Rune said, "I've got some things to do. Could you call

me if she wakes up?" She wrote Sam Healy's name, address and phone number on the back of a restaurant receipt she'd found in her purse. "I'm staying here for a while."

She nodded and Rune wondered if she was hearing the words.

"Who'd do such a thing?" Mrs. Weisman asked vacantly. "A robber? Claire didn't look like the kind of girl who'd have a lot of money. Do you think it was like what you hear about in California? You know, where they shoot people on the highway just for the fun of it?" She shook her head as if the answer didn't make any difference.

"I don't know," Rune said. Her mother would find out soon enough what happened. No sense in long explanations now.

But there *was* something Rune wanted to add. She wanted so badly to turn to this poor woman and tell her exactly what she was thinking right now. Which was that she didn't give a shit about the news story anymore, she didn't give a shit about the Lance Hopper murder. She cared about one thing, and that only: finding the two of them—Randy Boggs and his fat friend, Jack.

She'd get into the Network somehow—Bradford would help her—and steal her tapes and notes, get all the details on where Randy'd lived over the past ten years, where he liked to go, what he hoped to do in the future. Somewhere in that material would probably be a clue as to where he was running to right now. She'd find him and Jack and make sure they *both* went to Harrison prison.

But then, when it occurred to her that Claire might die and her mother would take Courtney back to Boston, she thought she might not turn them over to the police at all.

She'd kill them herself.

chapter 30

BRADFORD SIMPSON WAS UNEASY.

"The word is Piper wants you drawn and *eighthed*. Quartered isn't good enough."

"Look, I just need to get into the newsroom."

"If I were you I wouldn't be in the same *city* as Piper Sutton," the young preppy said. "The same *building* is a very, very bad idea. Very bad."

They were at Kelly's, a bar on the southern end of Columbus Avenue, around the corner from the Network. The shabby place couldn't make up its mind whether it wanted to be the home base for yuppies who traded insider information or for IRA sympathizers who argued politics.

Rune ordered Bradford another martini, a reporter's drink. And one calculated to make him agreeable. She asked him again to get her inside the Network and appended a heartfelt "Please."

"What for? Tell me what for."

"I can't. It's just really, really important."

"Give me a clue." He speared the olive expertly. Connecticutians are good with martinis.

"You know, that might not be the best question to ask. I don't think you really want to know."

"Now that's an honest response. I don't like it but it's an honest response."

"What's the worst that could happen?" she asked.

"I could get fired, arrested and sent to jail on Rikers Island."

"If anybody asks I'll tell them I snuck in. I promise. I wouldn't jeopardize your career. I know what it means to you. Please, help me out. Just this once."

"You're very persuasive," he said.

"I haven't even started trying yet."

He looked at his watch. "What am I supposed to do?"

"Nothing serious."

"Just distract the guard while you slip in?"

"No, it's a lot easier than that. All you've got to do is deactivate the alarm on the fire door downstairs, open it up and let me in. Piece of cake."

"Oh, Christ." The young man looked worried sick at this assignment. He poured down the last slug of martini.

"And look at it this way," Rune said. "If you *do* get arrested and sent to Rikers Island you'll be able to do a great exposé on what life's like in prison. What an opportunity."

IT DIDN'T GO QUITE THE WAY SHE'D PLANNED IT.

She got in okay, thanks to Bradford. She even managed to get to her old desk unseen.

The problem was that someone had beat her there.

Everything about Boggs was gone.

Rune went through every drawer, every shelf of her credenza, every wadded-up Lamston's and Macy's bag under the desk. But there was zip about Randy Boggs. All the files, the background tapes, the notes—gone.

Who'd done it? she wondered.

Rune sat at the desk until six P.M., when the first live Network newscast began. Everyone's attention was on the far side of the studio and not a soul noticed Rune walk up to a gaffer, a heavyset man in jeans and a white striped shirt. He wore a Mets cap. He was sipping coffee from a cardboard cup, watching the attractive Asian anchorwoman deliver a story about the mayor's press conference.

"Hey, Rune," he said, then looked back to the set. "Welcome back."

"Danny, I need some help," she said.

"Help?" he asked.

"You're on set here every day, right?"

"Yep. Working overtime to buy my boat."

"Somebody went through my desk recently. You see who it was, by any chance?"

He sipped more coffee, avoiding her eyes. "I'm off shift."

"Danny."

"Thought you were fired."

"I am. But I need your help. Please."

He stared at the newscaster, whose short-cut hair shone under the lights like a blue-black jewel. He sighed. "I saw."

"Who was it?"

"Oh, brother . . ."

RANDY BOGGS HADN'T BEEN ON AN AIRPLANE IN YEARS but he was surprised to find that they hadn't changed much. Seemed there were more men flight attendants and it seemed the food was better (though maybe that was just because of what he'd been eating off metal trays for the past thirty-three months, fifteen days).

He remembered what the United Airlines clerk who'd sold him this ticket had said about no one ever dying from getting asked out and he kept up that attitude on the plane, practicing a bit of flirting with the female flight attendants.

He'd dozed and had had a dream that he couldn't remember now and then the weather got rough and the seat belt sign came on. He didn't mind flying but he hated the insides of airplanes. For one thing, the dry, close air bothered him. But they also cheated you. Here you were moving at five hundred miles an hour! But what did the airlines do but try their best to fool you into thinking you were in a restaurant and movie theater. Randy Boggs wanted the planes to have picture windows. Man, what a thrill: seeing the clouds go past like they were trees on the interstate!

Thinking too about his hundred ten thousand dollars. His nest egg. What his father called a "stake" (Randy used to think the old man meant "steak"). And now that he had one he was going to do something with it. Something real smart.

Boggs wondered if he should invest the money in a clothing store in Hawaii. He'd really enjoyed going into that place in Atlanta. He liked the smell—he figured it was aftershave—and he liked the even rows of clothes on the chrome racks. He liked the way the men who worked there stood with their arms folded in front of the shiny counters. If it was slow you could wander outside into the forever warm weather and have a cigarette while you paced the sidewalk under palm trees. He wondered how much it would cost to open a clothing store in Hawaii.

Buying a store. That would be the kind of investment he'd be proud of. Not like those other dumb-ass ideas: like lobster farming and selling amazing water filters and no-money-down real estate and computerized sign painting, all of which he'd tried.

But then again, maybe instead of a store he should invest the money in the stock market. He felt exhilarated, thinking of himself being driven to work, wearing his tan suit and alligator-skin loafers, riding in an elevator up to some penthouse office on Wall Street.

The pilot announced they were landing and he looked out the window again.

Hearing his father's words:

You listen to me, young man, you paying attention? If you're not I'll tan your hide. Come here, son, come here. You remember this: Don't work for any other man. Don't lien the house. Get paid in cash, not in promises. . . .

Though the real advice from his father could be summarized much more easily. It was this: Don't be me.

Just then the plane banked sharply and the engines slowed to a growl. Randy Boggs shut out the overhead light and plastered his face against the window, looking into the night. In the distance he believed he saw a shoreline, he believed he saw water. He definitely saw the runway rising to meet him as if the land were rushing forward to greet him like a lover and welcome him to his new life.

THE BREAK-IN TOOK ONLY FIVE MINUTES.

The Network's personnel department was empty. Rune used a letter opener and fire hose nozzle to break the locks off two file cabinets. Inside, she found the bulky file she'd been looking for, examined it briefly then trotted out with it under her arm.

At an all-night coffee shop up the street she ordered dinner: a Greek salad—extra anchovies—and a large apple juice. (Which reminded her of Courtney and made her feel lonely. She canceled the juice and got coffee— the caffeine was a better idea anyway, she decided.) She sat at the counter, opened the stolen file and began reading. Her appetite had faded by the time she was halfway through the salad. But she drank all the coffee. Then she looked up, squinting, walked to the phone and got Lee Maisel's number from Directory Assistance. She punched the numbers in, noticing only then that it was midnight.

Wondering if she was going to wake him up.

She did.

The producer's voice cracked. "Yes, hello?"

"Lee, it's Rune. I've got to talk to you. It's an emergency."

"Emergency? What d'you mean? What time is it?"

"I've got to talk to you."

"You're okay?"

"I'm all right. I found out something about Lance Hopper's killing. It wasn't an accident. Randy and Jack were hired to kill him."

"What are you talking about?" The voice was sharper now; his mind was in gear. He was a journalist probing for facts.

"It was a professional hit."

"But who'd want Lance dead?

"It was—" Now Rune's voice cracked too and the reason it did had nothing to do with being tired. She repeated in a whisper, "It was Piper."

chapter 31

"WHAT?" MAISEL CLEARED HIS THROAT.

Rune heard the rustling of cloth. She pictured the producer sitting up, putting his feet on the floor, feeling for slippers.

"Piper hired them to kill Lance."

Again, a pause. He was waiting. She heard him clear his throat again then cough. "This isn't funny."

"It's true, Lee."

"Come on, Rune. Why would she want him dead?"

"Somebody took all the Randy Boggs files and tapes out of my desk. Everything was gone."

"Who?"

"Danny Turner, the head electrician on the set, told me it was Piper."

Maisel didn't answer.

Rune said, "And remember, she didn't want to do the story in the first place, she tried to get me to stop? She was going to send me to London? That was to get rid of me."

Maisel snapped, "What I was asking was *why* she'd want Lance Hopper dead."

"Because he was going to fire her. I went through her personnel file—"

"You what? How?"

"I just did. . . . Anyway, you know what I found? That Hopper tried to fire her a year before he died. Piper filed two EEOC complaints against him. They were both dropped but there's lots of memos—it was this huge war."

"Rune, people don't kill people for jobs."

"Maybe not usually—but you know Piper and her temper. You told me that her job was her whole life. And how much does she make? A million a year? That's enough to kill somebody for."

"But how is she going to find professional killers? This is just too—"

"What were some of her assignments?" She continued, "In Africa, in Nicaragua, the Middle East. She could've met some mercenaries. The fat guy—Jack—he looked just like a soldier. And he probably hired Randy to help him."

Maisel considered this. He was less skeptical than a moment ago. He said, "Keep going."

Rune felt like a juggler. It was tough to keep all the parts of the story in the air at once. "When Mr. Frost, the new witness, died? It wasn't an accident at all. Piper knew his name. She saw it from my story. She sent that fat guy to kill him. And then what happens? All the cassettes disappear. And she knew where I'd put the duplicate cassette of Frost. And she'd know how to get into the computer and steal the master."

She felt the silence from the other end of the line— his concentration as he weighed her words, the shock. But maybe also the excitement reporters must feel when they first sniff a lead to a hot story. When he spoke it was almost as if to himself. "And she was pretty smooth when she ad-libbed the broadcast."

Rune said, "Like she'd known all along she was going to have to do it."

A long pause. "This is a nuclear bomb we're playing with, Rune. You've got a lot of speculation. There's no direct evidence linking her to the killing."

"I *know* she did it, Lee."

"The way you *knew* Boggs was innocent?"

She said nothing to that. The producer continued. "Just let me ask you one thing. You're bitter because Piper fired you and ruined your story. If that hadn't happened, if you were an objective reporter, would you still be coming down against Piper?"

"Yes, I would. Maybe there're no eyewitnesses but there's plenty of circumstantial evidence."

Maisel was silent for a moment. "I'll have to call Dan Semple. I'll . . ." His voice was fading. "Semple . . ."

Rune asked, "What are you thinking, Lee?" She remembered Semple's picking Piper up in his limo after she and Rune had dinner at that French restaurant. "Oh, no, you think he's in on it too?"

"They had an affair, you know. Piper and him. Around the time Hopper was killed."

Rune said, "And after Hopper was killed Semple got his job . . . ! "What are we going to do, Lee?"

Maisel said, "Okay, stay on the line. I'm going to make some calls." She heard him use his cell phone to talk to Jim Eustice at home and tell him what Rune suspected. He then called Timothy Krueger, the Network lawyer who'd presided over Rune's unemployment. Then she heard a conference call as Maisel spoke to Krueger and, apparently, the police. She deduced that they were all going to rendezvous at the Network in a half hour—in Studio E, an old, unused space in the basement of the building where they could meet in private.

Maisel hung up his mobile phone and came back on the other line. "Rune, you there?"

"I'm here."

"I talked to Jim and our legal department."

"I heard."

Maisel confirmed that they were meeting two homicide detectives in Studio E.

"I'll be there," Rune said.

"Lay low until the cops get there. We don't want Piper to see you."

"Sure."

"Man, this's bad," he muttered. But that was the only

emotion he showed. Instantly he was Edward R. Murrow again. He said to her, "You did a good job, Rune. Whatever the fallout from this, you did good. See you in a half hour."

THESE WERE THE LONGEST MINUTES OF HER LIFE.

The hour was late but television networks never sleep and she was afraid that if she got to Studio E before Maisel or Krueger or the police, a security guard might see her and word would get back to Piper or Dan Semple.

So she sat in the booth at the Greek diner, bouncing her toes on the linoleum, feeling the terrible sting of betrayal.

Feeling fear too. Recalling all the time she'd spent alone with Sutton, inches away from her, a killer whose heart was as cold as her journalist's eyes.

After fifteen minutes Rune could stand it no longer and she left the deli and headed back to the Network. She slipped in through the door Bradford had doctored to let her inside then started down the corridor through a slightly more populated part of the studio.

A noise nearby. Rune froze.

But it turned out to be only Bradford.

"What's up?" he asked, noticing her troubled face.

She looked around. "Just between us, okay?"

"Top secret," he whispered.

"Piper Sutton had Lance Hopper killed."

"Are you serious?" the young man said.

"You bet I am," she answered. "He was going to fire her. She found out about it and hired Boggs and his friend to kill him."

"Jesus!"

"I'm going to meet Lee down in Studio E." Then her face broke into a smile. "And after she's in jail I'm going to talk Lee into letting me do the story for the Network."

"You?"

"Sure. Why not?"

Bradford apparently couldn't think of any reason why not and simply nodded. He said finally, "Brother, you've sure graduated from overturned ammonia trucks. Say, after your meeting, how 'bout that beer?"

"How 'bout some *champagne*?" Rune said.

"It'll be on me," he said.

THE NETWORK BUILDING WAS LIKE A WARREN — AS COM-plicated and big as a huge high school.

Rune got lost several times on her way to Studio E, which was at the end of a dozen dim corridors. At least she didn't have to worry about being seen now. The studio was in a completely deserted part of the Network building.

She pushed inside and waved to Lee Maisel, who sat at a battered swivel chair, engaged in a somber discussion with someone whose back was to Rune. This would be either Jim Eustice or the lawyer, Tim Krueger. The cops weren't here yet.

"Rune, come on in," Maisel said. He nodded at her hand. "You've got the files you found in Personnel?"

"Right here," she said.

"Good." Maisel stepped forward and took them from her.

Rune sat down at the table and turned to the other man as she started to ask when the police would be here. She froze.

The man was Jack Nestor.

He eyed her up and down and said, "There you go, Lee, I *told* you them girls look alike. No wonder I shot the wrong one."

chapter 32

IT WAS LIKE THE TIME SHE HAD THREE FROZEN MARGARI-tas, crazy drunk—her mind giddy and spinning, her body sick.

She tensed to leap up out of the chair. But Jack shook his head. "Naw, naw, don't bother." He showed her the butt of a pistol in his waistband.

She relaxed. He was right. There was no place to go even if she'd had the strength to get past Maisel, which she didn't. Maisel closed the door and leaned against it.

Her mind was racing, trying to pin down the speculation. "It was you?" she whispered.

Maisel sighed and nodded.

Rune said, "When I called you at home you just *pretended* to call Eustice and Krueger and the cops, right?"

"That's right, Rune. There won't be any cops."

"You did it just to get me here. So you could kill me."

Maisel didn't answer.

"You bastard," Rune hissed at him.

Jack wore a short-sleeved striped shirt over his huge belly and gray baggy pants and some kind of rounded, scuffed brown work shoes. He looked her over then picked up a cup of coffee, noisily drank from it.

"Sorry, Rune. I'm so sorry." Maisel gave her a grim smile but the disappointment and disgust in his face overwhelmed it. He blew air slowly out through his rounded cheeks. Rune could see he was suffering.

Good, she thought.

Maisel poured his drink down in one swallow. "I don't know what to say to you. I tried to stop it all without hurting you."

Jack said, "Yeah, he's right. We tried to kill Boggs in prison. That would've solved—"

"*You* tried to . . ." Rune looked at Maisel; he wouldn't meet her eyes.

"Paid to have a buddy of mine in Harrison kill Boggs. Then when you got him out I tried to do it myself. But that man just wouldn't die."

"It wasn't Piper? But she did everything she could to stop the story."

"Well, sure," Maisel said. "The story would've been bad for her image—she didn't want the EEOC suits coming to light. She hated having the courts to fight her battles for her. But just because she didn't *want* the story to run didn't mean she was going to stop it."

"*You* encouraged me to keep going with it."

"There'd been rumors that there was more to Hopper's death than just Randy Boggs acting alone. We needed you to find the evidence, witnesses. We knew we could control you."

Rune said to Maisel, "Why did you do it?"

"What does it matter?"

"It fucking matters to me!" she snapped.

"Beirut," Nestor said.

"Shut up!" Maisel snapped.

"The story where those people got killed?"

"Right."

"She doesn't need to know," Maisel muttered.

"Why not?" Nestor said. "You fucked up, Lee. You may as well admit it." To Rune he said, "You know Lee's big scoop a few years back? His big fucking award?"

She remembered his Pulitzer. She nodded.

"Well, it was all fake. He made up the interviews, he made up the names of the locals. Who understands all those raghead names anyway? He said they had machine guns and hand grenades and rockets. He scooped everybody."

"Jack . . . ," Maisel said angrily.

•But Nestor kept right on going. "Only the problem was the U.S. Army believed the story and when they went into this village they were loaded for bear. Some Arab kid shot a round at a dog or rabbit or whatever they got over there and, jittery trigger fingers, the whole platoon opened up. When the smoke cleared there were a bunch of dead ragheads and a couple of our own boys. All friendly fire. All courtesy of Mr. Newsman here."

"You made up the whole story?" she asked.

"It wasn't a big deal," Maisel said bitterly. "I mean, it *shouldn't've* been. I didn't even think anybody'd pay attention to it. You have to understand—there's so much pressure to get stories. There's so much time to fill and so little hard news. And always the fucking competition breathing down your neck. I started just adding a few quotes and the next thing I knew it got out of hand. I never thought it would have any consequences."

"But it did," Jack Nestor said, laughing cruelly. "And one of 'em was that Lance Hopper was going to investigate what happened."

"So you hired him." Rune nodded toward Nestor.

The killer said, "Mercenaries and journalists hang out a lot together in combat zones. Isn't much difference between them really, you think about it. Lee and me spent some time together over there, looking for the underground bars—fucking ragheads can't even drink—and hanging out. I go off to Sri Lanka and come back to California, where I do some funny stuff that lands me in Obispo for a while, doing easy time. When I get out Lee calls me and flies me into town to talk to him. The rest is history. . . ."

Maisel didn't look good. He was pale and sweating.

Beneath his salt-and-pepper beard, you could see his lips pressed together. She wondered what bothered him the most: That he'd nearly been caught violating journalistic ethics or that he'd had several people killed to cover it up.

Rune said, "What about Randy?"

"Boggs?" Nestor snorted. "That loser? We set him up. He didn't know anything about the hit. He couldn't kill anybody if he was about to get whacked himself. He lost his job in Maine and called me looking for work on a fishing boat in Florida. I had him meet me in New York. I made up some shit about a credit card deal. Lee and I were going to make it look like he hit Hopper then I'd waste him and leave the gun. There would've been a few loose ends but basically there's a perp and there's a vic so the cops'd be happy. But the son of a bitch ran right into a cop car. Well, he doesn't know we'd planned to kill Hopper so he plays stand-up guy and doesn't turn me in."

Nestor continued. "Everything was going along fine but then I read in the paper about you planning on getting him out. So I come to town and talk it over with Lee. We try to make the story go away and in the meantime I have this spic buddy of mine happens to be in Harrison try to move on Boggs but that doesn't work. Then you get him out and things go to hell. He's got his money and he's gone."

The shock wave passed over her like a fever. So Randy was innocent—to the extent he could be innocent after having been mixed up with people like these. She swallowed. "Please let me go. I won't say anything. I don't care about Hopper. Just let me go, please? I'll be quiet about it."

Maisel looked at Nestor, who was shaking his head no in a humorous, exasperated way. "Can't, Lee. You can't trust her."

Maisel said, "Rune, Rune . . ."

Her teeth were pressed together and she felt anger, hot and searing. Oh, what she wanted to say to him . . . But the words were logjammed in her mind and even if she found the strength and the calm to sort them out she knew he wouldn't comprehend them.

Nestor stirred. She understood. This was his show now. He'd seen Lee weakening and knew it was time for the pro to take over, before more mistakes were made.

Maisel said, "Jack, I don't think—"

The killer held up his hand, a patient school teacher. "It's okay, Lee. I'll take care of it."

Rune said, "No, please, I promise I won't say a word." Her eyes were in Maisel's. He opened his mouth to speak then looked away and sat down in his chair.

Nestor stood up. Pulled a gun out of his pocket.

"These're soundproofed rooms, right?"

Maisel, looking away from Rune, nodded.

The killer looked around and saw a large roll of dusty seamless: a ten-foot-wide paper used for backdrops. He dragged Rune toward it and shoved her down. Presumably to absorb the blood.

Then he looked down at the gun and pulled the slide back, aimed it at her head matter-of-factly. He hesitated. "Do you ever see pictures?" he asked. "Pictures in your head?"

Rune, crying, said, "What do you mean?"

Nestor shook his head. "Never mind." He started to pull the trigger.

"Don't move!" a man's voice called.

Bradford Simpson walked into the room, pointing a pistol at Jack Nestor. "Drop it!" he screamed.

Nestor glanced over his shoulder in disgust and when he saw the hysteria in the young man's eyes, tossed the gun on a nearby table. "Who the fuck're you?"

"Bradford!" Rune said, running toward him.

The boy's attention was wholly on Maisel now; he had no interest in Nestor, who watched the young man with some amusement.

"You son of a bitch," the young man cried. "You killed him! It was you!"

Maisel glanced at the pistol, which was feet from his chest. He said nothing.

"What're you doing here?" Rune asked.

"I'm going to kill him." Bradford said.

"Why?"

"Because Lance Hopper was my father."

chapter 33

"FATHER?" MAISEL ASKED, FROWNING.

"My mother," Bradford said, gazing at the reporter with angry eyes, "was one of the secretaries who worked at a station where my dad was a newsman twenty-two years ago. I was one of Lance Hopper's illegitimate kids the tabloids were so happy to start rumors about. Only in my case it wasn't a rumor. Four years ago my mother told me who my real father was. I came to see him.

"At first he thought I wanted money or something. But then he realized I just wanted to meet him, get to know him. We spent some time together. I liked him. He was a good man at heart. He had his vices and weaknesses—" Bradford laughed. "I guess I was the product of one of those vices. But he was somebody I started to admire. I decided to become a journalist and switched majors. He was going to get me a job here at the Network but I said no, I wanted to do it on my own. I applied for the internship and got accepted and that gave us an excuse to spend time together. We had different last names so no one ever knew who I was. But then he was killed . . . It just about destroyed me. I assumed the story about what happened was true and let it go at that. But a few weeks ago I was doing mailroom duty, going through all the unsolicited mail, and I found Boggs's letter. I read it a dozen times. I got to thinking that maybe there was more to my father's death than what came out in court."

"You're the one who put the letter on my desk," Rune said.

Bradford smiled. "You're a crusader, Rune. Nobody else here'd give a damn about finding the real killer. But I had a feeling you would."

"You were using me too!"

"Let's just say I was looking over your shoulder. The more you found, the more I got to thinking that it must've been Piper or Dan Semple who'd killed him. Lee, you crossed my mind too—that Beirut situation always seemed fishy to me." He nodded toward Rune. "When she told me you were going to meet down here—a deserted studio—I figured you might be the one so I hid up there." He glanced at the empty control booth.

"Look, kid," Nestor said impatiently. "Why don't you just let us walk out of here. And we'll forget everything. You go your way and we'll go ours."

But Bradford ignored him. He nodded at the control booth and said to Maisel, "I got everything you said on tape, Lee."

Maisel closed his eyes. He slumped in the chair.

Nestor sighed and shook his head. "Think you're on your own here, Lee. Nice doing business with you." The killer grabbed Rune by the hair and pulled her to her feet.

"No!" she cried.

Bradford pointed his pistol toward Nestor but the fat man paid no attention. He walked to the table where his own gun lay and picked it up.

"Don't!" Bradford said.

"Yeah, right," Nestor muttered.

"Shoot him!" Rune shouted to Bradford. "Now!"

But the young man froze. His eyes wide, his mouth open in fear as Nestor lifted the gun and fired at him as casually as if he were tossing coins in a wishing well. Rune couldn't tell whether Bradford was hit or not. He fell or dove to the floor. Maisel slid from his chair and rolled to cover under the table.

Tugging Rune after him, Nestor said, "Let's go, honey. May need some insurance, in case the kid called the police."

"No! Goddammit!" she raged, trying to pry his hand off her hair. But he simply got a better grip and dragged her more quickly behind him.

"Shut up," he whispered.

Maybe Bradford *had* called the police. Maybe Sam Healy and a hundred other cops were outside right now, their guns pointed at the door. Nestor'd see that and give up.

He pulled her in front of him and kicked open the door that led to the parking lot.

Please, she thought, let there be a thousand knights waiting here to slay the dragon . . .

They stepped outside. Nobody. She scanned the alley and the parking lot. Empty.

Oh, no . . .

Nestor squinted, orienting himself.

"Car's on the other side of the building. That way." He pointed.

"Let go of me!"

He released her hair but took her firmly by the arm and led her forward. She recalled what he'd said, about being a *mercenary* soldier. She said, "If you let me go I'll give you eight thousand dollars."

"No."

"I can get it for you right now."

Nestor was walking more slowly now. He seemed to be considering what she was saying. Finally he shook his head. "Not enough."

"Maybe I can get a little more." She thought desperately about where she might get some cash.

"How about fifty?" Nestor said.

"I don't have fifty."

"Forty-five."

Tears in her eyes. "I don't *have* that. I can get . . . maybe twenty. I don't know. From friends maybe . . ."

"Forty-three thousand," Nestor said.

"I . . ." She shook her head.

"Tell you what," he said. "You give me thirty-nine thousand five hundred and I'll let you live. I'll let you walk away."

More tears. "But I can't get that much."

"Thirty-eight two."

When she glanced at his face, a sick smile on it, she knew that he was just being cruel. He was playing with her, reciting the odd numbers. And whether she had fifty thousand or a hundred he wasn't going to let her go. This was business and the bargain he'd made was with Lee Maisel. Jack Nestor's job was to kill her.

They were on the sidewalk now, deserted except for a homeless guy in the middle of the block. The street was shimmering with a light rain that wasn't so much falling as hanging in the air.

Nestor said, "This way," and tugged her forward. Ahead of them, on Broadway, a few cabs and cars bounded up- and downtown. Maybe she could tear away and sprint the half block to the corner. She'd just charge right into traffic and hope she didn't get hit. Maybe she'd be lucky the same way Randy Boggs was *unlucky* at Lance Hopper's apartment building and a cop car would be cruising past.

But Nestor's grip was fierce and, besides, he still had his gun in his other hand, hidden inside his jacket.

He stopped at a car. He slipped his pistol in his pocket and reached into his other pocket to get the keys.

"Hey," the drunk called, staggering in their direction. His head drooped forward in his stupor. His clothes were drenched from rain and he looked like a straggly mutt. "Change? For something to eat. You got some change?"

"Shit. Fucking people in this town," Nestor muttered, pulling the keys out of his pocket. He leaned down and said to Rune, "I can feel you, honey. You're thinking the guy comes up and he's going to distract me and then you'll run for it. You think I'm stupid?" He shoved her in the car. "You think I'm not expecting that?"

Nearby now, the homeless man called, "Change, please?"

Jack Nestor, his eyes still on Rune, said to him, "Fuck you, mister."

The drunk suddenly stood up and became completely sober. "Fuck you too, Jack," Randy Boggs said and leapt forward, slamming his fist into Nestor's face.

"RANDY!" RUNE CRIED.

"Run!" Boggs shouted as he grabbed Nestor around the waist and tried to pull him to the sidewalk.

Rune scooted out of the car fast. She hesitated, watching them scuffle. It wasn't a fight—they were wrestling. Boggs was gripping the killer's shoulders, pinning his arms so he couldn't reach his gun. Nestor, blood streaming from his nose, tried to knee Boggs in the groin but couldn't get his leg up without falling over.

"Run, damn it!" Boggs shouted again.

She did. To the nearest corner, to a phone kiosk. Hitting 911 as she watched the men, on the ground now, a dark squirming mass, half in, half out of the street. She told the calm voice of the police dispatcher about the fight, about the gun. By the time she hung up, she heard sirens. Distant, but moving in close. She thought she should go back, distract Nestor, hit him with something. But she didn't move. For some reason an image of Courtney came into her mind and she thought, No, even if Claire's back, I can have *some* role in the girl's life and it wouldn't be fair to her to risk myself. This was their battle now.

Then Rune saw Nestor break free and scramble away. He had the gun in his hand. Randy leapt back into the street, scrambling beneath a car for cover. Nestor fired two fast shots at him then turned to run just as three blue-and-white police cars squealed around the corner. The officers poured out, shouting like madmen for Nestor to stop, to drop the gun. He fired at their cars twice and turned to run but he slipped and went down on one knee.

"Drop the weapon," a metallic voice came over the loudspeaker.

Nestor leapt to the side and lifted the gun again.

The big sparking explosion of a shotgun was like a thunderclap. The killer tumbled backwards. He tried to get up, muttering some distorted words. Something about "pictures," Rune thought. The fat man lay back. His body convulsed once. Then he was still.

TEN SQUAD CARS, WITH LIGHTS FLASHING, WERE PARKED in front of the Network building. Several EMS ambulances were here too and, for some reason, so were two fire trucks. Already the crowd of spectators was large. Rune noted with a laugh to herself that the three news crews on hand to capture the story on tape were all from the competition; no one at the Network seemed to have heard about the incident.

Rune was standing next to Randy Boggs, who leaned against a squad car. His hand and chin were bandaged. Nestor had missed when he'd fired those two shots at him but he'd cut himself in several places during the fight. (He seemed most upset because the ugly tan suit he wore was torn and greasy.)

Bradford Simpson *had* been hit by Nestor's bullet but only in the leg. He'd be all right.

Lee Maisel was in custody.

"How did you get here?" Rune asked Boggs, shaking her head in confusion.

"I went to your houseboat—saw what'd happened there. I'm plenty sorry about that. Did Jack do it?"

"Indirectly." She didn't mention that the actual arsonist was three years old.

Boggs continued. "I just came to the TV station here to see if maybe the guard or somebody could tell me where you were. I saw you and Jack coming out of the back door. Didn't know what was going on but I figured it wasn't good. And that I better do something about it. So I pretended to be a, you know, homeless man so I could get in close."

A detective came up to her and said, "Could you give us a few more details, miss?"

Rune answered, "Can we be alone for a couple minutes? Just him and me? Then I'll tell you everything."

The detective nodded. He walked over to the medical attendants, who were putting Nestor's body on a gurney.

"I thought you'd taken off," Rune told Boggs angrily.

He stared at the ground, not able to return her gaze. "I just went down to Atlanta for a day or two to get my money and then I was coming back. I was going to do that all along—I have some business to take care of here."

"Business?" she asked skeptically.

"I'm giving some of my money to the family of this friend of mine from Harrison. He got himself killed 'cause he was my friend. Anyway, I *couldn't* leave—remember, Mr. Megler said I had to stay in New York until the case was officially over?"

"When has obeying the law ever meant anything to you?" Rune snapped. "Why didn't you tell me about you and Jack?"

"Was a new suit," he said, studying his torn sleeve. Then he looked up, focused on the flipping lights atop a squad car. "Was the deal I made with him."

"Him?" Rune asked in disbelief. "That son of a bitch?"

"Way I was brought up is you don't snitch."

"He used you!"

"Know that now. Didn't then. Didn't until just a few days ago."

"Didn't you think it was kind of funny that he took

you along on this credit card thing then coincidentally somebody gets killed?"

"Not at the time I didn't think so. And then, when I started to think it *was* a little off, he give me all that money to keep mum. I needed a nest egg. A hundred thousand dollars—where'd I ever get money like that otherwise? Nowhere I know of."

Rune's head swam with painful emotions. She wanted to slap him, to scream, to grab his thin collar and shake him.

Randy Boggs said, "I'm sorry."

She didn't answer.

"I coulda just left. I'm thinking of going to Hawaii after everything gets settled in court, you know. I coulda just got my money and kept going there."

"Hawaii?" she asked as if he'd said, "Mars."

He nodded. "Buy me a store of some kind. On the weekends I could sit on the beach and drink those drinks that look like pineapples. With umbrellas in them. You could come visit. You like them drinks?"

She didn't answer.

"I wanta give you some money."

Rune said, "Me? Why?"

"It was on account of me that your house got burned down. How's ten thousand?"

"I don't want your money."

"Maybe fifteen?"

"No, forget it."

"Maybe your little girl—"

"She's *not* my little girl," Rune snapped.

Neither of them spoke for a moment. Then Boggs said, "I'm just trying to tell you I'm sorry."

Rune said, "I wanted to help you. That was why I did the story in the first place. Everybody told me not to. Everybody told me to forget about you, that you'd killed a man and that you deserved to be in jail."

Boggs said, "I'd appreciate it if you'd consider taking the money."

"Give it to Courtney's mother, Claire. She needs it more than me."

"I'll give her some, sure. But I'll give you some too. How's that?"

Rune slapped the top of the police car. She shook her head then laughed. Boggs was looking around, smiling too, though he didn't know what was funny. She said, "Hell, Randy, no wonder you never made any money— you give it all away."

"Haven't held on to it too good. That much is true."

She turned to him and said, "I need to do my story again. I'll have to interview you. Will you talk to me? And this time give me the *whole* story?"

"If I do that will you forgive me?"

She said, "I really don't know."

"Could we go drink beer some time?"

"I don't go out with felons."

"I've done some things that're *criminal*, I admit that, but I'm not sure I'm a felon exactly."

The detective returned and said to Rune, "Need to get some statements from you both now." He was in his politely firm civil-servant mode.

"Sure," she answered.

He took Boggs aside first and, for the moment, Rune was alone, surrounded by a pool of dull colors on the wet street—reflections from the streetlights, from apartment windows, from the emergency cars. She felt a huge desire to get home, to go back to her houseboat and to Courtney. But, of course, the boat was gone: And the little girl was with her grandmother.

Rune looked at the scene in front of her.

The news crews—at last joined by one from the Network—were busy taping their three-minute segments on the shooting. But they were virtually the only ones left on the street. Like the explosion of the shotgun that killed Jack Nestor the incident had erupted fast and then vanished immediately, pulled into the huge gears of the city and ground up into nothing. But for TV audiences throughout the metro area the events would live on in future newscasts until they were preempted by other stories, which would in turn be replaced by still more after that.

Rune sat down on a doorstep to wait for the detective, and to watch the young reporters, holding their microphones and gazing sincerely into the eyes of their loyal viewers as they tried once again to explain the inexplicable.

chapter 34

WRESTLE WITH IT, FIGHT IT.

Standing in front of Claire's hospital bed, Rune wore a white sleeveless T-shirt and black miniskirt. Beside her was Courtney—who was no longer New Wave preschool. No more black and Day-Glo and studs. She was in her new Laura Ashley cornflower-blue dress and lopsided hair ribbon (it had taken Rune ten minutes to get the red satin to impersonate a bow).

A sharp, sweet smell was in the air. Rune didn't know whether it was disinfectant or medicine or the smell of illness and death. She didn't like it; she hated hospitals.

"Where's your mom?" Rune asked Claire.

"At her hotel," the girl said. "She was with me all night. That's something about mothers, huh? Abuse 'em all you want and they keep coming back for more."

Courtney clumsily set a paper bag on the bed. "I got this for you."

One-handed, Claire shook it open. Out fell a stuffed dinosaur. Courtney made it walk across the bed. "Rune helped me buy it," her daughter told her.

"How'd I guess?" Claire examined the plush face with serious scrutiny. "He's like sensitive and ferocious at the same time. You can really pick them."

Rune nodded absently. "It's a talent."

Fight it. Fight it down . . .

Claire didn't look good. She could sit up okay, with some help, but otherwise she was pretty immobile. Her skin was paler than Rune had ever seen it (and Claire was somebody who went as a vampire on Halloween the year before and hadn't bothered with makeup or a costume).

"I won't see in my left eye," she announced matter-of-factly. "Ever again."

Rune looked her straight in the good one and was about to offer something sympathetic when Claire moved on to another subject. "I got this job. At a department store. It's kinda bullshit. I have a couple bosses and they're like, 'Well, we'll try you out,' And I'm like, 'What's to try?' It's not, like, the best thing in the world but it's working out okay. Like listen to this—I've got health insurance? I got it just before I left to come down here. Man, they're going to get some friggin' bill."

This room was better than the Intensive Care Unit where she'd been for a few days. From here Claire had a view of rolling Jersey hills and the Hudson and, closer to home, one of Rune's favorite hangouts: the White Horse Tavern, the poet Dylan Thomas's hangout, where Rune had spent a number of afternoons and evenings with a literary and artistic crowd.

Hospitals were pretty icky but here at least you got a view and sunlight and history.

Claire was talking about her mother's house in Boston and how weird it was that nobody in the neighborhood wore black leather or had shaved heads and how she hadn't met any musicians or short-story writers but the one guy she met who she liked was a salesman. Wasn't that the craziest thing you ever heard?

"Crazy."

Rune nodded and tried to listen. The muscles in her abdomen clenched against the crawly feeling, like she was possessed by a space creature that was getting ready to burst out of her. Fight it down. . . . Fight it!

Then Claire was into a travelogue, telling Rune and Courtney about Boston—Faneuil Hall and Cambridge and Chinatown and the lofts and antique stores around

South Street Station. "There's this one really, really neat place. It sells old bathtubs that must be three feet deep."

Rune nodded politely, and a couple times said, "Wow, that's interesting," in an uninterested way, which Claire seemed to take as encouragement to keep rambling. Rune found she was holding Courtney's hand tightly. The little girl squirmed.

Fight it. . . .

Rune didn't say much about Boggs or Maisel or the *Current Events* story. Just the bare bones. Claire must have known Rune was the reason she'd been shot and Rune wanted to steer clear of that. Not that she was racked with guilt—you could also say that Claire got hurt because she'd abandoned her daughter. But *that* got into the way gods or fate or nature worked and if you started thinking too much about cause and effect, Rune knew, it'd drive you nuts.

There was silence for a minute. Then Rune said, "I bought Court a new dress." Nodding at the little girl.

"Look, Mommy."

Claire twisted her body as far as she could so the un-bandaged eye got a good look at the dress, and the way the young woman's damaged face blossomed with love as she looked at her little girl clearly answered the single scorching question that had been consuming Rune since Claire had returned.

When she considered it now, of course, she realized there really had never been any chance that Courtney could stay with her and she was mad at herself for hoping things might turn out otherwise. After all, she'd read *The Snow Princess*. She knew how it ended. This business about fairy stories having happy endings—that was bull-shit. Sometimes people melt. People go away. People die. And we're left with the stories and the memories, which, if we're lucky, will be good stories and good memories and then we get on with our life.

Claire was reaching forward, awkwardly, across the bed with her good arm, saying, "Did you miss me, honey?"

"Uh-huh." Courtney let go of Rune's hand and tried to climb onto the bed. Rune boosted her up.

Rune said, "So you're going back to Boston, huh? The two of you?"

Claire said, "Yeah, like, we'll live at my mom's until I can get some money saved up but apartments are cheap there. It shouldn't take me much time."

Fight it. . . .

Rune swallowed. "You want, I can keep Courtney with me until you get settled. We're pretty good buddies, huh?"

The little girl was playing with the dinosaur and didn't hear what Rune said. Or didn't want to. In any case she didn't answer. Claire shook her head. "I kind of want her with me. You know how it is."

"Sure."

"Look, Rune, I never said it but I like really, really appreciate what you did. It was a pretty bad thing, just leaving like that. A lot of people wouldn't have done what you did."

"True, they wouldn't," Rune said.

"I owe you."

"Yeah, you do. You owe me."

"The doctor says I can be transferred to Boston in a couple of days. And, guess what?"

Rune's face burned. "A couple of days?"

"I'm gonna take an ambulance, like, the whole way. Is that cool, or what? My mom's paying for it."

And with that Rune realized it was no good fighting it anymore. She'd lost. She took a deep breath and said, "Well, ciao, you guys."

"Aw, come on," Claire said, "stay for a while. Check out the doctors. There's this cute one. Curly hair you won't believe."

Rune shook her head and started for the door.

"Rune," Courtney said suddenly, "can we go to the zoo?"

Pausing to hug the girl briefly, she managed, some-how, to keep her voice steady and to hold back the tears for the time it took her to say, "Before you leave, honey, we'll go to the zoo. I promise."

Rune remained steady and calm for the few seconds it took her to say this and walk out the door.

But not an instant longer. And as Rune walked down the corridor toward the exit the tears streamed fast and the quiet sobbing stole her breath as if she were being swept away, drowning and numb, in a torrent of melting snow.

"LOOK AT THIS. LIKE A DAMN DRAGON BURNED ME OUT."

Piper Sutton looked at her. "You and your dragons."

They stood on the pier, where the glistening, scorched hull of the houseboat floated, hardly bobbing, in the oily water of the Hudson.

Rune bent down and picked up a soggy dress. She examined the cloth. The collar was a little scorched but she might be able to cover it up with paint. She thought about the lawyer, Fred Megler, an expert at repairing clothes with pens.

But she sniffed the dress, shrugged and threw it into the discard pile, which looked like a small volcano of trash. Both the fire and the water from the NYFD had taken their toll. On the deck was a pile of books, pots and pans, some half-melted running shoes, drinking glasses. Nothing really valuable had survived, only the Motorola TV and the wrought-iron frames of the butterfly chairs.

"The 1950s were indestructible," Rune said, nodding at the frames. "Must've been one hell of a decade."

It was a stunningly gorgeous Sunday. The sky was a cloudless dome of three-dimensional blue and the sun felt as hot as a lightbulb. Piper Sutton sat on a piling she'd covered with a scrap of blue cloth—one of Rune's work shirts—before she'd lowered her black-suede-encased thighs onto the splintery wood.

"You have insurance?" the anchorwoman asked.

"Kinda weird but, yeah, I do. It was one of those adult things, you know, the sort that I don't usually get into. But my boyfriend at the time made me get some." She walked to the water and looked down at the charred wood. "The policy's in there someplace. Do I have to have it to collect?"

"I don't think so."

"I'm going to make some serious money there. I lost some really hyper stuff. Day-Glo posters, crystals, my entire Elvis collection . . ."

"You listen to Elvis Presley?"

"That'd be Costello," Rune explained. Then considered other losses. "My magic wand. A ton of incense . . . Oh God, my Lava Lamp."

"You have a Lava Lamp?"

"*Had*," Rune corrected sadly.

"Where're you staying?"

"With Sam for a while. Then I'll get a new place. Someplace different. I was ready to move anyway. I lived here for over a year. That's too long to be in one place."

A tugboat went by. A horn blared. Rune waved. "I know them," she told Sutton, who twisted around to watch the low-riding boat muscle its way up the river.

"You know," Rune said, "I've got to tell you. I kind of thought you were the one behind the killings."

"Me?" Sutton wasn't laughing. "That's the stupidest crap I ever heard."

"I don't think it's so stupid. You tried to talk me out of doing the story then offered me that job in England—"

"Which was real," Sutton snapped. "And got filled by somebody else."

Rune continued, unfazed, "And the day of the broadcast, when you ad-libbed, the tapes were missing. Even the backup in my credenza. You were the only one knew they were there."

Sutton impatiently motioned with her hand, as if she

were buying candy by the pound and wanted Rune to keep adding some to the scale. "Come on, think, think, think. I told you I was on my way to see Lee. *He* asked me if you'd made a dupe. I told him that you had and you'd put it in your credenza. *He's* the one who stole it."

"You also went through my desk after Boggs escaped. Danny saw you—the electrician."

"I didn't want any of that material floating around. You were really careless, by the way. You trust too many people. You . . ." She realized she was lecturing and reined herself in.

They watched the tugboat for a few minutes until it disappeared. Then Sutton said abruptly, "You want your job back, you can have it."

"I don't know," Rune said. "I don't think I'm a company person."

A brief laugh. "Of course you're not. You'll get fired again. But it's a peach job until you do."

"The local or the Network?"

"*Current Events,* I was thinking."

"Doing what? Like a script girl?"

"Assistant producer."

Rune paused then dropped a pair of scorched jeans into the trash pile. "I'd want to do the story. The whole thing. About the Hopper killing. And I'd have to include Lee this time."

Sutton turned back, away from the water, and stood up, looking over the huge panorama of the city. "That's a problem."

"What do you mean?"

"*Current Events* won't be running any segments about the Hopper killing. Or about Boggs."

Rune looked at her.

"Network News covered it," the woman said.

Rune said wryly, "Oh, that's right. I saw that story. It was about sixty seconds long, wasn't it? And it came after the story of the baby panda at the National Zoo."

"The powers-that-be—at the parent—decided the story should go away."

"That's bullshit."

"Can you blame them?"

"Yes," Rune said.

In her prototype Piper Sutton voice, Piper Sutton snapped, "It wasn't my decision to make."

"Wasn't it?"

Sutton took a breath to speak then didn't. She shook her head slowly, avoiding Rune's eyes.

Rune repeated, "Wasn't it?" And surprised herself again by hearing how calm she sounded, how unshaken she now was in the presence of this woman—a woman who wore suede and silk and bright red suits, a woman richer and smarter than she'd ever be. A famous commentator, who now seemed abandoned by words. Rune said, "You'd rather the competition did the story? *Prime Time Tonight* or *Pulse of the Nation*?"

Sutton stepped up on a creosoted railroad tie bolted into the pier as a car barrier. She looked in the water; her expression said she didn't like what she saw. Rune wondered if it was her reflection.

She said simply, "The story won't run on *Current Events*."

"What would happen if it did?"

"If you want to know I posed that exact question. And the answer was if it does the parent'll cancel the show." Then she added, "And I'll be out of work. You need a better reason than that?"

"I don't think I want my job back, no," Rune said. She'd found some of her old comic books; they'd miraculously survived both the fire and looters. She looked at the cover of a 1953 classic—"Sheena, Queen of the Jungle," who swung out of a tree toward a startled lion. The cat stared at her spear and radiant blonde hair and leopard-skin-clad hourglass figure—a physique that existed only in the luxurious imaginations of illustrators. "That's me." Rune held up the book. "Queen of the Jungle."

Sutton glanced at the picture.

Rune stacked the books in the small to-be-saved pile and asked, "Your conscience bothering you yet?"

"I've never had trouble sleeping at night. Not in forty-three years."

"You want my opinion?"

"Not really."

"You're caving, just to keep your paycheck."

Rune expected a tirade but what she got was a surprise—a small, hurt voice, saying, "I think you know it's not that."

And after a moment Rune nodded, understanding that Sutton was right. Sure, she'd bowed to the wishes of the executives. But the reasons were complex. She'd caved partly because she was hooked on the prestige and excitement that went with being a prime-time news anchor. Partly to keep a job that she'd fought hard for.

And partly—mostly—because Piper Sutton felt the world of journalism, and her ten million viewers, needed her.

Which of course they did. They needed the news handed to them by people like this, people they recognized, trusted, admired. An old boyfriend had once quoted somebody—a poet, she thought—who said that mankind can't bear too much reality. Well, it was the Piper Suttons of the world who cut reality into manageable little bites and set them out, pleasantly arranged, in front of the public.

"I put it in context." Sutton shrugged. "Boggs was innocent and you got him out. That's a good deed. But it's still a small story. There's a lot of news out there, a lot bigger news. Nobody says I've got to cover everything."

"I'll produce it independently." Rune sounded more threatening than she had meant to.

Sutton laughed. "Bless you, babes, and more power to you. All I'm telling you is the story won't run on the Network. Not on my program."

Rune turned to face Sutton. "And if I do it, I'm going to mention the part about how they wouldn't do the story on *Current Events*."

Sutton smiled. "I'll send you the files and all backup, the stuff I saved from your desk. Give us your best shot. We can take it."

Rune returned to her pile of salvage. "It'll be a son of a bitch to do by myself."

Sutton agreed, "Sure will."

"You know, I could use a business partner. Somebody who was smart and knew the business. And was, like, abrasive."

"*Like* abrasive."

"You wouldn't be interested, would you?"

"Wait—you mean quit my job and go to work with you?" Sutton laughed, genuinely amused.

"Sure! We'd be a great team."

"No way in hell." The anchorwoman walked over to the messy pile and began to help Rune pick through it. She'd hold up an object and Rune would give her instructions: "Save." "Pitch." "Pitch." "Pitch." "Identity-unknown pile." "Save." "Save."

They worked for a half hour until Sutton straightened up and looked at her smudged hands with a grimace. She found a rag and started wiping them clean. "What time you have?"

Rune glanced at her working watch. "Noon."

Sutton asked, "You interested in getting some brunch?"

"I can't today. I'm going to the zoo with somebody."

"A date, huh?"

"Not hardly," Rune said. "Hey, you want to come?"

Sutton was shaking her head, which Rune figured

was probably her reflex reaction to invitations of this sort. "I haven't been to the zoo in years," she said, laughing.

"It's like riding a bike," Rune said. "It'll come right back to you."

"I don't know."

"Come on."

"Let me think about it." Sutton stopped shaking her head.

"Aw, come on."

"I said I'll think about it," Sutton snapped. "You can't ask for more than that."

"Sure I can," Rune said.

The anchorwoman ignored her and together they crouched down in front of the pile of mystery artifacts and began picking through it, looking for more of Rune's damaged treasures.

about the author

JEFFERY DEAVER'S novels have appeared on a number of bestseller lists around the world, including the *New York Times,* the *London Times* and the *Los Angeles Times.* The author of fifteen novels, he's been nominated for four Edgar Awards from the Mystery Writers of America and an Anthony Award and is a two-time recipient of the *Ellery Queen Reader's* Award for Best Short Story of the Year. His novel *The Bone Collector* was a feature release from Universal Pictures, starring Denzel Washington as Lincoln Rhyme. Turner Broadcasting is currently making a TV movie of his novel *Praying for Sleep,* and his most recent novel, *The Blue Nowhere,* was recently sold to producer Joel Silver and Warner Bros. There are two other books in the Rune series: *Manhattan Is My Beat* and *Death of a Blue Movie Star.* Deaver is now at work on his next Lincoln Rhyme novel. Readers can visit his website at www.jefferydeaver.com.